Queen of the Hill

Genevieve Jack

Carpe Luna Publishing

Queen of The Hill: The Knight Games series, Book 3

Copyright © 2014 Carpe Luna Publishing

Published by Carpe Luna, Ltd.,
PO Box 5932,
Bloomington, IL 61701
www.carpeluna.com

FIRST EDITION: MAY 2014

ISBN: 978-1-940675-11-4

Cover design by Steven Novak

Formatting by Polgarus Studio.
www.polgarusstudio.com

v 1.0

BOOKS BY GENEVIEVE JACK

Knight Games Series

The Ghost and The Graveyard
Kick The Candle
Queen of the Hill
(and more to come!)

Contents

CHAPTER 1
Wake-Up Call

Sex is different with someone you love. New sex extinguishes a fire; old love stokes the embers. In a way, sex is a lot like wine—drinkable as soon as it ferments. But if you allow it to age, the result is a visceral experience—a nirvana of the senses.

When it came to Rick and me, we'd aged together for multiple lifetimes. Every touch elicited an irresistible array of memories. Each caress ignited a new flavor on the emotional spectrum. Sweet and aromatic. Complex. Layered. Having a long finish. An enticing intoxication of hormonal chemistry and raw heat.

I loved Rick.

In bed beneath me, he dug his fingers into the hair at the nape of my neck and tugged. I lifted my cheek from his chest to meet his gaze. His hooded stare held nothing short of reverence, his pupils almost black with need. "You must know you bewitch me in a way that has nothing to do with magic. I have crossed oceans of time to be with you. Lifetimes. I would do it again, but I hope I never have to."

"You won't," I promised. "We're together now, and I plan to be careful with myself."

I trailed my fingertips up the side of his chest and over the length of his arm. Iridescent purple magic followed my touch, markedly beautiful beside his dark hair and the silky red pillowcase under his head. The streak wasn't something I was consciously producing. Power poured out of me with so much love. At journey's end, my left hand linked with his, my engagement ring squeezed inside the web of his long fingers.

The blue and silver cushion of gems that marked our coming nuptials was both old and new. The ring itself was antique, commissioned in the 1700's, but its place on my finger was a novelty. Rick had asked me to marry him only a few short weeks ago, and I had said yes. I was engaged. To be married. To Enrique Ordenez—Rick. My caretaker.

I pressed my lips against the side of his neck. The heat of my breath brought his blood to the surface. Liquid ambrosia. My personal recipe for the elixir of life. During my first lifetime as a witch, I'd made the decision to store an immortal part of my soul inside Rick when Reverend Monk burned me at the stake in 1698. Of course, I don't remember all the details, having died and been reborn several times since. But I had pieced together this much: I didn't have to give Rick my immortality. I chose to. By using magic to create a symbiotic relationship between the two of us, I'd ensured we would be together forever. A lovely side effect was his blood healed me, and my blood strengthened him.

"I need to be inside you," he whispered into my ear. His hand found purchase between the dimples of my lower back. I obliged, shifting my hips to join with him. He groaned and rolled me over.

Nestled under his rock-hard body, his lips brushed my ear as he whispered a mellifluous string of Spanish syllables. The exotic adoration lulled me into a blissful state with each magnificent thrust. I had no idea what he said, but I knew exactly what he meant.

"Look down," Rick whispered.

"Down?" I tipped my face to the side. My hair swung below me in my line of sight. We were levitating above the mattress, suspended in midair.

"Me?" I asked.

"You," he whispered.

I sighed. The power from our connection flowed through me as Rick gently guided my chin back to center and his mouth crashed down on mine. His lovemaking became more fervent, and I was quick to respond in kind.

Knock-knock-knock.

We both ignored the sound at the door and came together in a mind-blurring crescendo. I clung to him fervently through airborne aftershocks. The internal

fireworks were still going off when the interruption came
again.

Knock- knock-knock. "I have returned twice. I shall not
return again," came Soleil's shrill voice.

We dropped like a two-ton weight. The bed groaned in
protest.

"She sounds pissed," I said.

Rick rolled off me, pulling the sheet over our spent
bodies. "Enter," he called.

The door swung open to reveal Soleil's tight expression
and ballerina-like physique. I was sure the lock had been
engaged from the inside, but then, as the madam of
Maison des Étoiles, Soleil had ultimate control. Each room
was enchanted to bring to life the desires of the patrons.
Soleil was celestial fae. In fact, her sunny disposition had
saved my ass from death by vampire in the past—the
winter solstice, to be exact. Fae magic played a big part in
the lure of her bordello, too, and was why Rick and I were
there. I'd had my first threesome in this room with Rick
and … Rick.

"Grateful, may I remind you that you have a dress
fitting today at noon?" Soleil asked. She tucked a stray
honey-colored hair back into her chignon with a set of
perfectly manicured fingers.

I yawned and stretched my arms above my head.
"That's tomorrow. Remember? On Saturday."

"It *is* Saturday."

With a flippant giggle, I said, "Very funny. That would mean Rick and I have been, uh, in this room for more than twenty-four hours."

Soleil's gracefully arched brows pinched together over her nose. "Exactly. Not only are we going to be late, I need the room."

Sheets clutched to my bosom, I sat up and grabbed my cell off the nightstand to check the time. "Shit!" I repeated the curse as I dispensed with modesty and leapt from the bed in search of my clothes. It was like an Easter egg hunt. My panties were hanging from the corner of the wardrobe. My jeans were in a heap under the legs of a Louis XVI chair. With my bare bum in the air, I bent over to pick them up, then glanced back to see if Soleil was staring.

She giggled, light and clear as silver bells, and averted her eyes.

"Sorry," I said sheepishly.

"This wouldn't be a problem if you allowed enough time for proper wedding preparations," she said between laughs. "A March date is too aggressive. It is already mid-January."

I sighed. "It has to be the afternoon of the spring equinox—Ostara," I said. "On March twentieth, the magic surrounding new beginnings will be at its apex. It is the perfect day to renew our life together and begin a new marriage. A metaphysical phoenix from the flames."

"Sounds superstitious," Soleil said.

Arms filled with clothes, I ducked into the bathroom to freshen up. Although I closed the door behind me, I could still hear Rick's reply.

"The wedding will come and go; the marriage is what's important. If Grateful wants to start our marriage on the day of new beginnings, so be it. I don't care if she walks down the aisle in jeans and a T-shirt and we eat her blessed Pop-Tarts for dinner."

I grinned. Good man.

"I doubt she would be pleased with such circumstances," Soleil said.

She was right.

"If something is not to her liking, she can change it," Rick said.

"You mean, use magic."

"She's getting stronger. Her power has blossomed and her magic is as good or better than mine," Rick said.

"I thought she was still learning her spells," Soleil said.

"Natural magic. She levitated just a moment ago, and you saw how she called the storm during the solstice. Learning the spells will come with time, but natural magic is more powerful than any potion or incantation." Rick sounded so proud. My heart swelled thinking about how he stuck up for me.

"Well, considering she might have a few things to think about on her wedding day other than magic, let's hope we can make it to the dress shop on time," Soleil quipped.

I bound from the bathroom, fully dressed and face washed. My hair was a wild mess, but I yanked the blonde waves into a bun at the crown of my head. "I'm ready."

"Great. We can still make it." Soleil opened the door for me. "Is Michelle meeting us at the dress shop?"

"Oh no, Michelle!"

* * * * *

"So, you forgot about me. No big deal. I'm just your matron of honor. There's no legal *requirement* that you invite your matron of honor to help pick out your wedding dress." Michelle crossed her arms over her chest and tapped her index finger on her bicep.

"Again, I am so sorry I didn't call you earlier. I'm just stoked you could make it on short notice," I said.

She gave me a tight smile. "Well, I'm here." She circled her hands in the air as if her presence was evidence enough of my forgiveness.

I sensed she wasn't over it.

"Schall I pull zee selection of dresses for you, Miss Knight?" Gertrude Evenrose, owner and proprietor of Carlton City's premier bridal emporium, Evenrose Bridal, stared at me over her bifocals, clearly perturbed that it was fifteen minutes past our appointment time, and I still hadn't tried on a dress.

"Of course, Gertrude. I apologize for the delay," I said.

"Vell, I haf a feelink you vill decide quickly," she said, a note of insistence in her voice. She took off like a whirlwind, sweeping through the store and selecting various styles from the racks. Her slight four-foot-nine frame was swiftly buried under yards and yards of white fabric.

"Do you need to know my size?" I asked.

"Nein. Zee dresses vill be ehltered to shpecifications post purchase. As you ehr khleerly a size eight, you shoult haf no problem vith zee samples."

"I'm a size six," I corrected.

She finished hanging the dresses on a trio of hooks in the dressing room and then turned to scan me from head to toe. "You ehr not," she said through her teeth. "Now, tryen sie das garment!"

I jumped like a dog at her command and raced into the spacious changing room. Geesh. I'd faced vampires, demons, shifters, and more in my role as Hecate, but Gertrude Evenrose scared the bejeebers out of me. I thumbed through the stack on the wall. Too poofy, too sparkly, too yellow (who wears a yellow wedding dress, anyway?). And then, *hello, gorgeous.*

Slipping the dress off the hanger, I pulled the pearlescent-beaded bodice on and zippered. I didn't need help. The plunging back ended just above my backside. A set of sparkling silver spaghetti straps slithered over my shoulders and crisscrossed just under my shoulder blades. Despite not having a proper back, the stiff boning across my ribs provided ample support for the girls. From the waist down, satin gazar draped to the floor in two layers, like the petals of an opening flower. More pearls were sewn in swirls along the hem and slit.

With a beaming smile, I paraded out of the stall and stepped up on the box in front of a three-way mirror to the *oohs* and *aahs* of my besties. Gertrude took one look at me and grabbed a pearl choker from her jewelry chest. In moments she had the necklace clipped around my neck, its drop pearl resting naturally in the groove between my collarbones.

"You look like a princess," Soleil said.

"A kind and thoughtful princess who would never forget about her best friend, or not tell her best friend important things about her life," Michelle added cheerfully.

I gave her a sharp look, twisting left and then right to get a better look at the plunging back. The dress seemed to defy gravity, like it was holding itself up by magic alone. My smile faded. I stared at my naked scapula in the mirror for a second, then at the pile of discarded clothing next to my purse in the changing room.

"What is wrong, Grateful?" Soleil asked.

"I just realized I can't wear this dress."

"Why?" Soleil pointed a graceful hand in my direction. "It is beautiful."

Lips pressed together, I turned toward them, my eyes filling with tears. "Nightshade. There's nothing on my back to conceal her. I don't want my father to walk me down the aisle knowing I have a sword strapped to my back."

Michelle rolled her eyes. "Don't you think you could go one afternoon without Nightshade? I mean, the wedding will be during the day, right? Rick will be there."

I bit my lip and shook my head.

Soleil tried to back me up. "She can't risk it. Not after what happened with Bathory."

Oh hell. I'd never actually told Michelle about Anna Bathory, the ancient vampire who had almost killed me in order to complete an invincibility spell from *The Book of Flesh and Bone*. The omission was a definite violation of our unwritten best friend agreement.

"What happened with Bathory?" Michelle asked. Her accusing stare darted from me to Soleil with an expression that went from questioning to disappointed pretty damn quick.

I spread my hands. "I'm sorry, Michelle. For your safety—"

"For my safety? For my safety, you didn't tell me what?" Michelle crossed her arms again and glared at me. If looks could kill, I would have burst into flames. Thing is, I still didn't think it was a good idea to tell her I'd almost been sacrificed on a stone altar less than a month ago. Bathory was still out there, along with her leprechaun sidekick, Naill. Neither would hesitate to destroy Michelle to get to me. I would protect her, but knowing she was vulnerable could ruin her life. Sometimes ignorance is bliss.

With a defeated sigh, I met Michelle's eyes but gestured toward Gertrude, who was busily straightening racks. "Later, okay?"

Michelle gave a curt nod. "Okay."

Contrary to her words, as her best friend, I was certain she was not okay. In fact, she was pissed at me. Pissed to the point of silence for fear speaking even one syllable might release a deluge of pointed criticisms.

"Perhaps you should try another dress," Soleil suggested, attempting to defuse the tension between us.

"Good idea." I jumped at the opportunity to change the subject. I did a quick change into a vintage style that was mostly layers of antique ivory lace with a black lace overlay at the top. It wasn't my favorite but would conceal Nightshade. I returned to the box in front of the three-way mirror. Michelle still looked like she wanted to kill me, and Soleil didn't even humor me with a pity compliment.

"What do you think?" I asked.

"I think the style does not do justice to your curves," Soleil said.

Michelle turned pursed lips toward me. "Beautiful," she spat, crisp and short with no resemblance to its proper meaning. "Hey, speaking of the wedding, have you figured out where you are going to live yet?"

Damn. Buttons successfully pushed. Michelle knew this was a touchy subject with me and no doubt intended the question as verbal retribution. I sidestepped. "I'm going to live in my house."

"No. After you're married. Is Rick going to move in with you? Or are you going to live with him?"

Ah, so she wasn't going to let it go. "It's complicated." My magic was fueled by the element of air, hence the importance of my attic. Rick's was fueled by earth, hence his stone cottage. Our differences made us stronger on the battlefield but made living together problematic.

"Right," Michelle said. "Because you need different things than he does. Funny how I know that because I can be trusted ... Because I'm your best friend."

"You are not going to live together?" Soleil interrupted, appalled.

A drum line kicked off in my heart—*lub-dub, lub-dub, lubidy dub.* My hands started to sweat. I didn't want to talk about this. I didn't want to think about this right now.

Michelle didn't quit. She was like a pit bull with her teeth in me. "Are you going to keep your nursing job when you are Mrs. Ordenez? Wait? Will you be Mrs. Ordenez? Are you going to change your name?" Michelle fired off the questions like bullets.

Soleil's gaze bounced between Michelle and me as if she were watching a tennis match.

The room grew hot. I took a deep breath. The walls swayed, and my stomach twisted. Saliva filled my mouth. I swallowed and swallowed again, but it just kept coming.

"Are you going to adopt kids?" Michelle asked.

That did it. I was going to be sick. I raced for the nearest door, one that led to the back alley.

"Nein! You khen not go out of dooers, Miss Knight," Gertrude shrieked, but I was already in the alley, the mid-January cold biting into my skin. I doubled over and heaved toward the pavement. Nothing came out. I hadn't eaten anything all day.

An arm slipped around my shoulders, and Michelle's dark head and concerned face appeared next to mine. "I'm sorry. I'm so sorry, Grateful. I was angry at you, but I didn't mean to make you ill."

"No. I deserved it. I should have told you everything. I just didn't want to burden you. My life is so—"

"Crazy?"

"You have no idea."

"It's okay, all right? You don't have to tell me about what happened with Bathory, and you certainly don't have to decide all that stuff I threw at you today. It's not worth getting sick over."

"You are not the reason I feel sick."

Michelle blinked at me curiously. "Then why are we out here?"

For a long time, I didn't say anything. Thoughts swirled loose and disorganized inside my skull. I leaned my back against the wall near the door, the sound of Soleil arguing with Gertrude reminding me I was on borrowed time. "You know how I told you Rick asked me to marry him at Christmas?"

"Yeah."

"I may have omitted part of the story."

She raised eyebrows at me.

"He actually asked me when he was about to die."

"What?" Michelle wrinkled her nose.

I took a deep breath. How could I explain this to her in a way she would understand? "Before our engagement, before I understood our history, I pushed Rick away. I took him for granted. He'd thought I didn't want him anymore and sought out another witch, like me, for help. She gave him a magic candle that could have broken our connection permanently by making him human. While the candle was burning, Rick sustained injuries that would have resulted in his death. I stopped the candle before it burned all the way down, halting the magic spell and allowing Rick to recover from his temporary humanity. I agreed to marry him on the floor of his stone cottage, amid a broken ring of skulls and magic. My answer in the affirmative was the only way to end the spell and make him immortal again. My 'yes' saved his life."

Michelle's mouth dropped open and a small disgusted sound came from the back of her throat. "Are you saying he extorted marriage out of you?"

I shook my head. "No. Well … Not exactly."

She narrowed her eyes and tipped her head, her arms crossed defensively across her ample chest.

"I love Rick." I met her eyes and made sure she knew I was serious. "I really love Rick. To my core. And I *want* to marry him. I'm happy about the way things are going."

"But?"

"Have you ever heard the expression, 'I'm not afraid of flying; I'm afraid of crashing'?"

"I love that one. Who's not afraid of crashing?"

"I'm not afraid of marrying Rick. I'm afraid it won't work out. We can't even live in the same *house*, Michelle. How are we going to build a life together?" I stared hopelessly at the snow-covered pavement, the cold seeping through my skin like a poison.

Michelle pondered my words for a minute, then squatted down next to me so her shoulder grazed mine. She nudged me slightly to get my attention. "You'll figure it out. One day at a time, together."

"Did you read that on an embroidered pillow?"

"I'm serious. If you are in love and committed, you will figure it out. People work out all sorts of arrangements. There's a nurse in ICU who works opposite shifts as her husband and only sees him on weekends. They have two kids. They're making it work."

"What if it doesn't?"

"No one promised you easy. Every couple has challenges."

I widened my eyes at her, my jaw dropping.

"I know your challenges are a bit more … unconventional, but you are blessed to be loved, Grateful. Rick's love for you has straddled lifetimes. Never forget that."

With an air of gratitude, I pulled her into a tight hug.

Clangorously, the door behind us opened, and Gertrude berated me in German. I didn't understand her words, but her gestures clearly meant, "Get inside my damn shop." The look on Soleil's face told me she'd done her best to detain Gertrude. I squeezed her shoulder as I re-entered the building to let her know I understood.

Slipping past Gertrude, I ducked into the changing room and checked to ensure the dress I was wearing was clean and dry, apologizing profusely while simultaneously changing out of it. Gertrude's German chastisement rose in intensity. I'm pretty sure the small fireball of a woman was throwing me out. I hung the antique lace number on the hanger, and pressed it onto the too-full hook. The pressure knocked a dress from the back to the floor. As I bent down to pick it up, a tingle ran up my arm. I lifted the dress and turned it this way and that, checking it out in the mirror. Fashion insta-lust swept over me.

"I'll take this one," I said, bounding from the changing room and handing the dress to Gertrude.

"Aren't you going to try it on?" Michelle asked.

"Gertrude will need measurements," Soleil said.

"I'm feeling lucky. I'll try it on at home. If I need any adjustments, I'll call."

Lips pursed, Gertrude shook her head. "No returns," she said, suddenly speaking accent-free English.

I nodded. "I'll take it."

She rang me up in record time and zipped the dress into a vinyl bag. "Six thousand."

"Okay."

The girls looked at me like I was insane, and maybe I was. Who bought a six thousand-dollar wedding dress without trying it on? Me, that's who.

I grabbed my purchase and led the way out the door. If every decision were this easy, this wedding would be a cinch. We'd just climbed into the back of Soleil's town car when Michelle completely ruined my sense of accomplishment.

"The way you hurled in the alley earlier reminded me of when I had morning sickness with Manny Junior." She snorted. "It's a good thing you know you can't be pregnant."

CHAPTER 2
The Test

Pregnant. *I could be pregnant.* I trudged into my kitchen with my new dress in one hand and a Red Grove pharmacy bag in the other. The first I hung in the hall closet. The second I stared at blankly while images and incantations swirled through my brain. I attempted to make sense of the emotions brewing within me, but couldn't sort them out.

As I stripped out of my winter clothes, my raven familiar, Poe, swept into the room on wide black wings.

"We need to speak, Witchy Woman," Poe said. He landed on the back of the couch.

"What's up?" I asked absently.

"Only that you have still not retrieved *The Book of Light* from the ghost-man Logan's home. May I remind you once again that the rightful place for your magical grimoire is in your attic?"

"Ugh." I tipped forward, conking my head on the kitchen island. "I know. I know. I know." I banged my head in time with the mantra. "I keep texting him, and he's always busy with the restaurant."

"Perhaps pick up a phone? Get off your spell-casting ass and take back what is yours? Grow a spine and stop taking 'later' as an answer?"

"It's not that easy. Logan gave me a key. Rick destroyed the key. Then, in the same conversation as I told Logan about the crushed key, I had to tell him I was engaged. I think I broke his heart."

"More than enough reason to demand your book of magic back," Poe insisted.

"I know. I know. I know." *Bang, bang, bang.* "I'm just hoping if I give him enough time, he'll get over it. I miss his friendship." I straightened, scrubbing my face with my hands.

Poe scrutinized me from head to toe. "This isn't just about *The Book of Light*, is it? As the kids say, what is up, buttercup? You have the pale malaise of a human suffering from the dengue."

"I threw up this morning. Still nauseous."

"The flu, perhaps?" Looking bored, he picked at his feathers with his beak.

I toyed with the corner of the bag on the counter. I was late. Not a lot late. Just about a week. "Can I ask you something?"

Poe shrugged his bird shoulders. "You can ask. I can't guarantee an answer."

"Do you think ... with the candle Rick used ... Do you think he was human? Like entirely human?"

"At the end? When you saved him?" Poe asked.

I nodded.

"As close to human as he could be. He was dying. If you hadn't put out the candle, you'd be up witch creek without a paddle."

The bag rumpled and ripped as I pulled it open and removed the pregnancy test.

"Bloody hell! You think you're pregnant!" Poe covered his beak with one wing.

Mouth gaping like a fish, I tapped the package down on the counter. "I don't know. I mean, I hope not. I haven't been on birth control since Gary, and Rick and I definitely did the sexual healing thing when he was human-like." I raised both eyebrows. "Plus, I'm late and perpetually nauseous."

"You said it yourself. Human-like. Not fully human." Poe gave a cynical snort. "The chances are ..."

I furrowed my brow as I stripped out of my puffy white parka. "What, Poe? You know nothing about the magic of that candle. Are you going to babble off some made-up statistic about the chances I could be preggers? I'll save you the trouble. It doesn't matter if it's one percent or ninety percent, I'm peeing on this stick."

Smugly, I marched into the guest bathroom. I was in there all of thirty seconds before I realized I never used the guest bathroom and marched back out. No toilet paper. With an indignant swagger, I jogged up the stairs to the bathroom off my bedroom, tearing into the box on the way. I tossed the package in my overflowing trash can.

What if I was pregnant? How could I raise a baby when I couldn't even empty my own trash or keep toilet paper in my guest bathroom? Michelle made her own baby food from organic produce. I could barely make a sandwich.

"Please don't let me be pregnant. Please don't let me be pregnant," I chanted as I took the test. I placed it on the back of the toilet while I washed my hands. Two minutes. Two minutes until I would know for sure if my life was over.

Into my bedroom I paced, heart thumping and mind racing. If I were pregnant, I'd have to keep the baby. This would be my only chance to ever have a child with Rick. Would the kid be normal? I was a witch. I had magic in my blood. What if the baby was born with horn stubs? Would electric lights flicker when it cried?

Poe flapped into the room and landed on my dresser. "By the goddess, breathe into a bag or something. You're going to give yourself an aneurism."

I laughed and wiped away the tears in residence on my cheeks. "What are you talking about?" Poe couldn't read my mind, but familiars, by nature, were intuitive of their witch's feelings. It bothered me a little that I couldn't hide what a mess I was about this from him.

"Whatever the outcome, it won't help the situation to have a magical meltdown. In the time I've known you, my worrying witch, in this life and the last, you've been uniquely adaptable."

"Adaptable. Not nurturing or intelligent. Not … parental."

"No one is parental until they become parents. But you've become a great witch in just a few weeks. You could become parental if you had to. You are … resourceful."

I plopped down on my bed. "I could learn to cook."

"Or hire a cook," Poe said under his breath.

My line of sight followed the trail of clothes on the floor to the dust on my dresser. "Also, someone to clean." Rick had money thanks to some wise investments in the early 1900's. What better use for it than improving his child's environment?

"Exactly. If by some miracle you are 'preggers,' as you say, you shall overcome." He blinked at me slowly.

I nodded, relaxing a little.

Poe rolled his eyes toward the ceiling. "It would, of course, be helpful if we knew the nature of the candle Rick used. What did he tell you about the source?"

"Nothing. Every time I mention it, he puts me off. On his deathbed he told me it came from Salem's Hecate, but whenever I ask for details, he changes the subject."

"Hmm. I'm afraid Salem's Witch has a reputation that precedes her." Poe narrowed his eyes like he was trying to choose his words carefully.

"Spill it." My demand went unanswered when the timer on my phone chimed. I tapped the screen to stop the alarm. "Hold that thought. Time to learn if I have a bun in the oven."

On shaky legs, I traversed the formidable space between my bed and the toilet. Lifting the test from the porcelain with both hands, my eyes focused on the little round plastic window. One line for not pregnant, two lines for pregnant. Simple. I blinked. Blinked again. Then, I tossed it in the garbage. It rolled off the top of the heap and clanked on the floor.

"Well?" Poe asked.

"You were right. Not preggers. Probably the flu."

"Ah. All is well then." He bobbed his head joyfully.

"Yeah." My spacey gaze found the gnarled branch of the oak tree outside my window. "Hey, Poe, I was up really late last night and I'm still not feeling the best. I think I'm going to lie down. Do you need me to let you out?"

"No. I've been using the flap in the attic window."

I groaned. He'd shattered a glass pane a few weeks ago, and I'd never replaced it. What was the point? He needed a way to go in and out during the day and the flap of plastic worked. I had more important worries, even if it did mean my heating bill was atrocious.

"I'm going to take a nap," I said. I removed my sweater and leaned Nightshade against the corner near my closet.

A raven's eyes are beady and black, but Poe's brimmed with pity. He transformed into a small black dog and curled up on the braided rug in front of my bed.

Instinctively, I knew he wouldn't leave until I was asleep. Poe could be a pain in the ass, but he was a good familiar.

As I climbed under my quilt and began to shed new tears, I took comfort in Poe's understanding presence. I'd just lost my last chance at a real family. For as much as I didn't want the test to be positive, at the moment, the negative was far, far worse. I closed my eyes, and slipped off to sleep, trying my best to forget losing the precious thing I'd never even had.

* * * * *

"*Mi cielo? Mi cielo?*" Rick's voice brought me out of a deep slumber, his hand rubbing my shoulder gently as he perched on the side of my bed. Maybe I was getting sick. Everything felt heavy. My body pressed into the mattress like I'd gained four hundred pounds. I struggled to shake the paralysis of sleep from my limbs.

"Hi." With some effort, I rolled onto my back so I could see him better. Black wavy hair that curled below his ears, gray eyes, full lips. Even exhausted and flu-ridden, the sight of him lit my fire. "What are you doing here?"

"I fixed your window."

"You fixed my window?"

"The one in the attic. I installed a pet door for Poe."

From the direction of the dresser came an offended caw. Poe was bird-shaped again. "Veritably, I am not a pet," he said.

Rick turned toward me so only I could see him roll his eyes. "They were all out of doors specifically for magical familiars," he said under his breath.

"Thank you," I said. "My heating bill has been ridonkulous lately."

"I began to worry when you did not wake. My work wasn't quiet."

I glanced toward the window. Late afternoon daylight streamed in, casting light against the far wall. I tapped my phone on the nightstand. Four o'clock. "Sorry. I'm not feeling well."

He placed a palm on my forehead, the tips of his fingers brushing my hair. "Do you need blood?" His wrist hovered in front of my lips.

"No." I threaded my fingers into his and lowered his offered arm to my chest. "Just tired, and I was nauseous this morning. I'm better now though."

"I discovered something on your bathroom floor." From my bedside table, he lifted the pregnancy test. "Can you explain this?" The concern in his voice tugged at my heartstrings. I hadn't intended to tell him about this afternoon, but I felt the truth press against the inside of my teeth, an unrelieved pressure. After all we'd been through, why keep secrets?

"I thought I might be pregnant with your baby," I blurted. The confession slammed awkwardly into the space between us.

The corners of his mouth twitched, and his eyes crinkled at the corners. "*Mi cielo*, I explained to you, I am unable to produce children. Immortals are sterile," he said kindly. He brushed my hair back from my face.

"The candle made you human. Maybe not completely, but I thought, maybe ..." The waterworks started again, and I turned my face away.

He placed a finger under my chin and returned my gaze to his. "You *wanted* to be pregnant?"

I sighed. Sitting up, I tried to put it into words. "Not really. Not initially anyway. But then I started to think about it. Now is not the best time, but when is? I just feel like I missed our only chance."

"If it is important to you, we can explore alternatives once we are married. Although, I beseech you to consider the inevitable hardships of raising a human child. We will live forever. Our child will not."

His point wasn't lost on me. Still, I picked at the corner of the quilt. "I was thinking, what if we bought another candle." I shrugged. "When we are ready, we could try again. We could make you human temporarily. I could use magic to improve our odds."

His face fell. "No."

"Why not?"

"I cannot obtain another." Eyes shifting away from me, he moved to stand.

"Why not?" I demanded.

With a groan, he placed his hands on his hips and shook his head. "Isn't it enough to adopt? Perhaps a supernatural infant?"

I shook my head. "Don't change the subject. Why can't we get another candle?" I gave him my strongest I-will-not-let-this-go look.

He sighed. "Will you walk with me? The story is not a simple one."

I nodded. "Give me a minute."

Ten minutes later, hair and teeth brushed properly for the first time all day, I wrapped myself up in my puffy white snowman parka and followed Rick into the woods across from my house. A thick layer of snow crunched beneath our boots as we wound between the dormant trees. The sky above was gray but bright. I couldn't see the sun behind the clouds.

"I need to tell you about the candle," Rick began. "When I saw you kiss Logan—"

"*He* kissed me," I clarified.

"So I have learned, but at the time, given the circumstances, I was convinced that you would choose him in my place if given the opportunity."

"I see."

"I visited Salem's Witch, Tabetha. She comforted me."

I stopped abruptly, my women's intuition perking ears at his words. "Define *comforted*."

He sighed, ignoring my request. "I've known her for hundreds of years. She offered to help me. To free me."

"She sold you the candle."

"She made me the candle. There has only ever been one."

Holy shit. This witch made Rick the candle from scratch. A custom spell was a lot of work to do as a favor or at any price. "How close were you two?" Jealousy crept into my voice, and I saw a muscle in Rick's jaw twitch. Oh my God, had he had an affair? "How close, Rick?"

He looked away. I had a feeling he was going to say more, but at that moment, the sound of splintering wood demanded our attention. I squinted, leaning forward to get a better look at the tree nearest us. "Is that—?"

A face formed in the bark, fine boned and feminine. The eyes popped open, sending me jumping back with a yelp. Rick barely flinched.

"She is coming," the bark lips said, and then a shoulder burst from the wood followed by a woman's body.

"Tree sprite," Rick whispered.

"Obviously," I deadpanned.

Once out of her tree, her skin took on the grain of birch wood; her hair, oak bark; and her dress, layers of green leaves. She bolted past us dancing, leaping, and twirling between the branches. She brought company. Sprites hatched all around us, giggling and bounding between the trees.

"She is coming. She is coming," they sang as they flit by.

"Isn't it early for them to awaken?" I asked Rick. It was twenty degrees outside. I wasn't familiar with tree sprites, but I was fairly sure they should be sleeping when the trees were sleeping. In fact, I was almost positive Soleil had told me as much when explaining why her fae cousins hadn't come to our aid during the winter solstice.

Rick didn't answer me. His brows knit, and his head dropped forward. I followed his line of sight and watched the snow melt beneath our boots.

"What the fuck is going on?" It was like spring was tearing through winter from the inside out.

"She's come," he said.

"Who?"

"Allow me to introduce myself, *sister*."

I turned toward the potent voice. A tall figure in a hooded cloak stood in a warm space of her making. A large scarab brooch fastened the cloth at her neck, the same scarab beetle I'd seen imprinted on the candle Rick was trying to tell me about. Her boots were tall. Her skirt, red leather. A black corset emphasized her sleek figure. As her long, graceful fingers brushed her hood back from her raven-black hair, my mouth fell open. The woman was stunning. She looked like Cleopatra—dramatically dark with flawless olive skin.

Her full red lips completed her introduction. "I am Tabetha."

CHAPTER 3
The Debt

"What brings you here, Tabetha?" Rick's voice was firm but not threatening. It resonated with professional politeness.

I was too taken aback to speak. Tabetha was everything I wasn't. To my short and curvy, she was tall and lanky, like a ballerina. I was blonde; she was dark. In her hand, she cradled a jagged twig that glowed purple at the tip. A wand. She had a magic wand. I didn't have a wand. Why did she get a wand and I didn't?

Pointing the purple glow in Rick's direction, Tabetha stated her purpose in a voice thick with power and lacking the politeness Rick had shown her. "We had an agreement, caretaker. I've come for payment." Her eyes flicked toward me. "When the magic of my candle called to me, I expected you to seek me out, as we agreed. I did not think I'd have to retrieve you."

Rick shifted a fraction of an inch, placing himself between Tabetha and me. "I apologize for the confusion. The spell was not completed. I am as I was before."

Tabetha stepped closer, sending the tree sprites swirling and leaping in the warm spring air that followed her. "That was not our agreement. Our arrangement was clear: if you used the candle, I would receive payment."

Finally, I found my voice. "What the hell is going on?"

"*Mi cielo*—"

"Sister," Tabetha interrupted, holding her wand hand up to Rick. I cringed at her familial label for me. While it was true the goddess Hecate was the mother of our magical selves, I had a family, and Tabetha was not part of it.

"What do you want here, *sister*?" I said the last through my teeth, like a curse. She didn't seem to notice.

"It is a shame such awkward circumstances have brought about our first meeting, Grateful Knight, but you should know your caretaker promised himself to me in return for the use of my candle, and I am here to collect." Power rolled off her, sending goose bumps marching across my arms.

My insides twisted at her use of my name, again an unearned familiarity in her tone. "What exactly do you mean by 'he promised himself'?" I asked.

"As my caretaker," she said with a throaty laugh. "Once he was human, I planned to claim him as my own."

My jaw dropped. I stared at her, waiting for the punch line. When she didn't say anything else, I turned to Rick.

He shook his head and faced her head-on. "You misunderstood. I never promised to be your caretaker. I never promised anything beyond helping you manage your new territory."

"And did you think you would do that as a human?" she snapped, voice rising in pitch.

"Yes," Rick said firmly.

"Well then, we have a problem. I am owed a great debt." Tabetha looked pissed.

"The contract is null, as the spell was not completed. I did not use it as intended," Rick stated.

Tabetha's perfectly shaped red lips pulled into a grimace and ripples of power blasted like sound waves from her body. Crocuses exploded from the ground, growing in fast forward. The atmosphere became warm enough that I was tempted to unzip my coat. But when the goddamn tree branches started to reach for us with their gnarled branch hands, I knew we were in trouble. We'd practically been transported to the dark forest in *Snow White* or the *Wizard of Oz*. It was freaking me out.

"Are you suggesting that I am owed nothing for my effort?" Tabetha seethed. "Are you going back on your word?" Her eyes burned into him. Worse, the look was familiar. Tabetha was a woman scorned. She had feelings for Rick. *Crap.*

"I will return the remaining candle to you," Rick said. This time he looked away from her when he spoke, as if he were ashamed. As if he recognized that he owed her something.

With a wave of her wand, Tabetha made it clear she did not accept his answer. She knocked Rick on his ass. Rick's eyes bled to black, and his beast exploded from his skin. The winged creature Rick shifted into had the scaly body of a dragon with tufts of hair protruding from the points of his ears and between his scales. Shifted, he was big—T-rex big—with jaws that could swallow a human-sized creature whole. His mere presence was foreboding.

I assumed his change would be a conversation ender. I was wrong.

One twist of Tabetha's wrist, and a blast of purple light hit Rick's beast. By force, his beast transformed, his bones bending and snapping painfully until he was human again.

"Rick!" I ran to his side. He'd collapsed to the ground, shocked and disoriented by the quick change. What a bitch! Fine, Tabetha didn't get the payment she expected for her magic, but she didn't need to get violent about it. I stepped in front of Rick and pointed a finger at her. "You say my caretaker made an agreement with you regarding the candle and that the price was himself?"

She nodded. "I have a contract signed in his blood."

Signed in blood! I glared at Rick. I desperately wanted an explanation, but now was not the time. "There's been a mistake," I said. "Rick had no right to make that agreement with you. As my caretaker, his soul is mine and not his to give." I glanced at Rick, who gave me a ghost of a smile. "However, I also understand that you worked hard on the candle's enchantment and deserve some compensation. What price would you consider suitable payment?"

She popped out her hip and shifted her jaw from side to side as she considered me. Finally, she avoided my question altogether. "Are you denying our agreement, Enrique? Are you denying that you begged me for release from your connection to her?" Tabetha's shrill voice made the surrounding tree sprites clutch at the bases of their throats and leer at Rick in silent union.

He looked her directly in the eye. "It was a mistake."

"Mistake or not, you are mine." Power, thick and palpable, rolled off her skin. The trees swayed, reaching for our heads. A gnarled branch gripped my bicep, bark digging in. Another wrapped around Rick's neck and squeezed. The tree sprites growled and closed in, wrestling Rick toward Tabetha. I tried to help him, but the goddamned forest restrained me. Pain tore through my ankle as a thorny vine sprouted from the earth and lassoed my calf.

That was it. This bitch had to go.

I reached for Nightshade with my one free hand. She wasn't there. *Fuck.* I'd forgotten to strap on my blade after my nap. She was still in the corner of my bedroom. "You can't have him," I yelled. "He's still *my* caretaker."

She ignored me. Rick's skin bubbled as the sprites dragged him toward her. Deep grooves formed in the dirt where his heels dug in. But Tabetha's magic was keeping him from shifting, and the sprites overpowered him by sheer numbers.

Without really thinking about it, my fear and adrenaline took over. As it happened on the night of the solstice, when my magic saved me from Bathory's vamps, the power came naturally, without an uttered word or any effort at all. The air sang to me, connecting to my will as if it were an extension of my body. Instinct and intuition took hold.

Wind and ice blew up between Rick and Tabetha, a hurricane of stinging snow and dropping temperatures. The tree sprites dropped Rick and sprinted for their trees, limbs sluggish. Rick staggered back toward me. With a little effort, I directed the storm to form a barrier between the two of us and Tabetha. Snow caked the ground, burying any sign of the warmth Tabetha had brought with her. The reaching limbs of the trees lost their animated properties and recoiled, falling back asleep in the dropping temperature. I rolled my shoulders, relieved to be free of their grip, then yanked my ankle from the dying thorns.

"Storm's a-brewin'," I said.

Tabetha narrowed her eyes at me. "Perhaps, sister, but I never did mind about the weather. You underestimate me, baby witch." She raised her wand. A blast of heat plowed into me, dissolving my storm, the snow, and the cold. I cried out as my power was forced back into my chest. Rick jumped between us again and held up his hands to her, but Tabetha was just getting started.

A new branch of thorns wound up my leg, shredding what was left of my pants. I howled in pain as thorns wrapped around my waist, sliced through my jacket, and scored my skin. When the vine reached my neck, I tried to turn up the volume on my magic to spare my trachea. The winter storm responded but not before the vine took hold. Warm and wet flowed over my throat and down my chest. I reached up and dug my fingers in, gasping for air. The plant tightened.

"Stop," Rick said. His eyes locked onto Tabetha's. I watched something pass between them and my heart broke. The look had meaning. The look had history. "Please."

"Do you give yourself to me?" Tabetha demanded, the power in her voice reverberating.

I strained to tell Rick no, but I couldn't catch my breath. My wheezing gasps had stopped, and nothing but gagging sounds came from my efforts to breathe. Black spots danced in the corners of my vision. My lungs burned. I slumped against the vines, and the thorns dug in.

"Stay with me," Rick said frantically, clawing at the vine around my neck. It was no use. Death was as close as a lover, and my magic was reduced to a faint and useless breeze.

And then, a miracle.

Thunder clapped above us—not my doing—and a sheet of lightning plowed into the ground near my feet. The vine retracted a fraction of an inch, and my lungs worked to pull in a trickle of oxygen. The earth shook violently, echoing the raging storm above and knocking Tabetha backward. Rick grabbed my shoulders to steady me, although he didn't need to, the thorns held me up like barbed wire. With fear in his eyes, he looked at the sky above and the ground below. Rick was rattled. I'd never seen anything shake him like this.

A booming female voice said, "You do not have permission." I could not place the source. It seemed to come from everything, every direction.

The thorny vine withdrew as if my blood were toxic, sinking into the ground from whence it came. I fell forward on hands and knees, wheezing as new air penetrated my pinched throat and filled my lungs. Rick's hands were on me in an instant, his wrist thrust between my teeth. I drank quickly and willingly of his blood. As soon as I was well enough, I got to my feet.

"I am due blood!" Tabetha raged toward the thunderous sky.

Another lightning bolt landed between us.

With a pained sigh, she straightened herself and fixed me with a threatening glare. "It appears Mother wants you alive. Very well. An alternative price for a caretaker requires some thought. It will not be insignificant. Both of you will come to my home when I call you forth. I will tell you my price then."

"Your home? No. A neutral location," I rasped.

Her dark eyes flashed. "Mother may spare your life, but even she will not deny me my due, sister."

I had nothing left. I could barely hold myself up, even after Rick's blood. Tabetha wasn't going to back down.

I nodded my acquiescence.

She sneered at Rick, her mouth twisting in disgust as if he repulsed her. With a flick of her wand, she dissolved into thin air, the overwhelming scent of roses lingering in her wake.

As soon as she was gone, I turned the full force of my stare on Rick. "Start. Talking."

CHAPTER 4
Tabetha

"Tabetha came to my aid in your absence. I couldn't have managed our ward for so long on my own without her help," Rick said. The snow began to fall again, this time on its own. My magic was spent, and my chest ached.

"In my absence?"

"After you died but before you returned. Twenty-two years is a long time."

"When you say she *helped you* …" My mind immediately went to sex. Caretakers fed on sex and blood. "You told me you'd never had sex with anyone but me."

He jerked back as if I'd struck him. "I did not have sex with Tabetha."

"Then why did she look at you like that? You obviously have a history. The way she addressed you, it was almost possessive."

"I can explain, but come. You need to sit down." With a sweep of his hand, he suggested we return to my house, and I agreed. The snow descended in earnest, big fluffy flakes that collected on our hair and shoulders. I followed him across the street.

"As I was saying, Tabetha helped in your absence with particularly difficult cases. A caretaker's magic is effective against the supernatural, but things become difficult when humans are involved. Some work requires a witch."

"For example?"

"A demon possession near Manchester around a decade ago. Tabetha had to expel the demon so that my beast could sentence it to hell. I can't separate the natural from the supernatural."

"I see. So Tabetha helped you because, as Salem's Witch, she's the closest Hecate to our ward."

"Not exactly. There was another—Polina, the Smugglers' Notch Witch—but she refused me. She was reclusive and wouldn't leave her ward. More recently, she's gone missing entirely."

"Missing?"

"Tabetha has been covering her territory for months. That was why she said she needed me, to manage Polina's ward. At the time, Tabetha was sure she would be given permanent power over Polina's realm."

"Why permanent? Polina will come back, right? If the Vermont witch is dead, she'll regenerate like I did."

He shook his head, holding my door open for me.

I stripped off my torn winter clothes and flopped down on the floral sofa. I didn't even bother attempting a seated position. I stretched across the cushions ragdoll-limbed and closed my eyes.

"Polina did not have a caretaker, which should have made her immortal, but unfortunately, even immortals can be neutralized."

My eyes popped open. "Wait, wait, wait a minute." I spread my hands in the air above my chest. "Explain. I thought most Hecates had caretakers."

Just then, Poe flapped down the staircase, swooped around the banister, and landed on the kitchen island. "Caretakers are rare, Witcherella. Very few witches would give up their own immortality for the sake of another."

I paused and let that sink in. During my first lifetime, when I'd put a piece of my soul into Rick, I'd made him immortal, but doing so had meant that my body would suffer death. Why had I done that instead of keeping the immortality for myself? Because I loved Rick and was afraid the angry mob that burned me at the stake would turn on him next. Only now did it occur to me that true love was unusual. Another witch might not split her soul to save her lover. Tabetha and Polina did not have caretakers. They were true immortals. They'd kept all their power for themselves.

"So Tabetha was an old friend and the acting witch of both territories. How does the candle come into play?"

"After I saw you with Logan, I went to see her. The times we'd worked together she proved a uniquely powerful witch. I told her you wished to dissolve your commitment to me. Who could blame you, Grateful? You are a new person. I thought I was doing the right thing by giving you a choice."

As much as I wanted to deny it, I couldn't. It was true. Before the candle, I'd felt trapped by my relationship with Rick. Choosing him in this life had made a difference to me. Still, I was furious. "I did *not* wish to dissolve our commitment," I snapped. "You had no right claiming to know my feelings without talking to me first. Your jealousy almost cost you your soul."

"I'm sorry." Rick turned his head away. "I could not bear to see you in Logan's arms."

I held up my hand. "Do not make this about him or me. You could have faced me. We could have talked out our problems. Instead, you did something incredibly dumb and dangerous."

He met my eyes and nodded his acceptance of my accusation.

"What happened next?"

"She agreed to help me." Again, his eyes shifted. He was keeping something from me.

"It wasn't that simple, was it?" I glanced at Poe, who quickly became obsessed with cleaning his feathers while clearly eavesdropping. Nice.

The muscles in Rick's jaw clenched. "No."

"Just tell me," I said softly. "It's done. All we can do is manage the consequences."

"She kissed me." The words tumbled over his lips all at once, as if he'd released them on one shaky breath. "The terms of her aid were wrapped in a proposition that I join her in Salem after I was free. True, she needed help managing her new territory, but the implication of her lips was that the partnership would go beyond business."

I cupped the base of my head. Where had all the air gone? Each breath stung and my eyes burned with the need to cry.

"You intended to take her up on her offer. You intended to leave me," I stammered.

"Never." He took a step toward me, but I leapt from the sofa and dodged backward, evading his touch.

"Then what *was* your intention, Rick?" I asked through my teeth.

"I intended to die," he said flatly. "Why do you think I lit the candle before our battle with the nekomata and Bathory? I knew what it would do. I battled your demons knowing they would kill me and set both of us free."

My gaze snapped to his. "But ... then you deceived her. Tabetha believed you were giving yourself to her to be her caretaker. You led her on. She was a victim of your vindictive suicide."

All at once his features hardened, and his soul seemed to leave the room. The man in front of me was an ice sculpture resembling my beloved. "Yes."

Lips trembling, I tried to focus. "Assuming you don't want to give yourself to her now, how do we get you out of this?"

Rick grimaced. His irises had gone black again, the beast coming to the surface. "Of course I do not wish to give myself to her," he spat. "I love you. You must consider the circumstances. Unrequited love is a particularly painful torture, Grateful. You were doling out that cruelty in spades."

"So this is my fault?" I said.

Poe chose that moment to interrupt. "May I propose the two of you focus on the problem at hand? The sun has almost set. Time to punch the clock."

My familiar was right. Rick and I had work to do tonight. "What was in the contract you signed? She said you signed in blood."

"I don't remember. I never thought it would matter."

"Well, it matters now."

The space between us widened into a black hole that sucked the life from the room. I'd thought he'd cheated on me, but in some ways this was worse. His jealousy had put both our lives in jeopardy. I didn't know what Tabetha would ask for to settle the debt, but I was willing to bet it would be no small thing. The worst part that I couldn't blame her. Rick had used her. She was as much a victim in all this as any of us.

A vibration from my back pocket pulled me out of the tense moment. My phone. I brought it to my ear and tapped the screen to answer the call. "Grateful Knight."

"Grateful, it's Silas."

Silas worked as a detective for the Carlton City PD. He was also a werewolf and dating my fae friend, Soleil. He rarely contacted me to chat though. A call from Silas usually meant a police case involving a missing or dead human by supernatural hands. "Is this call personal or professional?"

"Unfortunately, professional. There's been a murder. I need you and Rick down here right away."

I glanced at Rick and mouthed "Silas" pointing at my phone. "Sure. Hit me with the address," I said.

"You won't need an address. You've been here before and under circumstances I'm sure you'll remember."

"Where?"

"The Thames Theater."

CHAPTER 5
Murder

The Thames Theater was the current living quarters of the Carlton City free vampire coven. A little more than a month ago, the coven's leader, Julius, had almost drained me dry before Rick blasted a hole through the place and saved my life.

"They've renovated," I said as we pulled into the parking lot near the location of my rescue.

"Amazing what the undead can accomplish when their existence is at stake." He climbed from the Tesla and opened my door for me. It was a completely unnecessary gesture—I could open my own door. Hell, I could kick the fucker open if I wanted. But as someone born in the 1600's, it was a habit Rick wasn't keen to give up. Still, I avoided his hand as I rose in the small space between him and the door. There was unfinished business between us.

"Thanks for coming," Silas said from the entrance to the Thames. I navigated between the police barricades to join him. The theater was a recreation of a medieval castle, all old world stone and rough-hewn timber. Silas was a decent-sized guy, supernatural to boot, and he had to lean his shoulder in to hold open the front door.

"What's going on?" I asked, giving him a quick, one-armed hug.

"Girl was murdered. I need your help. Follow me." He led us through the foyer and down a back stairwell to another heavy wooden door crisscrossed with police tape. "Brace yourself. This isn't pretty."

He didn't have to tell me twice; I could smell the blood. I glanced at Rick, then nodded that I understood. The detective opened the door.

The only reason I could tell the victim was a woman was that her breasted torso was semi-intact at the center of the room. Her head and limbs were detached, although I saw the length of an arm near the foot of the silver bedspread. The wood floor was saturated with blood, the top of the puddle already coagulated, thick and shiny.

"This is Julius's room," I said. "I didn't recognize it from the hall. I was unconscious when he brought me here."

Silas rubbed his chin. "Are you okay to do this?"

"I'm fine." I stepped over the threshold.

"Don't touch anything without gloves," Silas warned.

I answered with a tip of my head, my lips tightly closed against the force of the stench around me. Rick moved in the opposite direction with the quick, graceful steps of the immortal. Slowly, carefully, I traversed the kill on heeled boots that clacked on the wooden floor.

Silas hovered near the door, hands in the pockets of his suit jacket.

"Why would he rip her apart like this? Why here?" I asked. "Julius is smarter than this."

"Good question," Silas said. "One my department has as well."

I stepped deeper into the room. I found the woman's bleached-blonde head under the bar where Julius kept his Scotch. The amber liquid I remembered him offering me was in a crystal decanter resting on the dark wood. "Who called this in?" I asked Silas.

"Vamp named Gary. He claims he found her like this."

I rolled my eyes. Great. My ex-boyfriend-turned-vampire. Was this Punch Grateful in the Gut Day? "Where is Julius? Have you questioned him?"

"Missing. Gary said Julius hasn't been seen or heard from since this happened."

"Do you think he ripped her head off and then ran for the hills?"

"I don't think anything yet. I'm investigating. Unfortunately, vampires don't leave fingerprints, which is why I called you. Frankly, I'm not sure we can trust Gary."

"I am certain we cannot trust Gary," I said adamantly.

Rick rubbed his chin. "There is too much blood."

"I know. It's gross." I covered my mouth with my hand.

"No." He shook his head and spread his hands toward the puddle near our feet. "A vampire perpetrator would not leave this much blood."

I looked at the room again with new eyes. When Julius drank from me, he hadn't spilled a drop, and when Rick saved me, he'd said I was ghost white, a few quarts shy of a full load. It was hard for me to believe an ancient vampire like Julius would leave this mess behind.

"The way she's torn apart, it looks more like the work of an ogre," Rick said.

Silas jotted something down in a notebook he pulled from his pocket.

"What are you writing?" I asked.

"Just some questions to ask Gary later."

"Yeah, I might have my own questions." If I knew Gary, he wouldn't tell Silas everything. My eyes fell on the bar. There were two glasses offset near the edge, one empty aside from a dried streak of amber at the bottom, the other a quarter full of Scotch. I glanced at the woman's head under the bar, then back at the Scotch-filled glass. "Looks like our victim wasn't a drinker."

"No lipstick on either glass," Silas said. "And there is definitely lipstick on the corpse."

Rick glanced in our direction and continued searching the room.

Next to the crystal decanter and behind the glasses, a plate with the remnants of some kind of flaky, fruit-filled pastry cradled a fork. "Looks like she had dessert though," I said. "Unless Julius ate the whole thing himself." A smudge of purple fruit with green seeds trailed across the plate. I caught myself wondering what flavor it was and realized I still hadn't eaten today. No wonder I felt weak and nauseous.

"Vampires don't usually go for sweets," Silas said.

"There's no lipstick on the fork either. Although I know plenty of women who can eat without losing their lipstick."

It was a common misconception that vampires only drank blood. They could eat; they just didn't need to. Nothing tasted better to a vampire than blood, so for Julius to finish an entire pastry when he had human flesh in the same room would be rare. Then again, I knew Julius had an affinity for expensive Scotch, so maybe he was the exception to the rule.

The entire situation struck me as odd. Julius had poured his guest a drink. They'd likely shared dessert. So when did he rip her apart? And why?

Carefully picking my way around the room, I found the victim's legs under the desk. "An arm is missing," I said.

"It is here." Rick pointed to the space between the headboard and the end table.

The path Rick took to reach the arm was narrow, and he returned the way he'd come to make room for me. When I saw what he wanted me to see, I frowned. Scotch and glass littered the space around the fingers in the crevice between the headboard and the wall. It was impossible to see from the door or even from the foot of the bed.

"A third glass," I said.

Silas's bushy eyebrows collided over his nose. He traversed the room to see for himself. I backed out of the spot and let him view what we'd discovered. After a long, hard look, he turned on his heel and caught my eye. "Grateful, why didn't you sentence Julius to the hellmouth when you had the chance? He tried to kill you. You had every right to judge him."

I startled slightly at the question. "Julius also saved me. He rescued me from Bathory, twice: once when she was torturing me, and once when she tried to sacrifice me. Honestly, I think the draining part was mostly an accident. Don't get me wrong, Julius is a vampire, totally driven by appetite, but he's also an important political figure in this coven, one who has benefitted me in the past. I thought it was a better idea to keep him around."

With a glance toward Rick, Silas ran thick fingers through his bushy brown hair. Even in his human form, his wolfy features were obvious—untamable eyebrows and perpetual stubble. "And you are absolutely right. Julius was the only vampire in Carlton City strong enough to stand up to Bathory."

"Where are you going with this, Silas?"

"Have you made any progress tracking down Bathory since we last spoke?"

"No," I scoffed. Was this an indictment on my abilities as a Hecate? "We've searched the entire city. I have a spell around the Mill Wheel; she can't return without me knowing. She's on the lam."

Silas bobbed his head. "I'm not interrogating you, okay? I just needed to make sure."

I retreated to the space near the door where all of us could stand without disturbing the evidence. "Why? Do you think Bathory's behind this?"

"I hope not." Silas held up one finger and pressed his ear against the door. After a second of listening, he began again. "When Bathory ran, she gave up control of her coven. The vampires she abandoned joined this one, Julius's coven."

"And now Julius is gone," Rick said.

"Exactly."

"Maybe Bathory exacted her revenge," I said.

"Makes sense. If she wants to return to power, she needs numbers to protect her—a vampire army. With the combination of the two covens, she stands to gain those numbers."

I laughed. "It's not as though she can just walk back in here and take over. Several of Julius's vamps ended up here after escaping her tyranny. She has a terrible reputation for torturing her own vamps. They hate her." I didn't mention that my ex-boyfriend Gary was one of them. There was no way he'd allow Bathory to take Julius's place without a fight. "Believe me, if Bathory was anywhere near this place, vampires would be ratting her out."

"You would think so, but make no mistake, our sources say that Bathory's ruthlessness is missed amongst the strongest and most brutal of vampires. It seems Julius has a reputation for following your rules. He doesn't allow feeding on humans without consent. Bathory, on the other hand, encouraged and enabled it." Silas shifted his feet and pointed emphatically at the floor. "If Julius does not return by the next full moon, his leadership will be challenged. Vampires will compete for his title and a new leader will rise from the ranks. It's in our best interest that the leader chosen is from Julius's camp."

The lesser of two evils. Silas was right. If Bathory's vamps took over the free coven, it would lay the groundwork for her return, and with a coven this size, Rick and I might not be able to get close enough to take her down. "How can I help?"

"Find Julius," Silas said. "And Bathory."

"I'm on it," I said.

Rick took my elbow. "*We* are on it."

His words burned. While I loved Rick, learning that he'd played Tabetha to get what he wanted didn't set well with me. He'd effectively given up on our relationship without talking to me about it. I hadn't had a chance to digest the storm of feelings I'd experienced today, but just now, that one tiny word *we* grated on my nerves.

"I need to talk to Gary," I said.

"Sun's down. I think he's gone for the night," Silas said.

I frowned, cursing under my breath. "Where's his room?"

"Down the hall and to the right." Silas motioned with his head.

With a nod in Silas's direction, I muscled the door open and moved into the hall. Rick followed. I stopped short.

"Hey, maybe you should run patrol while I'm following up on Gary. If I catch up to him, he'll be more open with me because of our history."

Ricks expression hardened. "I don't like you seeing him alone."

I scoffed. "You of all people have no right to pull the jealousy card with me tonight."

"Grateful ..."

Blood boiling, I opened the floodgates. "No. Don't try to downplay it, Rick. You can say you loved me, and I believe it. You can say you obtained the candle because you thought it was what I wanted, and I believe it. But what I don't believe is that you weren't attracted to her. I could see it in your eyes. And on some level, it made you feel like more of a man to know that another Hecate wanted you. You led her on. As much as you say you knew you would probably die, you also knew there was a chance you might survive, and you would have been happy to go to her if it hadn't worked out between us, like some supernatural consolation prize."

He staggered backward, eyes black and joints rolling unnaturally. For a second, I thought he was going to shift right there in the hallway. Instead, he seemed to fight the visceral response—lips parting, panting his way back to human. When he stepped toward me again, he looked strangely calm. He met my gaze, which must have been blazing with anger, and flashed a sad smile. "Isn't that exactly what you did to me with Logan?"

"Wha—?" It was my turn to step back. "How dare you turn this around on *me*!"

I had more to say, but with an expression bordering on pity, Rick broke apart into a dark mist and blew away. I hated when he did that. I slammed my palm into the stone wall and cursed.

"Everything okay out here?" Silas asked from the door to Julius's room.

I nodded. "Yeah, Silas."

His head disappeared again. I turned on my heel and trotted toward Gary's room. Or maybe I was running away. If I was, it didn't work. The heaviness in my chest came right along with me.

CHAPTER 6
Gary

Gary's room was surprisingly large for a newbie vamp, and I was surprised to find his penchant for literature had followed him into his undead existence. An entire wall of his chamber was filled with books, mostly hardcovers of the classics. Bram Stoker's *Dracula* caught my eye, and I laughed out loud. A poster of Virginia Woolf hung on the wall with the quote, "There is no denying the wild horse in us."

"Looking for something?" My ex-boyfriend-turned-vamp stood in the doorway to his room, green eyes bulging slightly like a nocturnal animal.

"Hey. I thought you were out for the night."

"I was. I circled back to see if you were here. I thought you might be looking for me."

"I need to ask you some questions."

"Thought so. Do you mind if we do this outside? I'm stuck in here all day."

I nodded. Vampires slept in coffins, even if they were disguised as fashionably decorated bedrooms with bookshelves. I followed him out of his room, up the stairs, and out the heavy front door. Cold night air slapped me in the face. I grimaced. Winter and I were officially at odds.

"Where's Julius, Gary?" I asked. "Did he run after he murdered that girl?"

Gary stopped short just outside the Thames. "First of all, if he'd killed the girl, I would never answer that question. Julius has been good to me."

"But you don't think he did it."

"I know he didn't."

"How?"

He started walking again. I buttoned my black wool coat (a poor replacement for my shredded white Patagonia) and shoved my hands in my pockets. Gary's light jacket was hanging open. As a vampire, he didn't need it, so it was just for show.

"I know who the dead girl is," he began. "Her name was Calliope. She was a regular with Julius."

"Fill me in on what you consider a *regular*."

"Calliope was a local singer and songwriter living on a shoestring. Unlike a lot of the artists around here, she was clean. Her gigs were usually at night, which meant she slept during the day. Julius gave her money in exchange for her blood about once a month."

"That's it?"

"Any more frequently and he could have killed her. There's a reason the Red Cross makes you wait eight weeks between blood donations. Four was pushing it, but Julius had it down to a science."

"You mean, he was an expert at keeping her alive."

"A pillar of restraint."

"Funny, he didn't show much restraint when his fangs were in my neck."

Gary frowned. "It's your blood. He said it tasted of honey and sunlight and gave him an orgasm."

I slapped my hand over my eyes. "Oh my God. He said that?"

"I can smell it all the way over here, pulsing under your skin." His fangs dropped a little when he smiled. "It's part of the reason I wanted to be outside."

"Gross. Put your fangs away, Gary. That is so not happening."

The offending teeth snapped back into his upper jaw. An awkward silence crowded between us while flashes of my history with Gary danced through my head like proverbial sugarplums. It was hard to imagine we'd been an item. He was a shadow of his former human self, and as much as I'd tried to let it go, I harbored negative feelings about our breakup.

We turned right on Main, heading toward the boardwalk near the river. Thankfully, Gary broke the silence. "I'm not lying to you when I say Julius would never drain Calliope. He had a longstanding relationship with her. It's hard to find a willing blood donor who will keep what we are in total confidence. Why would he mess with that?"

"She wasn't drained. She was ripped apart."

"Another good point. A vampire would never waste the blood."

"Unless he accidentally killed her and ripped her apart to hide the evidence."

"There's something else you should know, something I didn't tell Silas."

As I suspected. "Shoot. You can trust me."

"There was someone else in his room."

Part of me wanted to reveal the evidence of the third glass we'd seen behind the bed. By nature, I was a sharer, an extrovert. I liked to compare information. But the longer I was in this role, the more I learned to keep my mouth shut. People tended to say more to fill the silence. So, I pressed my lips together and simply looked at him expectantly.

He continued. "Vampires have excellent hearing, and my room is close to Julius's. Yesterday, before Calliope was murdered, I heard her and Julius in his room. But I also heard a third voice, a woman's voice."

"Did you recognize it?" I asked.

"No, and I was interested, Grateful, because, you know, I'm a man and I'm a vampire. I was half inclined to invite myself to the party, but Julius never liked to share."

Gross. "So you have no idea who she was?"

He looked me in the eye. "No. I asked around after I found the body. Julius was gone and hadn't said a word to anyone. No one saw or heard a thing. That never happens. The Thames is full of vampires with nothing to do but be in each other's business."

"No one saw anything?"

"Lots of vamps saw Calliope and Julius arrive at sunrise. No one saw the third woman. No one heard her but me."

"This is very important, Gary. Could the voice you heard be Bathory's?"

"Maybe."

"*Maybe*—you don't want to tell me? Or *maybe*—you don't know for sure?"

"I don't know for sure, which is strange. Really strange."

"Why so strange?"

He paused on the sidewalk and turned his back to me. "Move a finger. Any finger."

"What?"

Just do it.

I wiggled my pinky finger.

"Little finger left hand."

I tried another.

"Ring finger, right hand." He turned back around. "I can tell a human voice from a vampire voice, from a werewolf voice," Gary said.

"And which was it?"

Gary glanced at the street, the people passing by us in their warm cars on the way to who knows where. "I couldn't tell. Strange."

"Bathory has a leprechaun. She could have used magic to disguise her voice."

"True."

For a moment, the only sound was our footsteps on the gritty, salt-sprinkled sidewalk. "One more question. How did you find the body? Did you hear the struggle? Did the woman scream or something?"

"No," he said firmly. "That's the scary part. There was no struggle. No scream. I'd gone to Julius's door when I heard glass breaking. Then I smelled the blood. You saw what I found. He was already gone."

We'd reached the end of the block. From here on out, mostly abandoned warehouses and processing plants loomed. The types of places where people got murdered and nobody noticed for days. It was risky to go this way with a vamp, lots of dark spaces and no one to hear me scream. But I didn't want to interrupt him in case there was something more. Under the guise of scratching my neck, I brushed my fingertips over Nightshade's hilt. I'd have to trust in my ability to take off his head. I kept walking.

"What time did you hear the glass shatter?" I asked.

"Just after five, I think. I was up, getting ready for the night."

"But the third voice, when did you hear that?"

"Earlier in the day. Before I fell asleep."

"During daylight hours. You're not sure when they arrived, but they disappeared after sundown?"

He sighed. "Which suggests it was another vampire."

"Or working for one. Like we established, the perpetrator left a lot of blood for a vamp." Bathory had ways to compel people to do her bidding. She'd compelled Gary to consent to be turned into a vampire. It was very possible whoever murdered Calliope was completely under her control.

He nodded his head. "She might not risk coming back herself."

"Anything else you can remember? Besides Bathory, was there anyone who wanted Julius out of the picture?"

"No. That's it. But Grateful, you gotta find him."

"I'll try my best."

"There are vampires in the coven who will be happy Julius is gone. They'll want him to stay gone. A new leader will be elected on the next full moon. I can almost guarantee you won't like who it is. I know I won't." Gary scowled. He'd worked for Bathory once and described the experience as "tortured."

I placed a hand on his shoulder. "I'll find him, Gary. If he's still alive, I'll find him."

"Good," he said. "Now if you don't mind, I just heard dinner." With a swift goodbye, he disappeared into the nearest abandoned building.

My stomach growled. Even the thought that Gary was probably sinking teeth into a warehouse rat didn't sully my appetite. With plenty to think about, I circled back to the nearest diner for some sustenance of my own.

* * * * *

After I had drowned my sorrows in a greasy burger and fries, I caught up with Rick to finish our night's work.

"How did you find me?" he asked. A stray cat bolted out of the alley at the sound of his voice. "Did you follow our connection? I didn't feel you coming."

I held up my phone. "Not magic. GPS. I tracked the phone I gave you for Christmas. There's an app for that. Find-a-Buddy."

Rick pulled the phone from his pocket and looked at it in horror. "Are you saying this metal square allows others to know where I am?" He tapped the screen in frustration.

Smugly, I stepped to his side and slid his finger across the screen to unlock the phone. "I find it ironic that you have no problems bleeding a chicken within a ring of skulls to track someone, but this ... this amazes you."

"It is unnatural. Maybe dangerous. Does everyone know where I am?"

"Only those people with your number."

"Who has my number?"

I circled my wrist above my head and pointed at myself.

"Well then, I suppose my privacy is protected."

I nodded. "Face it. Life is better in the modern age. Why don't you try to text me sometime? You might like it."

"I highly doubt it."

My eyes darted around the alley, trying to remember what evil baddie our magic mirror had revealed to us here. The mirror was an oddly-shaped stretch of silver I'd enchanted in my second lifetime. Its magic pinpointed supernatural activity that could result in harm to humans. The mirror didn't exactly show the future, more like scenes of what was probable to happen. Rick and I used it to focus the location of our patrol on a nightly basis.

Tonight, I was anything but focused. All I could think about was Tabetha and what had happened that afternoon. The accusations I'd thrown at Rick lingered in my brain.

The weight of his stare settled on a spot between my shoulder blades. He wanted to continue the conversation we'd started at the Thames. Sometimes it was a pain in the ass to be able to read your lover's thoughts.

"I think we should ignore Tabetha's invitation when it comes," I said toward the brick wall.

Rick groaned. "A blood pact cannot be broken. She will come for us, and we are not strong enough to fight her off."

That was the understatement of the year. "The goddess Hecate protected me once. She might again."

"I suspect so. But she will not protect me. Tabetha will demand my blood one way or another."

I tipped my head back, staring in exasperation at the starless sky. "So the easiest way is to play nice and hope that she gives us an alternative."

"Yes," he said curtly.

"Fucking awesome," I said sardonically. I kicked an empty whiskey bottle into the wall and rubbed the spot on my neck where a particularly sharp thorn had cut deep. In the distance, a car backfired. An ambulance passed by on the street outside the alley. Rick said nothing for a full minute.

"I am sorry, *mi cielo.*" Rick's presence pressed against my frontal lobe. I didn't want him inside my head. I built a brick wall in my mind, cutting him off, but not before I registered what he was looking for in my brain. He wanted to know if I forgave him for Tabetha.

I wasn't ready to forgive.

Awkwardly, I paced the boundary of the alley, actively blocking our connection. I kept replaying our conversation in my head and coming to the same conclusion: Rick was probably underplaying his relationship with Tabetha. It was the only explanation that made sense. Why else would she want him so badly? Yes, she was promised blood, but she was willing to *kill* me for Rick.

True, Tabetha was a total psycho-bitch. But a powerful witch like her probably didn't crush on any man who came along. She could have turned him away entirely or asked for money. As beautiful as she was, she probably had men lined up at her door. But no, she wanted him. How many lingering looks or accidental touches had it taken for Rick to convince her he would become her caretaker?

To Rick's credit, he didn't ask me about the obvious mental block. He seemed to innately understand that I needed space to process what happened that afternoon.

"What are we looking f—" I didn't get to finish my sentence. A shrieking apparition flew out of the wall, her ghostly form passing like a cold wind right through me.

Rick exploded from his skin, his beast snapping at the figure before I could even draw Nightshade. He caught her in his teeth mid-shift, neck jerking with the effort of holding the wispy but formidable apparition. By the time he finished shifting, he couldn't open his jaws without risking her release.

I grasped for Nightshade, jumped over Rick's dragon-like tail, and with a swipe of my blade, sent the shrieking thing to hell. The smell of sulfur filled the alley. I brought the back of my hand to my nose.

Shifting back to his human form, Rick turned to face me, now completely naked. "Poltergeist," he said.

"You shredded your clothes."

"I had to. You were distracted."

"Sorry."

"Do you need the night off?" he asked.

I considered it. He was right. It had taken me way too long to draw Nightshade. I needed to get my head in the game. For tonight, I would save the Tabetha analysis for a safer time and place.

"No. I'm fine." I helped him pick up the pieces of his shredded apparel. None was salvageable.

"Good. I will go to the car for a change of clothes."

"Wait! Your cell phone!" I held up the pocket from his torn pants. "The screen's not even cracked."

He rolled his eyes. "Thank the goddess for small favors." He plucked the phone from my hand, and then dissolved into a mist and blew from the alley.

CHAPTER 7
The Invitation

I wasn't naive. Eventually, Rick and I would have to talk out the Tabetha situation. Keeping it bottled up was toxic. But even after a good long sleep and a few more nights of putting him off, I wasn't ready.

Three days later, a tree sprite arrived at my door with a rolled up parchment made of birch bark. How did I know she was a tree sprite? Picture a female Peter Pan wearing a dress of dead leaves and looking like she might pass out from fatigue at any moment.

"Her Highness Tabetha, Queen of the territories of Salem and Smugglers' Notch, requests the presence of Grateful Knight, Queen of Monk's Hill, to dine in her presence at six o'clock in the evening, the last day of January." She lowered her head in a deep bow and extended the parchment with both hands.

"Thank you," I said. As soon as I backed away from the threshold, the sprite limped slowly to the dormant oak tree in my yard and slipped inside. What a bitch Tabetha was. She could have sent a pine or fir sprite. Coming out of hibernation like that had to hurt.

I unrolled the parchment. Poe landed on my shoulder and read the invitation along with me.

"Six o'clock. After sundown," Poe said.

"Of course it's after sundown. It's a dinner party and we aren't over eighty."

"The cover of darkness is her advantage. You've never been to her residence. Taking away your ability to see clearly is a ploy meant for her benefit."

I pulled out my phone and texted Rick the details. "We need a plan, something to offer her in lieu of Rick."

"What did you have in mind?"

"I'm not sure, but it has to be something Tabetha can't do herself, something worth the value of Rick to her."

"May I suggest you move up the retrieval of your grimoire on your to-do list?" Poe asked.

I squeezed my eyes closed, kicking myself for waiting so long to force the issue with Logan. "You're right. I will."

* * * * *

I showed up at Logan's penthouse later that day, hoping his sunny disposition would pull me out of my funk. Things weren't exactly going my way. I had a date with a homicidal witch at the end of the month, and I was still holding Rick at arm's length.

"Hey, stranger," I said when he opened his door. "I was beginning to think you were avoiding me." I strolled inside, beaming with anticipatory gossip. I hadn't seen Logan in weeks, and our communication during that time had consisted of a handful of texts. I had so much to tell him, I was bursting at the seams.

"Uh, sorry about that. I've been busy at the restaurant. I bet you're here for your book." Logan closed the door behind me. Something was wrong. He wasn't making eye contact. I'd stored *The Book of Light*, my powerful magical grimoire, in his penthouse condominium to keep it safe during Bathory's attack on my home. At one point, I'd even had a key to his place until Rick squashed it in a jealous rage. I did need the book back if I wanted any hope of finding Bathory and Julius. But that wasn't the only reason I was here. Not by a long shot.

"It's okay. Lucky for me, I've been able to get by without it until now."

"Right. You have some of the spells on your phone," he said impassively.

"And Nightshade. She's handy with the supernaturals." Damn. This was like having a conversation with a block of ice. What happened to the former ghost who had haunted my house and made me hot chocolate? Shit, he hadn't even offered me a drink.

"What's going on, Logan?"

"I don't know what you mean."

"You avoid me for weeks, and now you're barely talking to me. You haven't even looked me in the eye since I got here."

He leaned one hip against an armchair in his great room. "Just tired."

"Are you angry about Rick?" I needed to understand the change. I was already feeling fragile due to the Rick/Tabetha situation. One thing I considered a constant in my life was Logan's friendship. Yes, he'd had feelings for me at one point, and I suspected he might take my engagement hard, but I thought he'd be over it by now.

He huffed and shook his head. "No. That's not it."

The answer came with ego-crushing speed and sincerity. It was completely unfair for me to miss being the focus of his affection, but it would have been nice to feel wanted. I smiled for his benefit. "Good. Then what's going on? You seem totally distracted."

A grin spread across his face, and his eyes took on the far-off look of daydreaming. "I met someone."

"You did?" My eyebrows shot up. "Tell me about her." Wow, he really had moved on.

He bit his lip and glanced at the floor. "I think I want to keep this one to myself for a while." He grinned like a child. "It'll jinx it. This is too perfect. I don't want to screw it up."

He was serious. The vibe he was putting off screamed "totally whipped." A weird emptiness expanded in my gut, a totally unfair feeling considering I was getting married in a couple months. Still, it stung. Logan had a secret I wasn't a part of. I was officially outside looking in the window of his life.

"I'm happy for you," I forced myself to say. "You look really, um, happy. Just ... blissful."

"I am, thanks. So, ah, you should get your book. I'll help you." He grinned that lopsided, boy-next-door grin.

"Yeah, the thing weighs a ton." I swung my arms awkwardly. Why did this conversation feel forced? "Hey, before I go, I need to ask you a question."

"Sure." He led the way toward his home office where I'd sealed the book behind a protective enchantment.

"Will you cater my wedding? I'd like to have the reception at Valentine's. It's March twentieth."

Logan's face fell, and his hands moved to his hips to support a defeated shrug. "I can't. The restaurant is booked."

"What?" Of all the things that could go wrong, I never thought this would be one of them. Logan always came through for me, always.

"We're booked for a private party. The entire restaurant and bar."

"Can you move it?"

He furrowed his brow. "No, I can't move it," he said incredulously. "The couple booked months ago. Why don't you move your date?"

"I can't. Spring equinox. New beginnings."

"Well, I can't do it."

Crossing my arms over my chest, I popped my hip out, my tongue poking into my cheek. "I got it. What if I rented another venue and you catered it? Then you could have your staff cater the one at the restaurant. Win-win."

Mouth dropping open, he looked at me as if I'd sprouted two heads. "You are not getting this, Grateful. The answer is no. I'm busy. I will not be catering your wedding. You will have to find someone else." He snapped the words at me like he was chastising a child.

I squinted in his direction. "Logan, I'm not some diva demanding my way, okay? I just wanted you to be part of my wedding. I thought we were friends. Good friends. I spent months nursing you back to health after I resurrected you. I stored one of the most powerful books of magic in the world in your home. Excuse me for expecting that you might want to be part of a major life event for me."

He sighed, head lolling forward on his shoulders. "Look," he said, spreading his hands. "We've grown apart, okay? You made it clear the last time we were together that you chose Rick over me. I've moved on. Yes, we're friends. But business is business. I can't do it. You need to find someone else."

I could understand the restaurant being booked. I could even understand him not wanting to be involved. But he was so cold about it, like he enjoyed telling me no. That wasn't Logan. Not my Logan. But then again, he wasn't mine, was he? The illusion that our friendship was indestructible shattered. Even when he thought he was in love with me, he wasn't really mine.

"Are you even planning to come to my wedding?" I asked in a hushed tone.

"Are you inviting me?"

"Of course."

"Then I will try to stop by." His eyes softened slightly, but they didn't warm to the twinkling green I was used to.

"Okay. I understand. Enough said." I didn't understand. After all we'd been through together, I expected more than "I will try to stop by."

"Cool." He opened the door for me.

I continued into the room where my giant leather-bound grimoire waited for me. The purple haze of my protective enchantment still surrounded the desk it rested on. No one could *see* my magic but me, of course. The purple was my own magical signature.

As I approached the barrier, I paused. "Hey, Logan."

"Yeah?"

"Did you try to look at my book?"

"No, why?"

"There's some damage to my protective ward." I ran my hand through the magic. "More than a little, actually. Have you had any supernaturals up here?"

There was a pause while he walked to the door and leaned against the doorframe. "No one's been in here since you. I keep this door closed."

"Huh." I waded into the magic, feeling the buzz of it against my skin. Whoever had tested it hadn't succeeded in getting through. The ward was still functional. But there was damage, which meant someone had attempted to reach my book. With the enchantments I had around his place, it was either Logan, another human, or a supernatural he invited inside.

I glanced back at Logan in the doorway. I wanted to ask him again if he'd had any supernatural guests, but his expression dissuaded me—a cross between impatience and annoyance, his jaw was tight and his lips a flat line. I needed to take a different tack.

"Has your mom stopped by lately?" Since I put Logan back in his body, he'd been in communication with his deceased mother. She'd helped me out a couple times.

"Actually, no. I'm not having the weird dreams anymore either. I guess my life is back to normal. Well, as soon as you get that thing out of my house." He smiled stiffly.

Jeez. The empty feeling in my stomach expanded to my chest. With a heavy heart, I drew Nightshade and cut through the space around me, breaking my enchantment. Then I placed my hands on *The Book of Light*. At least this was what I expected. My grimoire hummed to me. She was ready to go home.

Grudgingly, Logan stepped forward to help, but I shook my head. "Its okay. I can tell you're busy. I got this."

He tipped his head to the side. "That thing has to weigh a hundred pounds, Grateful. Let me help."

Rounding my lips, I blew out a deep breath. Wind circled and lifted the book. I placed my hands under it, but with my magic at work, it weighed almost nothing. Logan reached for it anyway.

"Stop,' I said, nudging him back with my power. We locked eyes for a second. I wasn't sure what Logan was trying to prove, forcing his help on me, but I didn't like it. "Maybe you can get the door."

Cracking his jaw, he led the way out. He opened the front door for me and tapped the button for the elevator. I stepped inside the compartment. With a hasty goodbye, he disappeared inside his condo. When the doors closed, something inside me broke, as if the heavy steel had severed the last frail spiderweb of connection I'd had to Logan.

CHAPTER 8
The Offer

I lowered *The Book of Light* onto the desk in my attic and ran the back of my hand across my forehead. Out of principle, I had refused Logan's help, but that momentary pride had taken its toll. The magic I'd used to move the gargantuan tome had drained me.

"Who are you?" A trembling voice came from behind me. "Where am I?"

I spun around to find the blurry outline of the murdered girl—Calliope—staring at me with wide green eyes. Her bleached-blonde head looked markedly different attached to her body.

"Holy fucking crow!" I scrambled to the other side of the desk.

Her face crumpled and her molecules broke apart and came back together.

"I'm sorry, Calliope. You just startled me."

"You know my name?"

I pressed a finger into my chin. "Yeah…" How did I put this in the gentlest possible way? Better to rip off the Band-Aid. "You were murdered, and you're here because your soul needs to be sorted. It happens sometimes when a soul is cut off before its time."

"Murdered?" She pressed a translucent hand into her chest. "When?"

"Yesterday."

She stared at the floor absently and then began to weep. "There was so much I wanted to do," she blubbered. Her frail shoulders bobbed with her sobbing. Her remains hadn't given me a full appreciation of how thin she was.

"I'm sorry to be the one to have to tell you about your death, but you're in the right place. I can help you get to the other side."

Her weeping intensified. Poor thing.

The sound of plastic on plastic heralded Poe's arrival. He barreled through the pet door Rick had installed along with a cascade of icy air that cut off quickly when the door sealed itself behind him.

"That's cool," I said, walking to the window and pressing on the flap. "It only opens for you?"

Poe stared with concern at Calliope weeping in the corner while he lifted a foot to show me a tiny metal band. "Chip in the bracelet unlocks the flap. Rick thought you would prefer this version as a fail-safe. Who's the dead girl?"

"Soul in need of sorting. She was the one killed at the Thames Theater yesterday."

Calliope paused her weeping. "The Thames? What happened?"

"I was hoping you'd tell me." She was freshly dead. Her memory wasn't going to get any better than this.

Her eyes narrowed. "I don't remember. I was on a date with Julius. We danced ... made love."

I tried to remain stoic but inside I gagged a little.

Calliope noticed my reaction. "Julius is a magnificent lover," she said, widening her eyes. "The best I've ever had."

"Okay," I said. It sounded dismissive despite my best efforts. "What happened after you made love?"

"He fed on me, like he always does." She rubbed her neck as she said this as if remembering the bite. "And then I fell asleep."

I waited a beat. "That's it? You fell asleep?"

"Yeah."

"When did the other woman arrive?"

"What other woman?"

"Are you saying you were alone all night?"

Calliope grinned. "Uh, yeah. The evening was ... intimate, if you know what I mean. No one else was invited. I am not into group sex."

"Hmm," I said.

"She might not remember," Poe said.

"Nightshade will sort out the truth," I murmured. Marching to my trunk, I removed my silver bowl and placed it in front of the ghost. Then I drew my blade.

"What the fuck?" Calliope said.

"Don't worry. This isn't going to hurt a bit." I threw my power into her and sifted her soul through it, straining out a series of memories.

Flash.

A platinum-haired ball of energy, six-year-old Calliope runs into a living room constructed of nothing more than a filthy couch and beer bottles. Her father, passed out on the couch, stirs, and she stops in her tracks, heart pounding with fear.

Flash.

She's twelve and the gym teacher is drilling her about the scars on her back. Burns. Her father put them there, but she doesn't want to tell.

Flash.

Calliope turns fifteen, now living in a foster home. Her foster father gives her a guitar for her birthday. She plays it until her fingers bleed.

Flash.

She's eighteen, on her own, and singing her first set in a hole-in-the-wall bar. Her stomach growls and she's afraid the audience can hear it through the mic. She'll need to finish if she wants to eat tonight.

Flash.

Julius introduces himself. Asks her to dinner. She eats until she's full for the first time in forever. He buys her a drink even though she's only twenty. Then he tells her what he is and proposes a deal. At first she's shocked, until they have sex. Then she's smitten. There's a new apartment, food in the fridge, and the wound on the inside of her thigh doesn't hurt a bit.

Flash.

She's holding a glass of Scotch, standing next to Julius's bed at the Thames, and sporting an ear-to-ear grin. He licks a bit of her blood from his lip then presses a kiss to her mouth. There's a knock at the door. "Who's that?" she asks. Julius looks her in the eye and says, "Relax." His pupils dilate. Blackness.

I tumbled out of her head, panting. Calliope's ghost blinked at me in confusion.

"Calliope North," I said in a clear, strong voice, "I release you to heaven." I sliced my arm. A drop of blood splashed into the silver bowl. Calliope broke apart into a column of light and disappeared through my ceiling.

* * * * *

"That wasn't the smartest thing you've ever done," Poe said. "She might have had information you could have used to find her killer."

I shook my head. "Julius had compelled her. She doesn't remember dying at all, let alone who killed her."

"You might have been able to undo the compulsion. Maybe unravel a subconscious memory," Poe said.

"Calliope North has been used enough in her short life." I darted a glance in Poe's direction. "Now she is finally at peace. The end." I shivered remembering the girl's life. Sadly, being a blood bag for Julius was the highlight.

"Understood."

"I did confirm one thing."

"What?"

"Julius didn't kill Calliope. Gary was telling the truth about that."

"There's a first time for everything."

A yawn forced itself out of me, and I stretched in reaction. "I better try to get a nap in before tonight."

The feathers of one of Poe's eyes arched higher. "You need more than a nap, Witchy Woman. You need a visit to the caretaker to recharge your magical battery."

"Rick and I are not exactly seeing eye to eye these days. I'm not sure I want to rattle that cage right now."

"Your undies are in a bunch over Tabetha and the candle." Poe pointed a talon in my direction.

"My undies are not in a bunch. I just have my reservations concerning what brought about the misunderstanding. Seems like Rick must have been stirring her cauldron to make her believe he'd become her caretaker."

"You think he had an affair while you were between lifetimes?"

I paused, rubbing my palms together. "I don't think he had intercourse with her. He told me he's only been with me, and I believe him. I can tell when he's lying or when he's blocking me mentally."

"But?"

"But I wonder if it was an emotional affair. Late-night dinners. Days prancing through fields of daisies, hand in hand, searching for eye of newt."

Poe cackled. "Fields of daisies?"

I spread my hands and shrugged.

"Well, if it is any consolation, Tabetha's reputation precedes her."

"You mentioned that before. What exactly is her reputation?"

"Let's just say, if anyone was acting the predator, it was Tabetha, not Rick."

I rubbed my chin. "Enjoys the boys, does she? A man-eater?"

"That's what I've heard," Poe said. "I think Tabetha gets what Tabetha wants."

"Maybe Rick wasn't underestimating their relationship after all."

"You can read his mind, dear witch. What do you think?"

Admittedly, Rick's thoughts were fairly clear on the subject of wanting me and regretting the entire candle fiasco. That wasn't the point. The point was … The point was … I had a right to be angry. Rick's hasty and jealous actions had put us at risk.

Tempted as I was to pursue this line of reasoning with Poe, I needed to focus on a spell to offer Tabetha. It had to be something exceptional. Exhausted, I started randomly flipping pages in *The Book of Light*.

"What would she want in place of Rick?" I asked Poe.

He looked at me blankly. "Who am I to get inside the mind of a witch?"

"You practically read my mind on a daily basis."

"That's different. I am your familiar, and you are nothing like Tabetha."

"Tabetha, Tabetha, Tabetha." I drummed my fingers on the desk and rolled my neck. "What do you want most in the deep recesses of your psycho head?" I straightened. "Wait. She's a psycho. I happen to know a great analyzer of psychos." I reached for my phone and poked a few buttons. Michelle's face popped up on the screen after the third ring.

"You were right to come to me with this," Michelle said once I'd brought her up to speed. "I know exactly what you should offer Tabetha."

I laughed. Of course my non-magical friend would have the answer. "Don't keep me in suspense.

"True love."

I glanced at Poe, then narrowed my eyes at Michelle's FaceTime image on my phone. "Are you saying I should find her another man to replace Rick?"

"Not exactly. What I'm saying is that if she was looking for love when she decided to help Rick, which makes sense since you say she appeared scorned by his rejection, then what she really wants is not him or blood, but true love. Also, Poe says she has a reputation for burning through men. A classic example of someone desperate for true intimacy and trying to fill the gaping hole in her soul with sex. Is there a spell to find true love? Love potion number nine?" She snickered.

"Let's find out," I said to Michelle. Approaching *The Book of Light*, I spoke directly to the grimoire. "Show me the spell to find true love." The pages lifted from the binding, light pouring out between them, and flipped forward and back repeatedly before coming to rest on the book's suggestion.

Turning my phone so that Michelle could see, I leaned over the book and read what was on the page. "The positivity potion. This concoction will change the drinker's chemistry to send out positively charged love energy that will attract his or her perfect balance with magnetic precision. Use sparingly. Works best in well-populated areas."

"Look at the footnote!" Michelle clapped her hands excitedly.

"Caution: the positivity potion cannot be concocted for oneself, as doing so could result in terminal narcissism. An extrinsic magical element is necessary for proper composition." I grinned. "She can't make it for herself."

Poe ruffled his feathers. "How long does it take to brew?"

"I can make it in an hour but it has to ferment for forty-eight. Should be ready in plenty of time."

"Do you think she'll go for it?" Michelle asked.

"I don't know, but it's the best idea I've got." I read through the ingredients. "It's fairly straightforward. I'll get started right away."

Poe squawked in approval. "May I suggest you visit Rick when you are done? If you are going to face Tabetha in a few days, you'll need your strength."

I ignored Poe and was about to say goodbye to Michelle when she yelled, "Wait."

"What's up?" I asked.

"Bridesmaids' dresses," Michelle said.

I groaned and closed my eyes.

"I know this is horrible timing, but if Soleil and I don't get sized and order them now, they won't be ready by the wedding."

"I can't go back to Gertrude's," I said.

She grimaced. "A hat and dark glasses?" she suggested.

"No."

"Grateful, woman up and meet me at the emporium. I guarantee, after spending six thousand dollars on a wedding dress, she will not kick you out." Michelle followed up with a string of pleading and a threat to walk down the aisle in something off the rack.

"Fine," I huffed. "Make an appointment and I'll be there."

Michelle squealed and promised to call Soleil for me. We said our goodbyes, and I got to work.

CHAPTER 9
Dinner and an Ultimatum

Three days later, I found myself in Evenrose Bridal, this time in the viewing chair. Thankfully, Gertrude didn't say a word to me, although that included any kind of a greeting. As long as the dresses were in on time, I'd get over the rudeness.

Soleil stepped on the box wearing a bright coral-colored sheath dress that made me shade my eyes.

"Too bright," I said.

Michelle agreed. "Way too bright."

Not to mention, on Michelle's squat frame, the dress completely lost its shape. I registered the disappointment on lanky Soleil's face and wondered if any dress was up to the task.

"I will try the violet option," Soleil said and disappeared into the changing room.

"Hey, are you okay? What's with the matching luggage?" Michelle asked, referring to the dark circles under my eyes.

I shrugged. "Stressed about the Tabetha dinner," I whispered. "Drained from work."

"Don't you have a supernatural fountain of youth across the street who you happen to be engaged to?" She waggled her eyebrows. "Go take a hit of the good stuff."

"Yeah." I pressed my lips together. "We're sort of fighting."

"About what?"

"This whole situation. How he jumped to conclusions about our relationship and almost died because of it."

Michelle's jaw dropped open. "Oh, come on, Grateful. You know as well as I do that things weren't nearly as cut-and-dried as all that. I mean, you and Logan ..."

"There was nothing going on between Logan and me."

She narrowed her eyes and held up one hand. "I am not even going to step on this landmine. Let me just say, mistakes were made all around, honey, and if you are too hardheaded to forgive his, you don't deserve him."

I frowned. "That's harsh."

"Not really." She placed her hands on her ample hips and shrugged her shoulders. "If you're asking me, I have a feeling your anger is more about self-protection than disappointment. You have an excuse to keep him at an arm's length, and the reward is you stay emotionally safe. It's becoming your M.O., Grateful, and it isn't pretty."

"Go try on the violet halter dress," I snapped. Who asked her anyway?

Still, my mind dwelled on Rick. All through deciding the violet halter dress was the one, Gertrude's measurements, and the entire ordering process, he was all I could think about. Part of me wanted to grip my anger to my cheek like a security blanket. Only problem was, Michelle was right. I didn't actually feel angry anymore. I just missed him.

On the drive back to Red Grove, I decided, quite formally and in conversation with myself, to get over it.

"I forgive you," I said when Rick opened his door. He was naked except for a pair of gray cotton pants that hung low, exposing the top of the raised muscle vee that hooked over his hips and blended into his back. When he looked at me, his eyes were heather gray, the beast within far from the surface, and his expression soft.

"Thank you. I *am* sorry, *mi cielo*. For everything. For doubting you, for disappointing you, and for the burden we now face to undo it." He shifted toward me, resting his arm on the doorframe. His bicep flexed to support his weight, and I had to swallow against the lick of desire that swept over me.

"Whatever it is, we will do what we have to. We'll move beyond this." I stepped into his body, the front of my coat brushing his chest. "Tabetha can't have you."

"Why?" He smirked, waiting for the words he desperately wanted to hear. His desire for my affection poured down our metaphysical connection like warm honey.

"Because I love you," I said. The words were barely over my lips before he was pulling me into his cottage and shutting out the cold and any lingering doubts with the slam of the door.

His fingers dug into the back of my hair, cradling the base of my neck. Lips brushed mine. He hovered over my mouth, teasing me with his breath. I thrust myself up on my tiptoes, kissing him gently at first and than in a more demanding way. Heat bloomed in my core. I needed this. I needed him.

I parted his lips with my tongue and stroked between his teeth, exploring his mouth while my palms eased down the skin of his back. With one hand, he reached between us and unbuttoned my coat. He pushed it off my shoulders, never losing the rhythm of our kiss, and tossed it toward the rack near the door. I heard it crumple to the floor. Neither one of us paused to pick it up.

My long-sleeved T-shirt was next. This time, he did pull back from our kiss to lift it over my head, but instead of removing it, he stopped at my hands, whirled me around, and wound my sleeves to bind my wrists together.

"What's this?" I asked.

"Give yourself to me," he whispered in my ear. His palm coursed over my abs to cup my lace-covered breast. With the position of my hands behind my back, I could feel his erection twitch against my palm through the cloth of his pants.

I understood what he wanted. This wasn't as much about binding me as it was about me showing I trusted him explicitly. Control was important to me. Giving it up would not be easy.

"Yes," I said.

He spun me back around to face him. One side of his mouth lifted into a devilish smirk, and my skin tingled in anticipation. His hands cupped my jaw, thumbs caressing my lips lightly. And then his mouth replaced his touch. The white-hot kiss made my head spin while he flicked his thumbs over the thin lace covering my raised nipples. A current of desire coursed through me. I arched my back to press my breasts into his hands, but he pulled away in response.

His low, heady laugh caught me off guard. "Oh no. I'm driving this time, *mi cielo*."

At first my instinct was to demand he step on the gas, but I forced myself to let him lead, go at his pace. I was rewarded with the return of his touch. His hands skimmed down my body, unbuttoned my jeans, and in one pass pulled them and my lace boy shorts to my knees. Kneeling before me, I groaned as his lips explored the space between my hipbones. He gripped my ass and squeezed, almost to the point of pain, but not quite. With my pants around my calves and my wrists bound, there wasn't much I could do but moan my approval.

My breath came in pants as his mouth neared the apex of my thighs. The wet ache there was raw; I thought a single touch might put me over the edge. I was right. His tongue darted out, licking my slit. I shattered.

For a moment I was lost to the intense pleasure. When I came down from the aftershocks, Rick was holding me up. I leaned into his shoulder while he worked to remove my boots and pants. "Safety first," he said, grinning.

In one easy motion, he stood and tossed me over his shoulder, holding me firmly by the back of my thighs. "Where are you taking me?" I asked.

His hand slapped my ass, hard. I moaned. It didn't exactly hurt, but the keen, sharp sensation brought the blood rushing to where his hand had been. The pulse of desire started anew. He hummed with satisfaction as the resurgence of my sexual appetite rushed down our connection. His hand slapped my cheeks again sharply, then rubbed the space between them, blissfully exposed by my position across his shoulder. I squirmed, my breasts grazing the muscles of his back.

All at once I was tossed in the air, and manipulated face down and bottom up on the bed. I turned my head to the side and arched, ready and waiting for whatever he had in mind. I didn't have to wait long. He entered me in one slick thrust, supporting my waist with his solid forearm.

He moaned, his need throbbing between us. One palm settled in the arch of my spine, stroked down, and rounded over my hip. For a heartbeat, he didn't move. "You are … exquisite." His breath rattled a little with emotion.

I turned my head, met his hooded eyes over my shoulder, and licked my lips. "I'm yours remember. Drive."

Hitching my hips up with his hands, he went to work. He pounded into me faster and harder, until I squeezed my eyes shut against the onslaught and bit my lip. We came together in a ripple of light.

When he finally pulled away, I rolled my wrist out of its binding and tossed the T-shirt aside. Flipping over, I straddled his lap and wrapped my arms around his neck so we were face to face. "My turn."

* * * * *

"Park on the side of the road," I said. Tabetha's home was in rural Salem, off a rarely traveled dirt road inside a stretch of densely forested land. I could see the driveway to her residence up ahead, complete with an ordinary mailbox. The house number reflected in my Jeep's headlights. I guess even ancient and powerful witches needed a way to get their electric bills.

"Seems an odd choice to hold a love potion," Rick said, glancing at the *Duck Dynasty* thermos in my hands.

I leaned my head against the headrest. "I know," I groaned. "It was the only one they had left at Red Grove Grocery and Pub."

"I doubt the container will make a difference one way or another." Rick frowned.

"I'm going to leave it in the car until she accepts our offer. Something tells me we should travel light."

"Agreed."

I shoved the thermos in the glove compartment.

We'd arrived almost an hour early. Twilight. I'd have plenty of time to check out Tabetha's domain before we were expected. I wanted to know exactly what I was getting into. We climbed from the Jeep.

"Poe," I said, "I need you to survey the property from the air. Try to stay out of sight, and only get involved if it's a life-or-death situation, understand?"

The raven bobbed his dark head.

"We'll meet back here when it's over." With a flutter of wings, Poe lifted from my shoulder and passed over the ten-foot privet surrounding the property.

Rick and I walked the length of the wall to the drive, where a monstrous iron gate barred our path. A scrollwork T graced the left side and a V, the right. "What does the V stand for?" I asked. I don't know why, but the idea that Tabetha had a last name seemed funny to me. I just assumed she only had one name, like Madonna or Eminem.

"Van Buren," Rick said. "She chose it for herself, of course. There are practicalities."

Electric bill, I thought. I pushed on the gate. Locked.

Rick tapped my shoulder and pointed up. "If I remember correctly, there's a switch inside the gate. It's automated, but there is a manual override."

"If I can't see it, I don't think I can bamboozle it," I said.

He bowed slightly. "Then may I suggest the old reliable method? It would be my pleasure to give you a ride." He started stripping out of his clothes. "Hold these."

When he lifted his shirt over his head, a zap of electricity traveled straight from my core to the surface of my skin. I swallowed as his muscles rippled in the indirect light of the setting sun. He reached for the fly of his pants and my heart did a jumping jack. Heat bloomed deep within me. I raised one eyebrow as my gaze settled on his ample endowment.

He laughed. "Work to do," he said with a sigh. My desire for him was burning up our connection, feeding his desire for me. That much was evident in the reaction of his body. I looked away and tried to think of unappealing things, like witches who wanted my caretaker. I turned back around at the sound of breaking bones and the rumple of leather on leather, his wings unfurling. A moment later, I was on his back and Rick was over the gate.

"Sweet ride," I said as I jumped from his back. My smile reflected in one of his large black eyes. He shifted quickly, landing a toothy kiss on my lips before lifting the pile of clothes from my hands.

While he was dressing, I took a good look at the place. A long driveway lined with fruit trees stretched a good mile or more toward the residence. I couldn't see the place clearly due to the trees and the mist that hung in the twilight, but the glimpses up the drive and above the foliage gave a definite impression. Tabetha's house was a Victorian English-style mansion, almost collegiate, all long stone steps and brick walls, with rows and rows of windows and multiple chimneys poking out of her many-gabled roof.

I stepped forward, stones crunching under my boots. "Is this pink granite?"

Rick shrugged. He joined me, fully dressed.

"I thought only Martha Stewart had a pink granite drive. Do you know how much this driveway costs?"

"Tabetha is very wealthy."

"Good investments?" I asked. It was how Rick made his wealth. When you lived forever, interest, growth, and dividends took on a whole new meaning.

"Yes, and consulting. As a wood witch, she has a knack for botanicals. She formulated the popular Zen line of cosmetics."

"Really?" I used Zen shampoo and conditioner. It was a miracle in a bottle. *Fuck.* I hoped this worked out. I did not want to have to find a new shampoo out of spite.

He nodded and started walking toward the house. I followed but stopped short when a pair of reflective eyes flashed at us from behind one of the tree trunks. I grabbed Rick's arm. "Look." I pointed needlessly. Rick was already facing that direction. "I think it's a deer." An albino deer. The animal was ghost white with red eyes under its long lashes that locked onto me. A few steps closer and the doe raised her head, turned, and darted away.

"The animals are eating the fallen fruit," Rick said, pointing at the grass around the trunk where the deer had been. The trees were laden with bulbous red fruit that reminded me of pomegranates but were darker in color. Near my toes, the fallen specimen left half-eaten by the deer had deep purple flesh with green seeds. The texture reminded me of kiwi but different, definitely an exotic variety, if related at all.

"There's no snow here," I said, absentmindedly reaching for one of the fruits.

Rick slapped my hand away. "She's a wood witch, Grateful. Do not touch the trees. They are surely enchanted."

I snapped out of it and continued walking up the driveway, looking in the direction the deer ran. I found the doe, waiting in the forested yard a few meters away, watching us watch her. "There's a bunch of them," I said, noticing her friends. "All albino. I've never heard of that before. Isn't it a recessive gene?"

He shrugged. "There are smaller animals, too. Likely attracted to the warmth as well as the bounty," Rick muttered. He wrapped an arm around my waist and ushered me toward the house.

I could tell he was nervous, and I couldn't blame him. The fog swirling between the legs of the animals was creepy for sure, as was the silence and the ever-darkening skies.

"It's because of the warmth," I said abruptly. I shook my head when he looked at me in confusion. "The fog.

When the cold air touches the warm plants, it causes the fog. The plants are warm from her magic, not the air."

"Oh," he said, uninspired by my revelation.

Fine. But I was pretty proud of myself for figuring that out. A few minutes later we reached the end of the drive and the base of the stairs. If possible, the place seemed even larger close up. Green and purple ivy climbed up the corners, branching like veins across the front of the place. If I were to describe it in two words, I'd say "looming" and "alive."

"I wonder why a wood witch lives in a brick house," I said.

Rick grinned. "A wood house is made of dead plants, but a brick house is made of baked clay. This house is like a giant terracotta pot."

"Ah, I see. Hey, I just thought of something. Where's her cemetery?"

"The backyard. It is small compared to Monk's Hill but significantly older. A Native American burial ground."

I turned to him in confusion. "She knocked you on your ass with a flick of her wrist and her cemetery is smaller than ours? How is she so strong with a tiny burial ground?"

"A Hecate draws her power from her dead, but a witch as old as Tabetha has had hundreds of years to find ways to amplify that power."

"Like a familiar?"

"Similar, yes. Although a familiar is one thing Tabetha does not have."

"What about the scarab beetle? It was imprinted on the candle and she wears a brooch."

"A symbol of power, yes. A talisman, maybe. But not living, not a familiar like Poe. Honestly, I'm not sure how she does it, only that she is considered the most powerful witch living in our time."

"Fabulous," I said sarcastically.

The front entrance was directly ahead of me, but I wasn't done snooping. I climbed the steps but shuffled right and tried to look in the window. Hand shielding my eyes from the glare, I pressed my face to the glass. "Oww!"

I saw a flash of green and then my entire body pitched into the air. I flipped over in time to face a giant sunflower as it repositioned me in its sticky green petals. When my shoulder touched the oozy center, my black wool coat smoldered, the stench of burning wool filling my nostrils. *Fuck!*

"Rick!" I yelled. The thing's petals folded in on me. "This thing is using me as Miracle-Gro!"

Rick cried out. He was fighting his own battle.

I yelled for Poe but didn't sense his presence. He must have been too far away to hear me. I'd have to get myself out of this one.

With effort worthy of a master Pilates class, I kept my face out of the acidic sap and reached for Nightshade. I barely had enough room to slide her off my back, but a yogi-contortion later, and I yanked her free. I hacked at the petal teeth of the plant, and then tried to use my blade to pry the jaws open. Nothing worked. Nightshade bounced off the bright green flower as if it were made of steel, and no amount of prying budged its bite. More than one way to kill a plant. I flipped the blade around and sank it under my arm, into the acidic goo under me. The thing emitted a screech like a dying animal.

I twisted the blade, grunting with the effort. Success! The flower spit me out on the stone steps ... at the feet of Tabetha Van Buren.

"Grateful Knight, I would request that you please do not damage my landscaping. Have you no manners?" Tabetha looked down her nose at me.

Speechless, I pointed at the sister-plant of the one that tried to eat me. Rick's leg dangled from between the petals and its sunflower-like head was waving to and fro as he battled it from within. A wave of Tabetha's wand later, and he was spit out right next to me, covered in steaming sap.

"If you are done playing, would you like to come in?" Tabetha swung a hand toward the open door.

"I don't suppose you'd have a towel," I said, watching the sap continue to burn a hole in my coat.

She sneered and with another wave of her wand, the sap disappeared. I had no idea how she accomplished that trick. As a wood witch, did she control every cell of every plant here?

"Thanks," I said flatly.

Rick helped me up, and we followed her into her home. The foyer was a tropical garden. Every type of plant known to man, and some varieties I was sure had never been discovered, grew from rows and rows of pots along the walls. Instead of a traditional chandelier, a multicolored blown glass sculpture in the shape of flowers glowed from above. It was covered in flowering vines, as were the walls and the staircase. The air was thick with humidity and an overly sweet floral scent.

"May I take your coat?" a man said from beside us. He was tall, young, handsome, with glassy eyes and a distracted expression. I supposed if I worked for Tabetha, I'd be distracted too. I handed him my coat, as did Rick.

"The dining room is this way," Tabetha said. She led us into an area as big as a gymnasium with a long table and straight back chairs. The walk-in fireplace near the back of the room housed a blazing inferno, guarded on either side by winged copper gargoyles. Not the modern decorative kind, but the medieval versions meant to scare people away—all horns and teeth, pointy wings and claws. The décor belonged in a castle. Oversized. Stone. Stained glass.

"Nice place you've got here," I said. I'd meant it to sound polite, but it came out catty. I guess I wore my heart on my sleeve.

"Please sit. Dinner will be ready shortly." Tabetha took a seat at the head of the table, the light of the fire dancing over her olive skin.

I glanced at Rick, who had pulled out a chair for me across from her. "Maybe we should get down to business," I said.

"Do not insult me, sister," she said. "A friend has prepared dinner for us this evening. We will eat like civilized adults, and then you will tell me how you plan to satisfy your blood debt."

Rick pushed the chair in slightly so that it tapped the back of my knees. I sat. The food did smell good. Rick took the seat to my right, leaving the two chairs on either side of Tabetha empty. She didn't seem to mind. Instead, she lifted her wineglass, the thick, dark liquid sloshing slightly, and looked directly at me. "To family. Wouldn't Mother be proud to see us like this, around the same table?" She tossed the wine back.

The service door behind Tabetha opened.

A man entered, an enormous domed tray balanced on his shoulder blocking his face. When he reached the table, he expertly lowered the food to the center of the place settings.

I gasped. "Logan!"

CHAPTER 10
Wicked

"What are you doing here?" I demanded, widening my eyes at Logan.

He glanced in my direction and then leaned over the table to kiss Tabetha on the lips. *Oh no, he didn't!*

"Hello, Grateful," Logan said. "When Tabby mentioned another couple was joining us for dinner, I had no idea it was you and Rick. What a terrific surprise."

He was smiling but his voice fell flat, and he wavered slightly on his feet like maybe he'd had too much to drink. As if to confirm my suspicion, he lifted his glass of wine and took a giant swig before removing the dome on the tray. "Venison roast with potatoes and vegetables," he announced.

I thought of the doe in the front yard and completely lost my appetite.

"So this is the new girlfriend you were telling me about?" I asked.

By his side, Tabetha was grinning like the Cheshire cat. "I stopped in to Valentine's for a bite to eat a few weeks ago. He gave me a free cupcake for dessert. The rest is history."

Logan stared at her like she was the rising sun. I'd never seen him so obviously smitten with anything or anyone ... even me. My jaw dropped.

He served Tabetha first, doling out slices of meat and an assortment of vegetables. Then he reached out a hand for my plate. When everyone was served, he sat down and had another sip of wine.

"Logan," Tabetha said, "tell us about the meal you've prepared. It looks delish."

My friend began to talk about his method of marinating and cooking venison, but I wasn't listening. Anger brewed within me; my head burned with it. Tabetha was Logan's girlfriend, the one he wouldn't talk about. That meant it must have been Tabetha who'd tried to get to *The Book of Light* in Logan's apartment, because she was the only one he would have invited in. Logan was different since he met her, distant. She'd turned one of my best friends against me.

Did he even know she was a witch? According to Poe, Tabetha was a dangerous man-eater. What if she used Logan and then spit him out?

Sure, Logan deserved happiness, and he certainly looked happy chatting about his cooking while his fingers tangled with Tabetha's on the tabletop. But something about this felt wrong. She'd met him at Valentine's a couple of weeks ago. Their relationship kicked off around the same time she'd come to Red Grove and been snubbed by Rick. Too convenient. This felt like leverage, like another way to get under my skin. Then again, how would she even know that Logan and I were friends?

I glanced at Rick, who met my eyes and gave me a guilty wince. The candle. Rick had told Tabetha about Logan when he came to her for help. Which meant that, while Logan may think this was real, Tabetha was using him.

"Enough," I said. "I know what you're doing. This is between you and me. Leave Logan out of it."

"I have no idea what you are talking about." Tabetha's sickeningly sweet tone came through a toothy grin.

"What is wrong with you, Grateful?" Logan asked, dropping his fork. "You're being rude."

"You don't know, okay?" I said to Logan. "There's more going on here than you think."

Logan stood, pushing his chair back with a wood-on-stone grind. "Do you mean that I'm in love with a powerful witch?" He placed a hand on Tabetha's shoulder. "One more powerful than you? Does it bother you that I'm happy without you, Grateful? Are you surprised that someone else, someone more beautiful, magical, and powerful than you, could appreciate me for what I have to give?"

A sick feeling overcame me. Was he right? Was I jealous that he was cooking for someone else? In love with someone else? It was true I missed his friendship. I missed having him in my life. But in my heart of hearts I wanted the best for him. It was just hard for me to believe that Tabetha was best for him.

Then again, he was an adult who knew what he was getting into. He could make that decision for himself.

"I'm sorry, Logan. You're right. I was out of line." I pushed my chair back a few inches from the table and glanced at Rick, who seemed markedly uncomfortable with the conversation. "I apologize that we can't stay any longer, Tabetha. But before we go, I'd like to offer you compensation for the magic you gave Rick."

She swirled her wine in her glass and leaned back in her chair. "Go on."

"In return for your spell, the humanity candle, I will give you the only spell you can't make for yourself—a spell to find and bind your true love. The positivity potion."

Tabetha's eyes widened. "Worthless to me," she said. "I've already found my true love." She waved a hand toward Logan. "What else can you offer me in exchange for *your* true love?"

My eyes flicked down to the table.

"I thought so." She tapped her fingers together in front of her chin, then turned toward Logan. "Darling, would you gather dessert while I talk business with our friends?"

He nodded, pecking her on the lips before shooting a nasty glance in my direction and disappearing through what I assumed was the kitchen door.

When her eyes turned back in our direction, they were as cold as ice. "I am owed blood, and blood shall I have. Positivity potion. Hah! You insult me." She stood, bracing herself on the table. Behind her, the gargoyles came alive, the copper melting, moving with her anger. Rick grabbed my hand. "I have not lived more than one thousand years to put my faith in such inconsequential emotions as love. There is only one thing that truly matters in this world: power. An experienced caretaker like Rick would have increased my power exponentially."

I recoiled with disgust.

"But since you find the idea to be so unsettling, there is only one alternative."

I was still speechless from her admission of using both Rick and Logan. She was a monster, a godforsaken fiend. The gargoyles bared their teeth in a silent growl.

Rick spoke up. "What do you want, Tabetha?"

She looked me straight in the eye. "Your territory."

"My territory?" I looked at Rick in confusion. "You mean, like my cemetery? I didn't know that was something I could give."

Rick straightened, his eyes darkening black as night, and the bones of his face shifting to take on an animalistic appearance, almost feral. "Unacceptable. Hecate will never allow it."

"She will." Tabetha pointed one long red nail at me. "Mother will allow it if you petition her to release you from your obligation."

I laughed. "You must be joking."

Her expression was as serious as sin.

"You want me to petition the goddess Hecate to relieve me of my territory and give it to you? Why would she agree to that? Why would I?"

Rick shoved his chair back. "It is not simply your territory, *mi cielo*. The source of a Hecate's power is the dead. Without your cemetery, you will lose your power. You will become human again, and she will gain what you have lost."

Human again. The thought of it wasn't as terrifying as you might think. There'd been lots of times I would have given anything to be a normal human being again with normal problems. But the power shift nagged at me. Tabetha's motivation went beyond my territory itself; I just knew it. She was after something more.

My mind flashed to *The Book of Flesh and Bone*. No, even she couldn't break Soleil's fae magic. Unless she planned to kill her.

"No," I said quickly. "Unacceptable. I made you a fair and equitable offer. If you don't want the love potion, that's your choice, but the terms of the contract are fulfilled. You turn your nose up at it, you get nothing."

Tabetha crossed her arms over her chest, drumming her nails on her forearm. The gargoyles behind her echoed her movements, their talons tapping on the brick hearth.

"You will petition Mother for release of your territory, or else," she said through her teeth.

"Or else what?"

"Or else you will find the head of the man who is about to walk through that door boiling in a pot on your stove."

I wobbled on my feet. Rick caught me around the waist and tucked me into his side. Tabetha was a wicked witch. I'd never been in the presence of someone as evil. With new eyes, I could see the darkness in everything she did. This had never been about Rick. The candle had always been about gaining power.

The gargoyles froze into their menacing shapes as Logan returned with a tray of pastries in his hand. "Are you all right, Grateful? You look pale," he said, the first notes of concern I'd heard in his voice all night coming through.

"Don't worry about her, darling. Have a pastry," Tabetha said. She ran the tops of her nails along his jawline and then cupped his chin. Before she removed her hand, she looked at me, her fingers making a subtle cutting motion across his neck before returning to her side.

Oblivious, Logan set the tray down and took a seat. He served her and then himself.

"You have until the spring equinox to convince Mother." She circled one hand in the air. "New beginnings and all. I know you can do it, Grateful. You're a strong woman." She smiled a broad, toothy grin.

I stared at Logan, my stomach clenching with fear for his life. "I'll try," I mumbled. I had to. If I didn't agree, she might kill him now, or tomorrow, or the next day. At least if I said I'd try, she might give me until the equinox.

"Oh, you will succeed, one way or another." Tabetha scraped a large bite of pastry into her mouth with her teeth. "Ba-bye now. Do be careful on your way out. I wouldn't want to have to rescue you from the landscaping again."

"From the landscaping?" Logan laughed around his pastry.

"It's a long story, darling," Tabetha said.

I wanted to kill her. I wanted to leap across the table and plunge Nightshade into her black heart. The fantasy played out again and again in my head. Rick ushered me back the way we'd come by the waist. "Easy, *mi cielo*. This entire house is her living weapon. We will never survive a fight with her here."

My fists balled with rage. I'd have to give her what she wanted. I had no choice. And I wondered once she had what she'd asked for, would that be the end? Somehow I didn't think so. Tabetha believed the only thing that mattered in this world was power, and like a drug, those addicted to power never had enough.

CHAPTER 11
Power Source

Poe met us at the door, landing on the porch railing with a noisy flap of wings. He'd opted to fly home while we drove. "How'd it go with the Wicked Witch of the East?"

I groaned as I turned the key and pushed the door open with my hip. "Crappy. She wants me to petition Hecate to relieve me of my responsibility for my realm so that she can take it over."

"Sacrilege." Poe shook his head. "She is violating the natural law."

Rick scoffed. "I do not believe Tabetha has any reverence for natural or any other law."

I grabbed an open bottle of Shiraz off the counter near the fridge where I kept it and poured myself a glass. "She says if I don't do this, she's going to kill Logan."

"Logan? How is he involved?" Poe asked.

"He's dating her. That's why he was acting so weird. They're an item, only he has no idea that she's using his life to bait me into doing her will." I sipped the wine, enjoying the dark symphony of flavors in the full-bodied red.

Rick rubbed his forehead and smoothed one eyebrow with his thumb. "This is my fault. This is all my doing."

"Stop," I said. "I forgive you, all right? We had a fight. You overreacted and pressed the self-destruct button. But I get it. I might have done the same thing in different circumstances."

He shook his head. "You don't understand. I should have known this was her true motivation. When she told me she was taking over Polina's realm, I should have suspected yours would be next."

"Are you saying that Tabetha played a part in Polina's disappearance?"

Rick paced to my cupboard and removed a wineglass. After rinsing the dust out in the sink, he picked up the bottle of wine. "Anything stronger?"

"Above the sink. I keep Scotch for Dad."

He put down the bottle and retrieved the Scotch, pouring a shot into the wineglass and tossing it back. I wasn't sure that alcohol did anything for Rick, but maybe he needed the burn in his throat to give him the courage to say what he needed to say. "Did you notice the gargoyles next to Tabetha's fireplace?"

"Yeah, they came alive when she got angry. Creepy as hell."

"That's not within a wood witch's natural power."

"Meaning?"

Rick's eyes darted around my kitchen. "Do you have a pen and paper?"

I dug a pen out of my junk drawer and grabbed an envelope from a stack of unopened mail next to the fridge. Electric bill. The great equalizer. "Here, use this."

He drew a five-pointed star with circles at each of the points.

"A pentagram," I said, thinking aloud.

"Yes. The symbol of ultimate power. Each point represents one of the five elements."

"Five? I thought there were four: earth, wind, fire, and water."

"For the children of Hecate, there are five." Inside the circle resting on the top point, Rick wrote *Wood,* then inside the circle to the right *Air,* then *Earth*, then *Metal*, then *Water*. "You are an air witch. Your power increases with the night air, you can control the weather, and you can create fire without using a spell—like when you light a candle with your breath."

I nodded. "Okay. And Tabetha is a wood witch. She can make things grow and animate plants to do her bidding."

"Correct. All witches have the power to manipulate all five elements. However, if the element is outside their natural source of power, they must use sorcery—spells, enchantments—and the result is weaker."

"But Tabetha could also create heat. She blasted me with it."

"Witches manipulate fire and ice as it relates to their element. Air is the only element that can produce true fire. The oxygen feeds the flame. But the spring follows Tabetha. Water boils and freezes. Metal melts. Tonight, the gargoyles animated with Tabetha's anger, not her enchantment."

"Let me guess, Polina was a metal witch," I said.

"Precisely. When Tabetha inherited Polina's realm, she inherited Polina's power."

Poe snorted. "She intends to absorb the entire pentagram."

"So, what you're saying is Tabetha always intended to acquire my realm, one way or another, to attain natural power over the air."

"Not just the air, earth too," Poe said. "When you made Rick, you gave him caretaker magic, which is based on the power of the earth. The combination has made you strong. She means to inherit both air and earth upon your abdication of your throne."

I looked at Rick. "She'd have everything but water. What would happen if she obtained all five elements?"

"The elements enhance each other." Rick drew arrows between the circles at the points of the star. "Wood feeds air, both by plants producing oxygen and burning in fire.

Air feeds earth by carrying natural matter from one place to another, and as fire, burning things to ash."

"Fertilization and pollination," I clarified.

Rick nodded. "Earth houses metal within it. Metal nourishes water. Water feeds wood."

"She'd be exponentially more powerful," I mumbled. "She's not just gaining another element, she's gaining the relationship between them."

"Yes."

Poe squawked to interrupt. "And she's losing balance. The elements are meant to keep each other in check. Wood parts earth. Earth dams or muddies water. Water extinguishes fire. Fire melts metal. Metal chops wood."

I pressed my fingertips into the sides of my head, feeling like my brain might explode sorting out the implications. "Is it even possible for one witch to house all that natural power within herself?"

Rick shook his head. "I do not know, *mi cielo*, but I do not wish to find out. Tabetha's heart is hard. If she succeeds in quenching her thirst for power, I fear there will be no stopping her."

I guzzled the last of my wine. "So what do we do?"

"I hate to be the bearer of bad news, but I believe your only option is to call her bluff and allow her to kill Logan," Rick said.

The base of my wineglass hit the counter, hard enough for the stem to break off in my hand. "Fuck!" I yelled as glass sliced my palm. I grabbed a paper towel and pressed into the cut. "I'm not paying her off with Logan's life. He's my friend."

Rick grabbed the garbage from under the counter and pitched the pieces of glass, then offered me his wrist. "Blood?"

"Not now," I snapped, pressing the wound. "It's out of the question. I'm not sacrificing Logan."

Poe exchanged glances with Rick. I knew that look. It was the if-only-she-understood-how-serious-this-was glare.

"I get it, okay? If we do nothing, she kills him. If I do as she asks, she absorbs our powers and probably kills us all, just as she probably killed Polina. So the question is, how do we stop her before she can do either?"

"How long did she give you?" Poe asked.

"The spring equinox. I need to hand over my territory by our wedding day."

"Of course," Poe said. "The spring equinox is the season when a wood witch has the most power. Everything sprouts. The trees come back from the dead."

"Great. So I'm supposed to give her more power on the day she already has the most?"

Rick took my hand. "I know Logan means something to you." He looked at me with pity and a well-concealed jealousy.

"He's just a friend. He used to be a good friend. I can't let him die to serve our purposes. It's too Machiavellian. I couldn't live with myself."

"No one wants Logan to die. But we can't give in to Tabetha. If she inherits our elements, only the goddess

Hecate would be more powerful. Tabetha would be invincible."

I scowled. "Then the question is, how do we remove Logan from the equation without giving Tabetha what she wants?"

Neither Poe nor Rick had any answers for me.

CHAPTER 12
Training

"Again," Rick commanded.

Arms laden with heavy stones, I concentrated on lifting from the frozen ground. Rick had brought me to the clearing behind his cottage to hone my skills in preparation for battling Tabetha. I'd already put in thirty minutes of swordplay, another twenty starting things on fire, and now was attempting to teach myself to hover. Levitating on command did not come naturally to me. Sure, I'd done it on accident when Rick and I were making love, but this, doing it again and again like some sort of endurance sport, hurt my brain.

True, I'd levitated my spell book, but working that magic on my own body was an entirely different animal. The intention had to come from within, from a hotspot deep within my heart.

The air around me buzzed against my skin. Eyes closed, I willed myself to become a part of it for the fifteenth time that day. I felt my boots leave solid ground. My toes dangled beneath me. I opened my eyes.

Rick smiled. "Good. More than a foot this time."

"A foot?" I made the mistake of glancing down. The ground rushed toward me, and I landed in a jumble of stones and limbs. "Ouch," I said, too tired to put any real emotion behind it.

"You must try harder, *mi cielo*. Tabetha says she'll wait until the equinox, but there is no guarantee. She cannot be trusted. You must learn to defend yourself."

"Do I look like I'm not taking this seriously?" I pushed a small boulder off my bruised abdomen and scrambled to my feet. "Besides, it's hopeless. No matter how hard I try, I'm not going to make up for a thousand years of missed experience. Even if I remembered all the magic from all my past lives, Tabetha has at least six hundred years on me."

"You can't think of it that way. You have access to two elements, just like her, and you have the larger cemetery. If she comes here, to your territory, you will be able to access that power. She won't."

I narrowed my eyes and pointed at my chest. "I can access the dead here and she can't?"

"Yes."

"A lot of good it did me when she came here before."

Rick rubbed his palms together. "It takes intention, *mi cielo*. I should have taught you the skill long ago. I thought we had time."

"Teach me now."

He knelt down and began to unlace my boot.

"What are you doing?"

"It is easier to connect with the dead when you are barefoot."

"It's twenty degrees out here. Does connecting with the dead require frostbite?"

"Do you want to learn to tap into this power or not?"

I toed out of my boots and planted my bare feet on the snow-covered grass.

"Concentrate. Send your intention into the earth below you."

I tried. I really did. I closed my eyes and reached out to my cemetery the way I often metaphysically reached out to Rick.

"How do you feel?" Rick asked.

"Cold. Like my pinky toe is going to crack off."

He tipped his head and pursed his lips like he was disappointed.

"Okay, okay, I'll try again." I closed my eyes and focused on the hotspot behind my breastbone. The wind buzzed against my skin and I channeled it down through my heels, into the dirt. I blocked out the cold, Rick's presence, everything. I breathed deeply.

An electric tingle pricked the arches of my feet. The power wormed through my ankles to my knees. "I can feel it," I whispered. I tried to will a stronger connection.

"Drink, *mi cielo*."

I opened my eyes. Flat on my back in the snow, I stared into the bleak afternoon sky with Rick's bloody wrist between my lips. I pushed it aside. "What happened?"

"You lost consciousness."

"But I felt it. The power was right there." Frustration made my words sharp and hard.

Rick grabbed my boots and lifted me into his arms. "You will keep practicing. It will come."

"What if it doesn't?"

"It always does." His words were soft and encouraging.

I leaned my head against his chest. He helped me put my boots back on.

"Up, *mi cielo*. We have more work to do."

CHAPTER 13
My Other Job

"Grateful, you are needed at the nurses desk," Berta, our unit secretary, said from the door. The ER was humming for the third night in a row, and I looked up at her from a sea of rubber gloves, bandages, and tape.

"I'll be there as soon as I start this IV," I said.

She nodded and closed the door behind her.

I slipped on a pair of rubber gloves and rubbed a disinfectant swab in swirls over the vein I'd chosen in my patient's forearm. The narrow ribbon of blue was barely visible beneath the skin. I checked her chart. "Mrs. Scott, can you tell me why you are here today?" It was always good to keep them talking while I inserted the catheter. The prick wasn't particularly painful, but people got weird around needles.

"I was grocery shopping, and I just passed out. One of the employees called 911, and here I am." The woman smiled. She looked about forty, neatly groomed, but pale and clammy.

I tied a rubber tourniquet just above the spot I had targeted and tapped the vein with my finger until it popped slightly. The reaction was less than I'd expected; she was definitely dehydrated, which would explain the syncope. Still, I was sure I could hit it.

"This might pinch a little," I warned as I positioned the needle at a shallow angle. She turned her head away. I was quick and accurate. A flash of blood, and I advanced the catheter and untied the tourniquet. "Do you have any medical conditions that might have contributed to your loss of consciousness? Has this ever happened before?" While she was distracted, I filled several vacutainers with her blood, and then carefully removed the needle. I had that puppy secured in a heartbeat with an occlusive dressing and connected to the saline drip I'd prepared.

"No. Nothing. I'm not on any medications. I've always been healthy."

"All set." I tossed the remnants of my procedure in the bin and removed my rubber gloves. "We'll send your blood samples to the lab and see what's going on." I used the sink in the room to wash up.

"Nurse?" Mrs. Scott said from behind me. "I think there's something wrong."

"Yes?" I turned around. A growing spot of blood had appeared on the blanket over the woman's pelvis. I looked at her arm. The insertion site wasn't bleeding. "Do you have your period?"

She shook her head, groggily.

Donning a new pair of gloves, I peeled back the blankets. The source was no mystery. A sloppy bandage over her femoral artery was soaked through. I hit the button on the wall to call for help and put pressure on the wound.

"Mrs. Scott, what happened here? Did you have an accident?"

Her eyes glazed over. "Nothing happened. There's nothing wrong."

Uh-oh. Was this? Could it be? I tugged the bandage out from under my palm and got a good look at the source of the bleeding. Vampire bite. *Shit.*

"Nothing's wrong. Nothing happened," she repeated. And then her eyes rolled back in her head.

Help arrived in the form of the trauma team and a crash cart.

* * * * *

Turns out the vampire had ripped open her femoral artery, then bandaged it and sent her on her way. The vamp had compelled her to believe nothing had happened. She could have bled to death. Thankfully, the surgeon was able to repair the damage.

The predominant theory was that she had suffered an animal attack. Yeah, an animal bite to the inner thigh. That made sense.

With all the drama, hours had passed since Berta had given me the heads-up to check the desk. I took my break and headed that way. On the corner of the desk, a bouquet of flowers in a crystal vase brightened the otherwise bland décor. Roses, lilies, and a few blooms I didn't even know the names of filled out the arrangement. It was gorgeous and exotic, and it had my name on it.

"Someone's a lucky girl," Berta said.

I plucked the card off the plastic prong and opened it.

> *Mi cielo,*
> *   Michelle has informed me you have not yet chosen flowers for our wedding. May I suggest these, although they will pale in comparison to the beauty of the bride.*
> *Love,*
> *Rick*

"How did your boyfriend even find a florist to deliver third shift?" she asked.

"He's my fiancé, and he's very resourceful," I said. Probably got help from Soleil. Flowers bloomed in her presence all year round. Plus, a fae florist would have no qualms about delivering in the middle of the night.

Berta huffed and mumbled something about "the honeymoon phase."

I pulled out my phone and sent Rick a text. *Thank you for the flowers.*

Nothing. He'd had the phone more than a month now and still didn't know how to text. I shrugged and dialed his number on my way to the cafeteria.

He answered on the first ring. "Why do you insist on typing the message?" he asked. "Isn't it enough that we can call each other at any moment we wish?"

"Thank you for the flowers."

"My pleasure."

"I think your choices will be perfect with the dresses I picked for the bridesmaids."

"Glad I could help."

"I have some bad news. I just saw a vampire bite come through the ER. Brutal."

"Brutal would be if you found a dead body. The vampire showed restraint if the person was alive."

"More like the vamp made an effort not to get caught. The victim was compelled not to realize she was bleeding to death. Probably so she could get far enough away from the scene before she died. Makes it impossible for us to trace the killer."

"It appears Julius's absence is already rippling through the coven."

"We've got a week and a half until the full moon. We have to find him. Can we do a locator spell like we did with Marcus?"

"We can try. The spell will have to be performed at the Thames."

"Tomorrow. I'll need sleep or I won't be strong enough."

"I'll make preparations."

"Oh, and Rick?"

"Yes, *mi cielo*."

"I texted you because you need to learn how to text." I stressed each of the words to make sure he knew I was serious.

He chuckled. "Why for?"

"Because someday you might be in a situation where you can't speak but you need to tell me something."

"When would that be? Give me an example."

"Say you were in a library," I suggested. "You must remain silent, but you might need to ask a question."

"Why would I be in a library?"

"Researching a spell."

"In what library could I research a spell?" he asked.

I closed my eyes and shook my head. "Okay, poor example. How about this? What if you were stuck in an alley and the only thing keeping you from being eaten by carnivorous elves was the ability to remain perfectly silent while texting me for help?"

"I'd simply use our connection to call you psychically."

With a groan of frustration, I said, "It's a life skill. I cannot be married to a man who can't text. It's impractical. I promise you'll like it if you try it."

He hummed skeptically.

I stopped at the entrance to the cafeteria and bit my lip. "How's this, Rick? I get off work at seven. I can either go home and sleep or stop by your house for sex. Text me which you'd prefer."

I hung up on his response and giggled with satisfaction as I slid the phone into my pocket.

CHAPTER 14
Logan

The next afternoon, I stopped into Valentine's for lunch. It was a Saturday, busiest day of the week, which meant Logan was guaranteed to be there. I needed to talk to him. I needed him to understand he was in danger.

"What can I get for you, Grateful?" Dustin asked as I bellied up to the bar. Dustin was Logan's assistant manager. Good sign. He only bartended when Logan was managing.

"Valentine burger, medium-well, and fries," I said, scooting onto a barstool.

He scratched my order onto his pad. "Coke?"

I nodded. While he filled a tall glass, I perused the restaurant.

"You looking for Logan?" he asked.

"I was going to say hello if I saw him."

Dustin slid the glass across the bar to me and leaned closer, his smile melting as he neared. "He's in his office." Dustin looked right then left. The bar was packed and Dustin had the reputation of being a huge gossip. I'm not sure what he was looking for because despite the crowd of people around me, he kept talking. "Between you and me, he hardly comes out of there anymore. He's changed."

I furrowed my brow. "Does he give a reason?" I was curious if Dustin had heard of Tabetha. Did they date publicly?

Dustin shrugged one shoulder. "I think you broke his heart."

"Pshaw," I protested. "Have you seen him in here with anyone new? Maybe a woman?"

He gave me a strange and curious look. "No. What have you heard?"

So, he didn't know about Tabetha. Interesting. "Nothing," I said. "I just didn't want to take all the credit for his weirdness."

Dustin nodded and held up my order. "I'll put this in. It will be a few minutes, if you want to say hello." He gestured with his head toward the office. "Leave your coat, and I'll save your seat."

I stripped out of my black wool trench and draped it over the barstool, noticing the slightly singed back and shoulders. I needed a new coat. Dustin disappeared into the kitchen while I navigated the bustling tables to the door to Logan's office and gave two sharp knocks.

"Come in," he said gruffly.

I hurried through the door, closing it behind me.

"What are *you* doing here?" he asked. He looked up from his lunch, an expression of disgust on his face that had nothing to do with the potpie he was eating.

"I need to talk to you about Tabetha."

"After how you treated us at our dinner party, I should throw you out of here on your ass. Lucky for you, Tabetha has asked me to keep our relationship discreet, for obvious reasons." He waved his hand in the air like he was directing an invisible wand. "Kicking you out would invite a lot of questions. I don't suppose you would consider leaving on your own?"

"Not until I say what I came to say."

He widened his eyes at me. "I'm all ears."

"You are in grave danger," I said. "Tabetha threatened to kill you."

He shook his head and rolled his eyes.

"When you left the room to get dessert, Tabetha demanded my cemetery. If I don't turn it over to her by the spring equinox, she threatened to kill you. She's using you, Logan."

For a moment, Logan simply stared at the wall, mouth slightly open, jaw sliding back and forth as if he were adjusting the joint. When he spoke, there was menace in his words. "Tabetha told me you would do this."

"What?"

He swiveled his chair to face me again. "You're jealous. You are finally realizing what a good thing you had, and now you want me back. You made your choice. Now you have to live with it."

My mouth dropped open. "I am perfectly happy with my choice, Logan." I stormed his desk and leaned across so that our noses almost touched. "What I'm not happy with is having your blood on my hands."

Hard eyes locked onto mine. "Then give Tabetha what she wants," he said through his teeth.

I straightened. Who was I looking at? Was Logan so smitten with Tabetha that he was willing to gamble his life for her cause? If he was asking me to give Tabetha what she wanted, he must understand on some level that the threat was real. But there was not one shred of doubt in his eyes.

"You love her," I said under my breath.

"Absolutely."

"She's using you, Logan," I repeated.

"I think you should leave now." He stood and pointed toward the door. "Go."

With a heavy weight in my heart, I did … as soon as I got my Valentine burger to go. You absolutely do not abandon a hot and ready Valentine burger.

* * * * *

The next day, I met Rick at the Thames Theater to perform the spell to find Julius. We'd done this magic before, when we'd gone searching for Marcus after he escaped the hellmouth. The salve was a little different this time. The goop at the bottom of the cauldron at the center of the ring of skulls still smelled of eucalyptus, but Rick had used more golden seal to counteract the additional time between Julius's last sighting and our search. I didn't understand how the spell worked exactly, but I hoped it was as effective as it had been when we'd used it before.

"Thank goodness they cleaned the room," I said. The area at the foot of the bed where we were performing the spell had been a puddle of blood the last time we were here.

"I am sure it was done as soon as Silas cataloged the evidence. All the spilled blood would have driven the vamps here mad." He removed the giant wrought iron swizzle stick he was using to stir and placed it on the floor next to the cauldron. "The salve is ready."

"Here goes nothing," I said. I scooped a glob onto my finger and smeared it on my eyelids. "Let me know when the minute is up." If the spell worked as planned, when I opened my eyes I would see a red dot in the direction Julius was taken. Rick and I would follow the dot to his destination.

"Open," Rick said.

Gradually, I worked against the heavy, sticky mess to lift my lids. I blinked and blinked again. "This is wrong," I said. I turned my head, right and left.

"Do you see the red dot?"

"Oh, I see it. Only, there isn't just one. There are thousands, all over the room, in every direction."

"What does it mean?"

"I have no idea." I stood and tried to focus my magic, willing the most ancient part of myself to interpret what I was seeing. "Maybe he's de—"

Rick's hand slapped over my mouth. In typical caretaker fashion, he'd crossed the room in a split second. "Don't say it," he whispered in my ear. His eyes flicked up toward the ceiling. "Once the coven knows, we will have no opportunity to influence who is chosen as his successor."

I nodded. He dropped his hand. "But do you think I'm right?"

"It's possible. I have no explanation."

I grabbed a towel from our equipment bag and wiped the salve from my eyes. "Let's try again, this time for vampire suspect number one."

"Bathory," he said, agreeing with my course of action.

Scooping another glob of salve, I spread it over my eyelids and concentrated on the vamp who'd tried to kill me. When I opened them again, I shook my head in frustration as I looked around the room. "Nothing. No red at all."

"She wasn't here."

"She was behind this, Rick. We both know she was."

He nodded. "I agree, *mi cielo*, but perhaps she compelled another to do her dirty work for her. The injuries to the victim were more consistent with ogre activity."

Again, I wiped the salve from my eyes. "This spell only finds vampires. If we don't know what or who took Julius, and I can't track Julius, how do we find him?"

Rick grimaced. "We will have to think of something else."

"In the meantime, we need to learn who plans to challenge Julius's position, and try to win that person's allegiance."

"Or groom our own candidate." Rick looked at me and lowered his chin.

"I know what you're thinking, and he'll never agree to it," I whispered. Oh, how I hoped he wouldn't agree to it. My stomach sank. He was thinking of Gary. Gary, who I'd dated in a past life—his past life. Gary, who I tried my hardest to forget on a day-to-day basis, not because I still had feelings for him—I didn't—but because of how our relationship ended. For me, it was an ego-shattering, financial train wreck.

Rick pressed the issue. "No one else hates Bathory and loves you more. He'd be the perfect coven leader."

"He doesn't love me."

Rick raised an eyebrow. "As vampires go, his feelings for you are close enough to serve our purposes."

I couldn't argue with him there. "If the challenge is physical, Gary doesn't have a chance of winning. Vampire or not, he's forever stuck in a poet's body."

He dropped his chin and looked at me through his lashes, a sexy smirk turning the corners of his lips. "Tsk,

tsk, tsk. Always underestimating your abilities. When will you see yourself for the powerful witch I know you to be?"

"Excuse me?" I was slightly offended at his perception that I lacked confidence.

"You are magic, *mi cielo*. A sorceress of the dead. I believe with the right spell, you could greatly improve his odds."

* * * * *

"No. Definitely not," Gary said.

I'd cornered him in his room and carefully revealed our suspicion that Julius might be permanently detained.

"You don't know what you are asking me to do," he whined.

"If you are worried about the challenge itself. I can make you a potion that will render you practically invincible for a time. I can make it so you can't lose."

He ran his long tapered fingers over the spine of a book on a shelf in his room. "Do you want to know what the challenge entails?"

"Yes."

From the bookshelf, he selected a purple book with a gargoyle image on the spine and symbols where the title belonged. Vampire language, I supposed. "Is that the secret vampire manual?"

"Something like that." He opened the volume to a page near the back. "At midnight, during the full moon, the Druherand, the coven leader's second, will announce the abdication of the leader and ask for a challenger for the throne. If no challenger steps forward, the second-in-command inherits the throne." He looked up at me from the book. "That's the normal procedure, only this time, Julius's second is the demon Padnon. A demon cannot rule a vampire coven. So in this case, his request will not be to challenge him directly."

"Okay. So anyone can toss their hat into the ring?"

"Yes. There is no limit on the number of challengers, but if there is only one challenger, that vampire will inherit Julius's role because Padnon can't."

"Seems like more than one vampire would want the honor of leading this coven."

Gary groaned and plopped down on his bed. "There's this guy," he whispered. I leaned in so I could hear. "A vampire called Kace, one of Bathory's. Rumor has it the guy was a serial killer Bathory saved from the chair. He's a badass, Grateful, and he has not been happy feeding on animal blood and willing humans. This guy likes to be a predator, you get me?"

I straightened and nodded. "You think he will be a challenger?"

"He's already talking about it. No one is going to want to fight Kace, especially since the ring itself is so deadly."

"What's deadly about the ring?"

He opened the book again. "The challengers shall be confined to 'the ring.' The place where the challenge shall take place shall be no more than twenty-five feet in diameter with posts to the north, south, east, and west.

The north post shall be covered with silver spikes soaked in holy water, the south, a chained werewolf, the bite of which is deadly. The east post shall be the site of a Vladimir's guillotine—that's a machine designed to cut off your head if you get too close—and the west post will be a coffin."

"A coffin?"

"The competitors are bound to the ring by magic. They cannot leave unless a winner is proclaimed. The challenge continues until there is one survivor or the sun comes up. Only one coffin means only one vampire can survive the sunrise in the ring. It's a fail-safe."

"Nice."

"Two go in but only one comes out," Gary said. He slammed the book shut and got up to return it to the shelf. "Or at least that's how it usually plays out. You can see why I'm not interested in being a challenger, with or without your help." He ran his fingers through his chestnut brown hair. "I'm a lover, not a fighter, Grateful. It's not going to happen."

"Answer me this." I clasped my hands behind my back and rocked back on my heels. "What happens if Bathory returns and becomes a challenger? What if she wins and is your coven leader?"

"She can't." Gary shook his head.

"Why? Julius can't stop her anymore, and we think she's behind his disappearance. All she needs is a coven large enough to protect her and she's back in the game."

"If she comes out of hiding, you will sentence her to the hellmouth."

I shook my head. "Even if you share the location of the challenge with us, would we be able to get close enough? Or would her supporters protect her?"

Gary frowned.

"Whether it's Kace who takes over or Bathory, do you think the new king is going to allow Julius's vamps to live? After your attack on their coven during the solstice, do you honestly believe you are safe once Bathory's supporters are in charge?"

His green eyes narrowed, and his arms crossed over his chest. "It's the middle of the day. I need sleep, and you need to go."

I was in serious danger of pushing too hard. I gave him a curt nod and turned for the door. As I left, I said, "Let me know when you come to your senses."

CHAPTER 15
A Good Night's Rest

I flopped into bed in the wee hours of the morning, my limbs bouncing on the mattress from the intensity of the collision. What a night. Two demon possessions, a vampire rapist, and a twelve-year-old girl attempting to open a portal to hell with a book she picked up at a yard sale. Malice mitigated. The baddies were snuggled in their hellmouth beds, and the book was burned in a cauldron of spirit-infestation-sanitizing herbs.

"The house is going to smell like Thanksgiving dinner for weeks," Poe said, sniffing at the burnt sage in the air.

"Better than the alternative. You'd think a kid these days would have seen enough horror movies not to reenact a scribbled ritual in a garage sale novel about necromancy of all things."

"Is the girl going to be okay?" Poe asked. He'd waited outside during the entire confrontation.

"Yeah, Rick hoodwinked her brain." I yawned. "She'll stay away from the occult from now on."

"Where is the caretaker, anyway? Don't you too usually, er …"

"Engage in post-patrol coupling? Not tonight. I gotta get some sleep." It wasn't just the night's work. I'd practiced levitation every day this week and was semi-successful in drawing my cemetery's power a time or two. But between our training sessions, managing our ward all night, and my nursing job, I was licked.

The problem was we couldn't take our foot off the accelerator. Tabetha could strike at any moment, and the vampire challenge for Julius's position was just around the corner. As a newbie witch, I was still waking up to my power. I needed to ready myself. I needed to evolve.

"G'night, then," Poe said, nesting in a discarded shirt on my dresser.

"Goodnight, Poe."

Despite the night's excitement, I drifted into a deep sleep almost instantly, my body's desperate need for rejuvenation trumping the ceaseless race of thoughts through my mind. The "should haves" and "could haves" were swept away by the "must have" of physical exhaustion. The luxury of guilt and anger was not one I could afford.

The dream started well into my rest, near the coming of dawn. How I knew this, I can't say; I had no way to measure except for circadian intuition. I experienced the dream lucidly, aware I was dreaming but vividly entrenched as if I were awake. My mental world turned green. Plush grass tickled the sides of my bare feet, and the sun glinted through a rich tapestry of forest canopy. A bird called overhead and the colorful curved beak of a toucan soared past me.

"A banana would totes rock right now," I said. "Or a bowl of fruity rings." I followed the flight of the toucan. The bird landed on a bunch of bananas hanging from a tree. "Ask for a banana. Get a banana. I love this dream."

I stepped forward, plucking the fruit from beneath the bird's talons and opening it under its watchful eye. The fruit tasted sweet and perfectly ripe. As I swallowed, a stone wall appeared behind the tree. The wall didn't erupt from the ground or shimmer into existence. One moment it wasn't there and the next it was.

The wall was made of stone and mortar with an open metal door just a few feet from me. Two torches on either side of the doorway blazed to life. I stepped back to get a better view.

A dark and dangerous woman stepped over the threshold. Something was seriously wrong with my vision. For a moment, it appeared she had three heads—one streaked with gray, one with ebony waves, and one plaited down her back. I blinked rapidly against the triple vision, and the faces blended into one.

The power of her presence was overwhelming. It filled the garden with a soupy humidity that weighed on my skin like a cloak. I recognized her. I'd met her once before, when I'd conjured my familiar. This was Hecate, my mother. Well, my first mother; the mother who'd made me a witch. My physical presence came about via human mothers, but the feminine power coursing toward me now was the source of my wild and eternal soul within.

"Mother?" It was the only word my lips would produce.

Her toga shifted unnaturally as she approached, defying gravity, while her black silky hair contrasted her full ruby lips. The intensity in her eyes made me look away. A snake dripped down from the tree beside her, and she offered it her arm to wrap around with a warm smile, as if the thing was a long-lost pet.

"Do not be afraid. I have not come to hurt you," she said to me. Her voice echoed as if three women were speaking at once. Only the echo wasn't of the same voice. I heard the thready, deep tones of an old woman, the heady confidence that matched the middle-aged woman before me, and the high-pitched clarity of a young innocent. "We must speak, daughter."

"Okay," I said tentatively. It wasn't every day that a goddess asked to have a chat. I could guess this was about Tabetha, but I wasn't presumptuous enough to speculate on her opinion on the matter. Fortunately, I didn't have to wait long to find out.

"Your sister Tabetha displeases me," she began. Her black eyes blazed, and her lips moved in an exaggerated fashion reminiscent of silent movies. I resisted the urge to cover my ears against the intensity of her voice.

"Funny, I feel the same way."

Hecate's dark eyes drilled into me, and a sensation of being squeezed by a massive hand left me breathless. She did not say a word, but I got the sense this was meant to be a one-sided conversation. I buttoned my lip.

"Tabetha is attempting to obtain the five elements. I cannot impart to you strongly enough how vital it is we thwart her efforts. She has asked you to renounce your throne. I will not allow you to do so. You are the Monk's Hill Witch, the ruler of your realm. If you allow Tabetha to have the air, the elemental source of your power, she will become too mighty, a monster. Already, absorbing Polina's territory has left her mind unstable and withered her soul."

A monkey cried, leaping between two trees in Hecate's garden, and the weight of an expected response settled upon my shoulders. I could feel her staring at me, like a hot ray of sun on my face. Apparently, she wanted an answer.

"I won't let her have my territory, but I need help. She has my friend Logan, and she says she will kill him if I don't turn over my ward."

"And so he must die," she said coolly. "Tabetha is owed blood. Your friend will fulfill the debt against your caretaker." A butterfly landed in her palm and she whispered to it in another language as it opened and closed its wings. An uninvited tension gripped me wondering if the snake coiled around her opposite forearm would make a snack of it, but the reptile didn't move.

I cleared my throat. "Uh, I can't let Logan die. Like I said, he's my friend. A close friend. Well, he was until Tabetha poisoned his mind."

Her eyes narrowed in my direction. "He is human, yes? Resurrect him if you must, once his blood has fulfilled the contract."

"Resurrect him?" I shook my head. "I'm not going to turn Logan into some sort of zombie. I got him into this. Tabetha knew we cared for each other and is using him to blackmail me. I won't let her get away with it."

Thunder cracked above us, and the sky darkened. Mother was angry. The butterfly in her hand fluttered away to safer ground. "Your human feelings impair your immortal judgment."

I bit my lip, thinking fast. How could I put this in a way even a self-absorbed deity might understand? "Logan is a medium who helped me keep *The Book of Flesh and Bone* out of vampire hands. I need his alliance to protect my territory." It was true to an extent. I'd left out a few details like he'd actually only channeled his mother and his power didn't seem to be working anymore.

Her eyes narrowed. "A medium? A human who communicates with souls who have crossed over? Yes, his talents could be useful. Souls on the other side are beyond even my reach." She played with the snake between her hands, allowing it to crawl and twist around her wrists and between her fingers. Her jaw hardened. "There is only one alternative."

"Yes."

"You must challenge her for her territory and kill her before she kills you. I give you permission to kill Tabetha."

I widened my eyes in shock. "Um, she's immortal!" I shook my head. "I'm ... not. How do you suggest I do that?"

"An immortal cannot die, but can be permanently incapacitated. To destroy her, you must turn the source of her power against her. Remember Kronos?"

No, I didn't have a clue about Kronos, but I nodded my head anyway. I was still reeling that she'd just given me permission to kill my sibling, her daughter. I had no love for Tabetha, but I was not a murderer. It was one thing to kill a few vampires and nekomata in self-defense, but quite another to hunt down a witch and kill her in cold blood because "mummy said so." All I wanted was Logan's safety and Rick's freedom, without having to give up my world to have it.

"How do I turn her power against her?" I shook my head.

Hecate sighed. "Tabetha is not like you. The source of her power is not her own anymore."

"I don't understand."

Brow furrowed, her black eyes fixated at something over my right shoulder. "You are required by your familiar." Focusing again on my face, she raised one hand in a silent blessing. "I give you permission."

Pressure on my belly button drew me back into my sleeping body. "Wait? How do I protect Logan? How do I destroy Tabetha?"

Too late. I awoke with a jolt to talons digging into my chest. Poe dropped my ringing phone onto my neck. "What the hell, Poe?"

"She keeps calling back. I fear it is important," he said.

I grabbed the ringing phone from the sheets above my shoulder and answered it.

"Grateful, you've got to come to the hospital right away," Michelle said into my ear.

"Michelle? What's going on? Why?"

"It's your father." A beat of silence passed, long enough for me to pray he was her patient in the ICU and not a resident of the morgue. Her answer came whispered into my ear. "He's been bitten."

CHAPTER 16
Dad

Nothing prepares you for seeing your parent in a hospital bed. As a nurse, I'd been on the other side of this coin, but I never really understood. Parents are with you from the day you are born—protecting, teaching, and guiding you. Seeing my father clinging to life in the ICU was knowing that someone I loved unconditionally and who reciprocated that love, a rare guardian angel of a man, could be taken from me in an instant. He was a constant in my life, and I'd failed him.

Dad's eyes were closed, and he was on a vent. His chest rose and fell rhythmically with the machine. Propofol dripped creamy white into his IV, a sedative meant to keep him from fighting the vent while his body healed. A bandage covered most of one side of his neck.

"Dr. Hastings was able to fix his larynx and close the wound. He's going to have a scar though. The flesh was torn from his neck. They gave him ten units of blood." Michelle stared at her tangled fingers.

"Ten. My God, he's lucky to be alive."

"Understatement. If he hadn't been brought in as quickly as he was, I'm not sure they could've saved him." Michelle cleared her throat. "Grateful, I've got to ask … Is he going to turn?" She inflected her voice on the word "turn."

"You want to know if he'll become a vampire?"

She nodded.

The idea hadn't occurred to me. I thought about it for a minute and shook my head. "In order to turn a human, the vampire must drain the person to the point of death and then bring them back by feeding them their own blood. Dad was drained, but if he'd been changed, he'd be fully healed. He wasn't fed vampire blood. He's still human."

Michelle placed a hand on her chest. "Thank the lord."

"Do you know who found him?"

Michelle frowned. "I asked. I knew you'd want to know. The man didn't leave a name, but Berta said your dad was carried in, Grateful. Carried." She met my eyes.

"You think it was a vampire who dropped him off?" I whispered.

"Your dad is a big man, and once he was on the stretcher, the guy who carried him disappeared."

"Did anyone get a good look at him?"

"No. Do you think it was the same vampire who bit him?"

"I don't know. With this type of damage, it looks like the vamp lost control. It's hard to believe it then regained enough control to carry him to the hospital. Something doesn't add up." I stared at my father, his image blurring through my tears.

Michelle ducked her head into the hall, looking both ways, then returned to my side, squatting down until her dark head was level with my own. "Do you think the vampire knew who your dad was?"

I blinked at her, my overwhelmed brain feeling like it was crowded with cobwebs.

"Maybe the vampire wanted your dad to live. Maybe this was a warning or message of some kind."

The tears in my eyes dried in the mounting heat of my anger. I glanced between Michelle and my father and knew, without a doubt, she was right. This wasn't a random feeding. This was a warning.

"Gary knows," I said. "We dated. He knew my father. I don't think it was him, but maybe he told someone."

"But why? Why would they do this to your dad?"

A chill coursed through the room, and I hugged myself. "When is the full moon?" I'd been so busy, I'd lost track of the date.

Michelle's eyebrows did a nosedive. She pulled her phone from her pocket and tapped an app on her screen. "Tomorrow night. Can I ask why that matters?"

I stood and tossed my coat over my shoulders. "I've got to go. Text me if there's any change."

Before I made it to the door, Michelle's hand shot out and grabbed my wrist. "Are we safe here?" she asked me.

My eyebrows inched toward my hairline. How could I be so stupid? She needed protection, and lucky for me, I'd performed this spell before. "I'll place a ward on this room. It's strong. It's the same one I used on my house and at Logan's to protect *The Book of Light*. But Michelle, it won't protect you outside of here. If you sense danger, come into this room."

She nodded.

I began pacing the periphery, muttering the enchantment I'd repeated so many times before. A silver mist formed near my feet and spooled out in every direction—up the walls, over our heads—until the entire room sparkled with my magic. The silver shifted when the spell was complete, maturing into a purple haze.

"It's done," I said. "Nothing preternatural can cross the threshold."

"Thanks, Grateful."

Guiltily, I nodded and said my goodbyes. She shouldn't be thanking me. I was the reason she was in this mess and my father was in a hospital bed. I needed to make this right, and I knew just where to start … Gary.

* * * * *

On the way to the Thames Theater, I checked my messages. Rick had been trying to reach me all morning, but I'd been distracted with Dad. His voicemail sounded urgent. I felt his anxiety through our connection, a general buzz under my skin like an alarm you are trying to sleep through. I'm sure he could feel mine too. I tapped the call back button.

"What is going on?" Rick said by way of answer.

"Dad's been bitten. I'm going to the Thames to interrogate Gary."

"I'm on my way."

"No. Don't come. It will be better if it's just me. He'll be more open."

"*Mi cielo?*"

"I'm serious, Rick. I'll call you later." I ended the call as I pulled into the parking lot.

The Thames was as dead on the outside as on the inside. At high noon, most of the vamps within would be sleeping, which made the place the equivalent of a giant mausoleum. I knocked loudly on the front doors and wasn't surprised when no one answered. Drawing Nightshade, I placed the tip of the blade over the lock and said, "Otevrano." There was a click and with a shove of my shoulder, the heavy wood gave way.

Darkness enveloped me as I allowed the door to shut. There was no natural light in the foyer. Where there should have been windows, red velvet drapes hung thick and heavy. Since the outside of the theater was solid brick, the drapes were likely for show. Vampires wouldn't risk the glass.

By the light of Nightshade's faint glow, I moved toward the staircase that descended to Gary's room. On the landing a floor down, I almost tripped over a pair of legs.

"Watch it," the vampire hissed. Her fangs dropped, and she lurched for me, but once she saw Nightshade, she eased back against the wall. I gave her a warning look.

As I passed Julius's room, I noticed the door was propped open. The place looked like a museum, pristine and soulless. The Scotch was gone, as was the large mahogany desk. Clearly, the vamps had moved on. I wondered how long until they redecorated.

Down the hall, I didn't bother knocking on Gary's door. As far as I was concerned, my father in a hospital bed was all the invitation I needed. I opened the door and stepped into his room, coming face to face with Virginia Woolf. The poster gleamed in Nightshade's glow. I patted the wall and flipped the light switch.

A gasp broke through my lips. Gary lay sleeping on his bed, covered in blood. He'd washed his face and his hands, but his shirt and pants were soaked. Even the blanket under his body bore the stains of his night's activities. Shaking with anger, I lowered the tip of my blade to his throat.

"Give me one reason I shouldn't kill you," I growled.

Gary stirred, eyelids lifting slowly. I watched him startle under my blade, his emerging consciousness turning to horror. "Grateful?" he asked tentatively.

"Did you drink from my father?" I asked, pressing the blade until a drop of blood boiled up under the tip.

"No!" he said quickly, holding up both hands. "No, I found him!"

I narrowed my eyes. My witchy sense told me he was telling the truth, but I'd been wrong before. Still, I lowered Nightshade and stared at him expectantly. "Start talking."

He sighed and pushed himself up on his elbows. For a vampire, he looked remarkably human, even exhausted. "I think it was Kace."

"Bathory's vamp?"

"Yeah, the challenge is tomorrow night. He knows, Grateful." Gary's voice was barely a whisper and his eyes were wide and fearful. "I didn't tell anyone that you asked me to be a challenger, but Kace got in my face and said, 'Don't be a traitor to your race.'"

"He said that?"

"Yeah. And then I find your dad unconscious in the alley behind the Thames. He knows, Grateful, and I didn't tell him. But I swear, when I dropped your father off at St. John's, he was still breathing." Gary's face looked tortured.

"He still is. He's alive, just unconscious."

Gary scrubbed his face with his hands. "Thank the goddess."

"So do you think Kace wanted to send us a message to back down?"

"I think he wants to scare us off. And honestly, I think he's succeeded. I can't do it. Find someone else."

"Shut up." I pushed him hard in the chest. "You can't give up. The challenge is tomorrow night. I'll never find someone else to work with before then."

"He'll kill me." Gary shook his head. "He'll kill everyone you love. You do not know this guy. He's working for *Bathory*. What kind of evil bastard maintains a relationship with a sadist like her?"

I had to give him that much. The fact that Kace admitted he was still a proud, flag-flying member of the Bathory fan club said something about his character and his sanity. "I'll keep you safe. I'll load you up with enough enchantments that he will bounce off you like a rubber ball."

Gary took a deep breath and blew it out his nose. "Okay, tell me your plan. What types of spells are you thinking?"

Sheathing Nightshade, I racked my brain for something to say. The truth was, with the whole Tabetha sitch I hadn't had time to research a plan for protecting Gary. I was sure I could do it. *The Book of Light* was brimming with protective spells. I just wasn't sure which ones would help in this situation … yet. "I, uh—"

"Tell me you have a plan." He shook his head angrily and scooted away from me. "Tell me you didn't intend to send me to my death on a wing and a prayer."

"I, uh, I have a plan. I just haven't fully developed the plan."

His mouth dropped open, and he stared at me incredulously.

"Only because I didn't have you with me. If you come to the house tonight, I will make you powerful enough to take on Kace."

His expression shifted, the corners of his mouth curling into a suspicious grin. "Will you invite me inside?"

Damn. Once a supernatural being was invited past my protective ward, there was no going back. If Gary came inside my home once, he would always have access. Physical barriers like doors and locks weren't ultimately useful against vampires without magic to back them up. What Gary was asking for was a level of access into my life I wasn't comfortable giving him.

"Fine," he said, looking away. "I'm out. Find someone else."

"Wait," I said. I needed him. With Julius gone, we could not have Kace running the show. As much as I hated the idea of trusting Gary, I had no choice. "Come at sunset. I'll invite you in."

Gary nodded and held out his hand. "Then we have a deal."

Hesitantly, I reached out and clasped his icy fingers within my own. We shook on it, even as a weight at the pit of my stomach told me it was a bad, bad deal.

CHAPTER 17
The Search

"You agreed to what?" Rick growled. He'd ignored my request to stay away and was waiting in the parking lot when I finished with Gary. "You cannot allow Gary over your threshold."

"What was I supposed to do, Rick? We need Gary. Who is going to face off against Kace if he walks?"

"Kace. Yes, the presumed progeny of Anna Bathory." Rick stepped closer to me, eyes narrowing. "Have you ever actually met Kace?"

I placed a finger on my chin and thought back. "No. I guess I haven't."

"Then how do you know he exists?"

"Gary." My face tightened.

"Gary, who was covered in your father's blood. Gary, who stands to gain leadership of the most powerful coven in Carlton City. Gary, who has never been known for his honesty."

Hands on hips, I became defensive. "It was your idea to enlist Gary as a challenger. You suggested I use magic to strengthen him."

"Yes, but these matters must be handled with a degree of caution. If he's asking to be invited in, we must suspect the worst."

"He had no desire to get involved. He told me no repeatedly."

"The trick of a savvy salesman. Make the buyer believe the product is not for them, that you are considering pulling it from sale, and psychologically the customer wants it all the more."

"But why would he lie? Why not just tell me he planned to engage in the challenge?"

"Because this way, he has lured you to his cause. If you give him protective enchantments, he is much more likely to win the challenge. Plus, how much more powerful will he be when he has access to Hecate's home?"

I stopped for a moment, turning the facts over in my head. It was possible Gary was telling the truth, but even more likely he was lying. I'd like to think I could tell, that my witchy sense was infallible, but I hadn't been the witch long enough to know for sure.

"Shit. Shit. Shit. Shit." I stomped my feet and pumped my fists in the air. "What are we going to do? He's coming tonight. I promised him protection."

The corner of Rick's mouth turned up slightly at the sight of my tirade. He reached out and cupped my elbows in his palms, pulling me near. "You are an amazing and powerful woman, *mi cielo*. You will think of something."

"I'd turn him away, but we can't know for sure if he's telling the truth." I looked up into Rick's eyes. The weather was icy, but the sun shone behind his head, warming my face. He had such confidence in me. There was no contempt, no I-told-you-so in his expression. Rick believed, to the center of his soul, that I would fix this. If I told him at that moment that my plan would require us to dump hot soup over our heads, he'd do it.

"Maybe the answer is not found in Gary but in another. We could try to find Kace. If we had a trace of blood, saliva, or magic from your father's attack, we could trace it back to the perpetrator."

Straightening, I checked my watch. Only a few hours until sundown. I thought about what Rick said. Would there be blood or saliva on my dad's clothes? Or magic? "Wait, we can trace magic?"

"Yes, it leaves a residue."

My heart beat faster. "We need to split up. Rick, see what you can find out about Kace. I'll text Michelle and have her meet you with my dad's things. Maybe there is something you can use."

He nodded but asked, "Where will you be?"

"I'm going to try to find Anna Bathory."

* * * * *

To be specific, I didn't plan to search for Anna herself—we'd tried that before—but Anna had a sidekick named Naill, a leprechaun with a bad attitude. Both were fugitives. Both were on the lam. And I was willing to bet my lunch money they were laying low in the same hidey-hole, probably with an imprisoned Julius.

When Rick said it was possible to trace magic, I remembered that I had some of Naill's, and I was more than happy to use it against him.

"Ugh," Poe said. "You haven't washed that?"

I held up the bloody slip I'd worn when Bathory had tortured me and Julius had almost killed me. The fabric was stiff, and I was careful not to distress the dried blood. "I never planned to use it again, but I wanted to keep it as a memento of how far I've come as a witch," I said.

"Seems unsanitary," Poe said with disgust.

"You eat maggots."

"The maggots are clean, it's just the flesh they are feasting on that is questionable."

I stuck out my tongue. "Anyway, it's not the blood I'm after but the wine stain." I pointed to a small splash of maroon at the neckline. "Naill poisoned my drink the night Bathory kidnapped me. I spilled some on the green sweater dress I was wearing that night. Bathory took the dress, but a little of the spill soaked through to the slip."

"You'll be lucky to get a whiff of magic off that thing after all this time. Not to mention it is undoubtedly polluted by all that blood," Poe said sourly.

I shrugged. "Good thing I have a familiar capable of magnifying my power."

He followed me up the stairs and through the door to the attic. "Even I have my limitations," he said.

"You're in an exceptionally chipper mood today," I said sarcastically. "Did something happen to get your feathers in a bunch?" I crossed the attic to *The Book of Light* and opened it to a random page.

"Just nervous about becoming Tabetha's biotch. If she takes your territory and with it the source of your power, what will happen to me? Will I become hers? Go back to Hecate's garden whence I came?"

"I'm not going to let that happen. Tabetha will have to kill me first."

"Somehow I don't find that reassuring."

Offended, I widened my eyes in his direction. "Poe! Are you saying you don't believe in my mad magical skills?"

"I'm saying, Tabetha has been around a long time and doesn't appear to have a conscience. That's a dangerous combination."

"There's something I have to tell you Poe." I sank into the chair behind the desk that held *The Book of Light*. It was a suspiciously cubicle-like arrangement for an ancient magical artifact, but it worked for me. "The goddess Hecate, my mother, came to me in a dream. She confirmed Tabetha is after my power and forbade me from giving it to her."

Poe rolled his eyes toward the ceiling. "I don't suppose she offered a suggestion for stopping her from taking it?"

Biting the corner of my lip, I admitted, "She suggested I let her have Logan."

"Popular opinion."

"Not doing it," I said firmly. "Anyway, she gave me an alternative."

He widened his eyes expectantly at me.

"She gave me permission to kill her."

Poe's beak dropped open. He gawked at me for a moment and then belly laughed.

"Thanks for the vote of confidence." I stood to dig out my silver bowl from the trunk where I kept my magical paraphernalia. Poe followed me.

"Don't take it personally," he squawked. "Tabetha is—"

"Older, more powerful, immortal, devious. We've covered this. Just shut up and help me gather ingredients."

Water, vinegar, lemon, powdered lamb bone (left over from what I'd borrowed from Rick's stash). "I need a live grub."

He nodded his head and exited the window through his pet door. A few minutes later, he was back in the attic, an extra large grub wriggling in his beak. I'd mixed the other ingredients in my silver bowl. Once Poe dropped in the grub, the potion started smoking. "Is this supposed to happen? What's the spell say?"

"Hold the slip over the smoke," Poe said after checking the spell.

I did, and the results were breathtaking. The steam sifted through the silk, the wine stain, and my blood, and projected a full-color picture of a cavernous region on the wall.

"Do you know where this is?" I asked Poe.

"Looks like Pawtuckaway State Park," he said without hesitation. "Fabulous place to find small, meaty rodents."

"I'm looking for a small, meaty leprechaun. Come on. Let's go."

* * * * *

Hours later, Poe and I entered a less traveled section of Pawtuckaway State Park. Poe was frustrated I couldn't keep up with him as he soared overhead. He huffed and groaned as I traversed the rocky, forested landscape.

"Your element is air," he whined. "Couldn't you join me up here? The spot is so close."

"Keep it down," I whispered. "As far as I know, I can't fly. Although, I hovered a few times during my training sessions with Rick." I groaned and climbed the cliff wall in front of me the hard way, digging my toes and fingers in the nooks and crevices to pull myself up. I thought about the morning in Maison des Étoiles when I floated above the bed, and the times I'd practiced with Rick. I might be able float if I tried, but I couldn't move once I was in the air. Not yet. Also, sometimes I dropped like a rock when I least expected it. That would be particularly undesirable given the terrain below me.

"How is the training going, anyway? Do you feel more prepared to face Tabetha?"

"To be honest, not really," I said, blushing. I tossed a knee over the edge of the cliff and squirmed on my belly until I was on terra firma. Thankfully, the ground evened out up here. I pushed to my feet and gestured with my chin for Poe to lead the way in silence. Minutes later, I recognized the topography as the one the spell had shown us.

I drew Nightshade, her blade glowing blue in the shadow of the forest. We were close; Nightshade only glowed when she detected a supernatural nearby. I stepped toward the grouping of trees and cave opening. "Alligo corpus meum impenitribility meorum mucro," I muttered. A swirl of darkness slithered over my body and sank through my clothing, making my skin feel heavy. I'd used this protection spell once before. Naill was a powerful leprechaun. I hoped it would be enough.

A green blur raced by us. A shock ran up my body, and the hair on the back of my neck lifted.

"To your left!" Poe yelled.

I spun and threw Nightshade like a spear, completely trusting my witchy instincts. My bone sword plunged into the bark of a tree, the hilt reverberating with the impact. I thought I'd missed until Naill's struggling form blinked against the bark. He'd made himself invisible, but I'd hit him in the shoulder. Nightshade's magic was draining his power, thus the blinking. The flashing became a flutter, and then Naill appeared fully formed in front of me.

As I approached, I noticed his red hair was dirty and matted, his gold vest and green pants stained with mud and other things.

"Ugh. You smell like a sewer," I said.

He growled at me, showing his gold teeth. A bit of lime-colored blood oozed from the place Nightshade pinned him to the tree. "If you are going to judge me, do it." He squirmed painfully against the bark.

"First tell me where Bathory is," I commanded.

His green eyes narrowed. "What are you trying to prove, Hecate? You caught me. Why play games?" His high-pitched, raspy voice reminded me of a munchkin from the *Wizard of Oz*. It made it hard to take him seriously, but I'd learned the hard way that deadly things could come in small packages.

"We can end this if you tell me the location of your mistress."

"She's gone," he said through his teeth. "She's been gone for weeks."

I rubbed my chin. My gut told me he was telling the truth. "Where did she go?"

His squat face twisted. "How should I know?" he spat. "I thought you'd caught up with her."

Confused, I exchanged a glance with Poe. "What do you know about Julius's disappearance?"

Naill met my eyes with a hateful stare. "Haven't seen or heard anything since the solstice. Anna left me in this hole and never came back."

"Do you have any idea where Bathory might have gone?"

He cackled. "No." He annunciated the word through his wicked sneer.

"Fine. You don't know anything, which means you are no longer useful to me." I grabbed Nightshade's hilt.

"Wait!" he said. "I could work for you. I could help you the way I helped Anna."

"I doubt it," I said. Naill was evil, and I didn't need the help of evil. "Naill, I sentence you to live out the remainder of your days confined to the hellmouth."

He screamed as purple fire blasted from Nightshade's blade and folded around his body, transporting him to his new prison. The sound of a bubble popping ushered him to hell. I yanked my blade from the tree bark.

"That was disappointing," Poe said.

"You can say that again. Without Julius, I have only one choice." I sheathed Nightshade on my back and started retracing my steps to the car. "I'm going to have to trust Gary."

CHAPTER 18
Vampire Games

As expected, Gary arrived on my doorstep at twilight, the winter wind biting into my skin as I joined him on the porch.

"Please tell me you have a plan," Gary said nervously.

"I do. An armor spell, enhanced speed. I think I can even hide a wooden stake inside you."

"Then invite me in," he said. "Let's get started. We don't have much time."

I needed to know Gary wasn't lying to me, and there was only one way to do that. I drew Nightshade and pulled a vial of potion from my pocket.

With super speed, Gary retreated from the blade to the center of the yard. "What gives!" he said.

"I'm not going to hurt you," I said. "I just want to perform a truth spell to ensure you are being honest about

Julius and Kace. Here, drink this." I held out the truth potion.

Gary shook his head. "Fuck that." He flipped me the finger. "I want no part of this. I'm trying to help you, and this is the thanks I get? Forget it. You can live with Kace." He took off, running for the woods but stopped short when Rick formed in his trajectory. Gary ran right into him.

"A moment of your time," Rick said, holding Gary's elbow in a firm grip. He dragged the vampire back to my stoop.

"Aww. Come on," Gary whined. "What the fuck?"

Rick raised his black eyes to mine, his beast close to the surface. "What Gary says about Kace is true. I saw the vamp myself. He is preparing for the challenge."

"Of course it's true! Why would I lie?" Gary said. "Now let me go. Find some other pawn."

"Gary!" I yelled to get his attention. He stopped fighting Rick and stared in my direction. "Stop talking and get inside. We have work to do." I opened the door to my house.

My heart was drumming in my chest. This was it. No going back. I was torn in two, knowing it was a bad idea but also that it was the only chance we had.

"Are you inviting me in?" he asked, standing taller and looking toward the open door. Rick slowly dropped his hand.

"Yes," I said.

Gary was inside before I could finish the word.

* * * * *

"This way," Gary whispered.

We were deep within the forest behind Carlton City, the full moon directly overhead providing just enough light to navigate through the trees and underbrush. Still, I hung on to Rick's hand. He could see in the dark, and I wanted the added protection. My intuition was itching with the vibration of supernatural power.

Above us, Poe soared between the branches. "We're close," he said from just above me. "The coven has gathered straight ahead."

A clearing came into view, a snow-covered meadow. Rick stopped me at the tree line. The place was lousy with vampires. I stretched on tiptoe but could barely see over the heads of the hundreds crowding the area.

Poe landed in the tree closest to us. "Up here."

Rick pointed to a branch above my head. I nodded and was swept up in his arms. In one lithe jump, he'd pulled himself up onto the branch below Poe and gently sat me down beside him. From here, I could see the challenge zone clearly.

The vamps had shoveled out an area slightly larger than a boxing ring and arranged the area as Gary had described it: to the north, a post of silver spikes; to the west, a coffin; to the south, a chained werewolf even larger than Silas's; and to the east, Vladimir's guillotine. The blades of the last whirred steadily in the moonlight. On a platform behind the ring, the wrinkled face of Padnon smiled from a throne that appeared to be made of human bones. Skulls topped the decorative spikes of the straight back and bottomed the legs. Human skulls. My stomach recoiled at the sight.

"Relax, Grateful. The throne is more than one thousand years old," Gary whispered from below my feet. "Nothing recent. Practically a historical artifact."

"Did I say anything?"

"No, but you're throwing off power like a thousand-watt bulb."

I cast him a dark glance. "I'll relax. Get on with it."

He motioned for us to stay where we were and bolted forward to blend into the crowd.

"Do you think they know we're here?" I asked Rick, so quietly he might not have heard if not for our metaphysical connection.

"They can't smell me, and Nightshade offers you some protection. She makes you harder to sense." Rick pulled me in close to his side.

"But Gary can sense me."

"Gary came here with us and stayed within close proximity. Plus, you let him in."

I'd let Gary into my house, but I sensed that wasn't what Rick meant. The implication was that I'd let Gary into my inner circle, behind my wall of magic, so to speak. I hadn't meant to, and the idea disturbed me.

"They're starting," Poe said from above me. I turned my attention back toward the ring.

Padnon stood from the throne, the moon and candles casting competing shadows across the platform and emphasizing the deep wrinkles in his skin. He raised his stubby arms, revealing the yellow underarm stains on his sleeveless T-shirt. It was February, but demons didn't mind the cold. "We gather today to call forth the best within our ranks to replace our fallen leader Julius Octavianus." Padnon's voice was all gravel like a long-term smoker, a side effect of being a demon. "Any vampire may challenge for the position, but be warned, many may compete but only one will survive to rule."

The crowd of vampires whooped and howled their excitement. Padnon bent to retrieve a carved alabaster bowl. I would have assumed it was bone except it was gigantic, larger than any bone in the human body. Perhaps it was a carved elephant skull. I couldn't tell. He placed it on a stone pedestal near the top of the stairs leading from the crowd to the platform.

With a snap of his fingers, a blaze erupted inside, the fire tinged with green. I'd seen this type of fire before when Rick had used the circle of bones to try to force Logan's ghost to the other side. This kind of fire wouldn't just burn you, but bind you.

"Whoe'er shall challenge for the privilege to lead, cast thy blood into the sacred fire." Padnon held up a silver knife and scanned the edge of the crowd of vamps.

"I so challenge!" a baritone voice said. The largest vampire I'd ever seen shouldered through the crowd. The guy looked like a linebacker with a Mohawk ponytail. A tribal tattoo curled from his face, down the side of his neck, over his shoulder, and disappeared into the waistband of his pants.

"That must be Kace," I whispered.

Rick nodded in the affirmative.

"No wonder Gary was afraid. That vamp must be three hundred pounds."

Kace swaggered up the three stairs to the platform and accepted the silver knife. Positioning himself in front of the bowl, he sliced his forearm and thrust it over the flames. A glob of red fell into the fire, and to my surprise, the tribal symbols from his tattoo erupted from the flames, curled around themselves, and scattered into the cold night air.

"I give you Kace Bloodgrain as first competitor." The crowd erupted into cheers. "Do any among you wish to challenge Kace?"

Silence. The fire flickered. Padnon scanned the crowd. For a moment, I thought Gary flaked on us. Maybe he'd never intended to help us at all, that bastard. Then the crowd parted and his chestnut-colored head emerged. Next to Kace, he looked scrawny and emaciated. Gary had no visible muscle under his wide-striped Henley. Slowly, like he could barely force his legs forward, he climbed the stairs and accepted the knife from Padnon.

A murmur rose up from the crowd with the occasional snicker. Gary paused next to the bowl, knife in hand. He grimaced as he considered the act required of him.

"The impenetrability charm," Poe said with alarm.

"Oh shit!" I yanked Nightshade from her sheath and muttered the counterspell, concentrating on Gary's right arm. I'd never done this so specifically before. I focused my intention on the small patch of skin he'd have to cut. Licks of magic coasted down from my perch, traveled quickly across the snow, and wrapped around my target. Gary must have felt his arm grow lighter because he glanced toward our tree before cutting into his forearm. His blood dropped into the bowl. The smoke rose up.

It was shaped like a raven.

CHAPTER 19
From Dusk to Dawn

The vampire coven closed in around the platform, a collective gasp rising up as the smoky raven rose, then broke apart. Gary cleared his throat and stepped into line next to Kace. A rumble erupted among the vampires, several clearly unhappy with the turn of events. Padnon scrutinized Gary and Kace for longer than seemed necessary, slapping the knife against his palm.

"I wasn't expecting that," I said.

"They know the raven is your symbol," Rick said.

I glanced at Poe, who shifted nervously on his branch. "How?"

"Every free vamp knows their Hecate. I'm sure word traveled quickly the first time one of them saw you with Poe."

Poe had buzzed past Gary the night he'd returned my
money and been a fixture at my side almost every night
since I'd conjured him. Of course the vampires would
recognize the symbolism. Funny, up until now, I'd only
thought of Poe as my familiar, but seeing him as a symbol
of my power made total sense. If I'd flown a flag from my
gable, a raven would be the likely choice for the
embroidery. My element was air, and what represented
that better than the bird who magnified my power? "So,
they all know I'm helping Gary."

Rick's face moved from shadow into a strip of
moonlight. "Do not worry yourself. There is no law
against what we have done. Although discretion might
have been to our advantage."

"I'm sure I could have concealed it, had I known," I
said. I stopped talking when Padnon raised the bowl from
the stone column and placed it on the seat of the throne.

"I proclaim these competitors worthy of this trial," the
demon said. "Let us begin."

Gary stepped down into the ring, followed by Kace
who seemed unruffled by the revelation I was helping
Gary. I didn't know Kace, but I assumed he was either
ignorant of what my raven meant or too big and proud to
be afraid of Gary or me. The two competitors positioned
themselves face to face at the center of the clearing. A
group of vampires rolled the platform away from the ring.
The coven closed in, circling the ring and forming a
barrier around the perimeter.

Two go in but only one comes out, I remembered Gary saying.

From the platform, Padnon raised one arm toward the moon. Silence fell across the coven. "Begin!" he commanded. His arm swept down, and the crowd burst into cheers.

Gary sank low, circling Kace with arms outstretched as if he were hugging an invisible tree, an effort, I suspected, to make himself look bigger. Kace grinned, the muscles of his chest and shoulders flexing and relaxing. Was he testing his weaponry? My stomach clenched.

"Why didn't you tell me Kace was a gargantuan freak? I should have layered more enchantments on Gary."

"I did not think it would help our cause to share his size with you," Rick said. "Gary knew what he was getting himself into, and you could not have layered one more spell in the time we had."

"Fuck. Let's hope Gary has some skills."

As Gary danced in a circle, Kace's massive fist shot out and pounded him in the center of the chest. Gary's body soared back, directly into the silver spikes to the north. If not for my impenetrability charm, he'd be impaled for sure. Instead, his body bounced off the razor-sharp points and he landed on his feet.

Kace's eyes widened, and a cheer rose up from a subset of the crowd.

"Well, if they didn't know I was helping him before, they do now," I said.

Dropping low, Gary took advantage of Kace's surprise to charge. His shoulder caught the giant in the stomach. Without my help, I was sure Gary would have never been able to move the vamp, but I'd given him potions to magnify his speed and strength. Kace's back barreled toward the werewolf. The beast growled and snapped. Nine-inch, razor-sharp claws dug into Kace's shoulders. Massive wolfie jaws clamped down on the giant's Mohawked head.

Werewolf bites were fatal to vampires. Gary receded, a smug grin spreading across his face. The werewolf tore into Kace, growls and cheers rippling through the crowd.

"There's no blood," I said, alarmed. In fact, after a moment to collect himself, Kace shrugged off the wolf like a cheap coat, slamming its body into the frozen ground. The werewolf whimpered and stayed down.

Whoops and hollers filled the night. Kace's supporters pumped their fists in the air and yelled their encouragement into the ring. Kace cracked his neck.

"Another witch is helping him," Rick muttered. "No vamp survives a werewolf attack like that without help."

I turned my head to look at him. "Who?" I shouldn't have had to ask. I grabbed the branch above my head, the one Poe was on, and pulled myself into a standing position, scanning the crowd. I was looking in the wrong place. She wouldn't be in the crowd.

I raised my eyes to the edge of the forest, just inside the tree line opposite our position. A figure in a dark cloak watched the action from atop a branch similar to ours. I couldn't see her face clearly from this distance, but if her dark hair and red lips weren't enough of a clue, the bright green of the forest around her would have given away her identity. My nemesis.

"Tabetha," I said. "Poe, do a flyby and see if she's alone."

My familiar took flight.

A growl rumbled deep in Rick's chest. "It appears we are not the only ones who care to influence the outcome of this event."

"Her symbol is the scarab beetle. Why did Gary's blood produce a raven and Kace's, his own tattoo?"

"She must have known and used a cloaking spell."

"That takes preparation."

"Another way to pressure you to turn over your territory," Rick said solemnly.

Furious, my gaze darted back to the ring. Kace and Gary grappled for the upper hand. Kace lifted Gary off his feet and slammed his back into the ground. Gary didn't hesitate. He hooked an arm between Kace's legs and twisted, knocking Kace off balance. In the blink of an eye, the two became a rolling, twisting mass of vampire flesh.

"How do we help him win?" I asked Rick.

He shook his head. "We don't. Not yet. He's doing well on his own."

Gary was on top, fists flying in super speed, using Kace's face as a punching bag. Kace's legs lifted. He twisted his torso, knocking Gary onto his side and grasping his neck. A dark object appeared in Kace's hand.

"What is that?" I asked Rick. His caretaker vision was more acute than mine.

"It looks like a walnut," he said.

As Gary struggled beneath the chokehold, Kace thrust the nut into Gary's throat and held his mouth closed. Gary reflexively swallowed.

The werewolf was up again, snapping and snarling just short of Gary's head. Gary raised his knees to bring Kace's face closer to the beast's jaws. Planting a foot, Kace dug a heel in, stopping his forward momentum, and bared his teeth as he squeezed Gary's throat. Fangs extended, Gary gripped Kace's wrists, trying to pry his meaty hands from his neck. Vampires didn't need to breathe, but Gary's eyes bulged ominously. Kace wasn't trying to strangle Gary; he was trying to rip off his head.

Gary opened his mouth, I assumed to scream, but instead a thick vine erupted from his throat.

"Fuck!" I clutched the branch above my head until my fingers turned white. "That isn't fair. Tabetha is directly interfering," I said. Red-hot anger spread through my torso and settled in a spot behind my breastbone. How dare this bitch come to my territory and try to influence my vampire coven?

Poe swept past me, landing on a branch near my head. "The witch of Salem is alone," he said. "And grinning like she's already won."

My previous levels of anger were replaced with a sure and certain fury at Tabetha's sickening arrogance. A swift wind picked up over the clearing, my natural magic coming to the surface, and before I could reconsider, I'd jumped down from my branch and was walking toward the action.

"Wait," Rick said. "What are you doing?"

"I'm claiming what's mine. This is my territory. This coven is in my jurisdiction. No fucking way am I letting Tabetha's dupe win." I drew Nightshade.

The power coming off me thickened the air and dropped the temperature a good ten degrees. It was enough to turn the faces of the vamps nearest me. They made a path for Rick and me to stand at the edge of the ring. Across from us, Tabetha made her own entrance, a few vamps bowing slightly as she approached the ring across from us. Her lips peeled back from her teeth as she looked at me.

Gary was in dire straights. His abdomen roiled as if roots tangled within him, and the vine had thickened to the point of straining his jaw.

"Use it, Gary," I commanded.

We had one last trick up our sleeve. One last chance to use it. Gary released Kace's wrist and contorted his body to plunge his hand into his calf. For a moment, blood spewed, and then his fist swept into the air clutching the enchanted stake I'd sealed inside his flesh. He plunged the bloody weapon toward Kace's heart.

My stake was soaked in a grounding potion meant to neutralize supernatural flesh. It was the only way we could seal it inside Gary's leg without his body expelling it. But now the spell had an additional benefit. It cut through

Tabetha's enchantments and entered the soft spot between Kace's collarbones. Kace's hands recoiled from Gary's neck to scramble for the end of the stake before it could conclude its magical journey to his heart. Gary wriggled out from under him.

Freed from Kace's clutches, Gary gripped the vine growing from his mouth and yanked. I had to look away as he tore the thing out by the roots, with what I imagined was a large chunk of his entrails. When I looked back, blood was gushing from between his lips, but the vine was dislodged, and he was already healing.

Kace, on the other hand, writhed in pain from my enchanted stake. I glanced at Tabetha. She seethed at me, her wand raised in warning.

"She underestimated us," I whispered to Rick. I could see it on her face. She'd thought this would be an easy win. She was wrong.

Gary stumbled toward Kace, lifted him by his hair and waistband, and tossed him toward Vladimir's guillotine. The blades struck the mammoth vamp's neck. Tabetha's spell was strong enough to keep him whole, but the enchantment of my stake left a spot of vulnerability. The flesh near the entry point split. Kace tumbled to the ring, bleeding profusely.

With a wicked grin, Gary moved in for the kill, hand reaching for the wound. Would he rip out Kace's throat?

Tabetha had other plans. A root shot up and wrapped around Gary's ankle. He flopped to his stomach and was dragged away from Kace.

The crowd went wild, pressing in around us, but none seemed to go as far as to attack or retaliate. Instead, the coven looked between Tabetha and me with equal parts excitement and disgust. Their instinct for self-preservation kept them at bay.

Kace plunged a hand into his chest and with a howl, pulled out the stake. His flesh healed itself as he walked his muscular frame to the place where Gary struggled against the roots and vines that bound him to the ground.

I turned up the volume on my power, a winter storm moving in like a tornado of ice. Tabetha did the same, her side of the ring blasting me with heat. The vampires struggled to steady themselves against the tug of war between fire and ice. Cries rang out as the vamps on my side clung to each other to stop from blowing away in my icy tornado. The ones closest to us stepped back in fear. I circled Gary with my storm, forcing Kace to shield his eyes from the spinning hail.

Tabetha waved her wand. A blast of spring forced me back a step. My power withered in the heat. Every cell in my body begged me to give up.

Gary was still tethered, and Kace had the stake. If I didn't help him, he'd be dead in one swipe of Kace's hand. This was my territory, damn it. I ground my teeth. No bitch kills my ex-boyfriend in my territory.

I toed off my boots and planted my bare feet in the snow, casting my power through the earth, calling on my graveyard. I'd only ever tried this during the day and with mixed results. Poe landed on my shoulder, amplifying my efforts. Rick grabbed my hand. The night air and the light of the moon pressed in around me, giving me strength. I drew on their energy, and I rallied. The power of the dead snapped into me like an overstretched rubber band. I didn't have to coax it out as before; it came of its own accord, slamming into me, filling me.

Focused, I punched my power toward Kace with a forward motion of my chest, straight from my heart. The vampire stumbled back in the wind, dropping the stake as he fended off the storm of ice. The vines around Gary froze, snapped, and fell away.

On her side of the ring, Tabetha struggled to retaliate. She flicked her wand again and again. Blasts of power bounced into me, but the elements were already in my control. I owned the air. I owned this earth, thanks to the power of my caretaker. I owned the power of the dead. All the forces of hell, my graveyard, fed into me, through me, until I became the power. My limbs throbbed with it. The air around me hummed. I. Was. Invincible.

Tabetha stumbled.

Gary sat bolt upright in the eye of my storm. His eyes bulged and his fangs extended to the point he couldn't close his mouth. I'd never seen any vampire look as feral or as deadly. He attacked in super speed, scooping the stake from the ground and pounding it into Kace's chest.

In a last-ditch effort, Tabetha wielded her new power, her stolen power. She melted the silver spikes and directed the molten metal toward Gary. It hardened, harmlessly, in the icy power of my hurricane before it ever reached him.

"More elements won't help you, Tabetha. They *all* belong to me here." My voice reverberated in the space between. I opened the floodgates and let the power pour through me.

Blood filled Kace's lungs, and he gurgled up at Gary. The power of the stake leached into him, cutting off Tabetha's protective charms. Gary had missed his heart, but I got the sense that was on purpose. My ex-boyfriend clamped one hand around Kace's ankle and dragged the vampire across the ring, flinging his massive body at the werewolf. This time, the beast's teeth sank into Kace's flesh around the stake. The enchantment I'd placed on it in order to keep Gary's vampire flesh from expelling it now ate away at Tabetha's magic. It left Kace vulnerable. A sharp scream escaped the massive vampire's lips, and then the werewolf ripped out his throat.

While Kace's blood soaked into the ground, I turned the full force of my intention on Tabetha. She looked drained. Her nose was bleeding. I hit her with a blast that blew back her hair.

"This isn't over," she said, backing into the night. Her body melded with the darkness.

"Oh yes, it is," I said.

I pulled the power of the circling storm back inside myself. My nose was bleeding, too. When had that started? I wobbled on my feet. Rick held me up by the shoulders. Poe clung to me but hung his head like he might be ill.

Gary turned toward Padnon and the platform. The coven parted to allow him access. He climbed the steps to the throne. On the seat where the alabaster bowl had been was now an alabaster crown. I didn't know if the bowl had magically changed or been replaced by Padnon during the fight. Gary lifted the prize and turned, extending it above his head.

It was done. To the cheers of the vampire coven, Gary lowered the crown upon his head and sank to the throne of human bones.

My work here was done. I turned in the circle of Rick's arms. "Poe, you're free for the night."

Poe lifted from my shoulder on lethargic wings and flew toward the woods, no doubt hungry from his night's work.

I raised my eyes to Rick's. "Take me home."

He scooped me up into his arms. "Of course, *mi cielo*."

CHAPTER 20
Consequences

Nestled in Rick's arms, I slept as he carried me home. I was tired, exhausted even, but I didn't pass out. Instead, I allowed my mind to drift. Something had changed tonight. I'd tapped into the power of my graveyard in an organic and terrifying way. For a moment, I'd almost lost myself to it. But I hadn't, and I was sure I could harness it again. For the first time, Tabetha had feared me. I'd seen it in her eyes. After tonight, I was sure she'd think twice about messing with me, especially in my territory.

"She'll still want payment," Rick said, reading my thoughts.

I opened my eyes. "She'll take the love spell I offered her. If she doesn't, I'll kill her."

Rick sighed. "What about Logan?"

"She's threatened to kill him by our wedding day if I don't hand over my territory. That means I have a few weeks to find a way to save him."

We'd arrived home, my porch light casting a welcoming warm glow over my yard. "She could change her mind and kill him sooner."

"If she does, she loses all leverage over me. She won't. She'll hang on to her ace for as long as she can."

"Sounds risky," Rick said. "I hope for Logan's sake Tabetha acts out of logic and not passion."

"You're right." I wriggled out of his arms, landing on my own two feet. "We should abduct him now while she's weak. We might be able to sneak him out of Valentine's before she regains her strength."

Rick shook his head. "You need to regain *your* strength, *mi cielo*. The magic you performed tonight wasn't simple. It could've destroyed you. You are not ready for a second run-in with Tabetha."

"But Logan …"

"As you said, there is time."

I always scowled a little when Rick said there was time. He was immortal. For him, there was always more time. For humans like Logan, not so much. I was too weak to argue. I allowed him to lead me into the house and lift me again to carry me up the stairs, ending our journey in my bedroom.

"Rest," he said, helping me remove Nightshade.

"My face is covered in blood," I slurred. I was holding on to consciousness with both hands.

He lowered me to the bed and brushed my hair back from my face. If he said anything else, I missed it as I drifted to sleep.

* * * * *

"I'm going to run you a bath," Rick said.

I'd spent most of the day in bed with a wicked magic hangover. Rick had been babying me all day, feeding me tea and toast and watching over me as I drifted in and out of sleep. The sound of running water preceded billows of steam through the doorway to the bathroom.

I started to get undressed. The squeal and thump of a cabinet door opening and closing raised my eyebrows.

"What are you doing?" I asked.

"Cleaning up a little," Rick said.

I sighed. "You don't have to do that. I'm a terrible housekeeper, but I'll get to it eventually."

"I'll help you."

My cheeks warmed with embarrassment.

He poked his head out of the doorframe and tossed a tied garbage bag toward the hallway. I'd never seen him look so domestic. Warmth bloomed behind my breastbone at the simple human gesture.

My eyes misted, and I sat back down on the bed dressed only in my bra and underwear.

Before the first tear could drop, Rick was there to catch it. "Why are you crying?"

"You really do love me, don't you?" I asked. "I know it seems like a stupid question. We're getting married; it should be obvious. But, as my caretaker, maybe you, sort of, *have* to love me."

The corners of Rick's mouth sank. "I am not compelled to love you, *mi cielo*."

"I know. That's why the tears. If you were, you wouldn't be cleaning my bathroom." I smiled weakly. "Cleaning means a lot to me."

He kneeled between my thighs and wrapped his hands around mine. A subtle smirk turned his full lips. He looked at me through his impossibly long lashes. "Wait until you see my dust and polish."

"Oh?" I raised an eyebrow.

"No one polishes like I do." He shifted his hands to my hips as if to drive the point home, then cupped my ass and jerked me forward until I was pressed against his chest.

Mouth parted, I searched his face. There wasn't one shred of defensiveness. He wasn't guarded or confused about the future or dwelling on the "what ifs" of our relationship. Rick's heart was open and exposed, as it had been for hundreds of years. He loved me.

I lowered my mouth to his, gently melding our lips. He tilted his head and the kiss went deeper. I dug my fingers into his dark waves, wrapped my legs around his back. My tongue stroked his.

Just when things were getting good, he gently pulled away. "It's almost five. You should eat something," he said.

I narrowed my eyes but didn't break eye contact. "Stand up and I will."

He swallowed hard enough that I could hear it. "You need your strength. Eat, have your bath——" Rick jumped up and ran into the bathroom where I heard him curse and turn the water off. I followed, laughing when I saw the half-inch of water on the floor around his feet. He reached into the tub and pulled the plug.

"You think this is funny?" he asked through a smile. "It will ruin your floor."

With a smug grin, I tipped my head to the side and snapped my fingers. A strong wind coursed down the wall and blew the water across the floor and up the side of the porcelain tub. The toilet paper roll spun in the warm blowing air. Rick's hair blew back, and he leaned against the sink to lift his feet. I ran my toe across the linoleum. Bone dry.

"See? No problem," I said. My nose began to run, and I reached up to wipe under it. My hand came away bloody. "Oh."

I swayed on my feet. Rick caught me around the waist and pulled me to him. "You're still drained," he said. "You need rest." He propped me against the sink and re-plugged the now half-full tub of steaming water. He poured in a heavy dose of bubble bath and churned up a thick foam. "Come."

Taking his hand, I stepped toward him. His fingers traced the strap of my bra, then knocked it off my shoulder. I reached behind my back and unhooked the band. It dropped to the floor. "*Mi cielo*, please. You need rest. There will be time later." His eyes pleaded with me.

Reluctantly, I kept my hands to myself and finished undressing. He tied my hair up with a clip from my drawer and lowered me gingerly into the tub, folding a towel to support my head and neck. The water was cathartic, warmth seeping into my muscles. I moaned with pleasure and closed my eyes. When I opened them again, Rick was slipping from the room.

"Where are you going?" I asked

He leaned back through the door. "Relax. I'll be right back."

I closed my eyes again, and this time I allowed the warmth to carry me away.

* * * * *

When I woke again, my fingers were pruney and the water was lukewarm. Rick stood next to the tub with a puffy white towel in his hands.

"How long have I been out?" I asked.

"Maybe an hour. It took me longer than I expected."

"Longer than you expected to do what?"

He extended his hand.

I took a moment to wash my face, then rose from the water and allowed him to wrap the towel around me. As I did so, I tried to meet his lips, but he planted a kiss on my forehead.

"Not yet," he murmured.

"Why?"

He steered me out of the bathroom. Rick had transformed my bedroom into something out of a dream. Every surface was covered in red candles, the flames flickering and filling the room with warm light. He'd moved a small table into the room with a vase at the center filled with the same flowers as he'd sent me at the hospital—roses, lilies, protea, and liatris.

"I love the flowers. How did you know?"

"That you weren't a fan of carnations? I've spent lifetimes with you, remember?"

I crept toward the table, taking it all in. Two plates rested on either side of the flowers—lasagna, garlic bread, salad. The smell of garlic and oregano made my mouth water.

"What is this?"

"Do you know what day it is?"

I narrowed my eyes. "The night after the full moon?"

"Valentine's Day. Our first Valentine's Day as a couple since you've been back."

I snatched my phone from my dresser and confirmed. It was February fourteenth. "I didn't get you anything," I said. "I didn't even know."

He swept into me like a dark wind. One of his hands pressed between my shoulder blades, the other my lower back. "All I want is you. All of you."

"You have me." I searched his face. "It scares me sometimes. If you left …" I shook my head.

"I'm not going anywhere."

"I know. It's just, there's a vulnerability that comes with loving someone. You hold who I am now—how I see myself, how I define myself—you hold it in the palm of your hand. You could crush me."

His lips hovered over mine, the warmth of his breath against my mouth. "I'd only be hurting myself. You see, I hold you not in my palm but deep within my heart, and if I crushed you, it would ruin that vital vessel and surely kill me."

I dropped the towel I was holding and dug my hand under his shirt and up his back. "Then I guess we're stuck with each other."

His lips collided with mine, wanting and hungry. I shifted to take the kiss deeper. This time he didn't stop me. I paused, breathless, to peel off his shirt, then worked my hand into the front of his pants. When I wrapped my hand around his shaft, he inhaled sharply. I allowed him to breathe in my kiss, working on his button and zipper.

In a way no human man could accomplish, he wriggled from his jeans with a shiver of his skin I barely noticed. He stepped from them, standing fully naked before me, all lean muscle and taut skin. My breath hitched in my throat. My pulse raced. Quivering desire slithered from my nipples to the apex of my thighs.

Grabbing his hips, I pulled him toward me as I sank to sit on the bed. I took the length of him into my mouth, hot and slick, easing my tongue over his flesh. He moaned, digging his fingers in my hair. He thrust to the back of my throat. Pleasure rolled through my body, my nipples tingling, my thighs spreading to draw him closer. His lust became mine thanks to our metaphysical connection, and I sucked and stroked, losing myself in the rhythm.

His hand coursed over my shoulder to cup my breast, kneading and pinching the nipple, while mine toyed with the heavy weights at the base of his shaft. We were close. I could feel the edge of my orgasm coming fast.

In super speed, he shoved my shoulders back, slamming me onto the soft bed. Anticipation traveled over me, cool fingers on hot skin. Before I could draw my next breath, he'd dropped to his knees and buried his face between my thighs. Warm, wet pressure. I shattered, the orgasm causing my arms to tremble and my hands to grip the sheets. He slowed, kissing the inside of my thigh while I came down.

Standing, he ran his hands up my legs, over my stomach. He braced himself on an elbow and teased one of my breasts. I bit my lip. With a shift of his hips, he aligned himself with me. One swift thrust filled me almost to the point of pain. I whimpered with pleasure, and ran my nails over the muscles of his back.

Hands cradling my hips and face buried in my neck, he unhinged me. We collided in a pillar of soul-shattering light. Just when I'd caught my breath again, his lips brushed over my skin and his teeth sank into the flesh of my neck and shoulder. The air around thickened with power, sending the flames of the candles blazing three inches high. Rick drank of me, and I bit down on the flesh of the wrist he offered. Liquid orgasm, warm and intricate, coursed down my throat. I swallowed. I healed. I curled my body tighter against his.

He didn't disappoint. Ready again, he began to move with me.

CHAPTER 21
The Gilded Rooster

"They're going to try to wake your dad this afternoon," Michelle said. She sat across from me at the Gilded Rooster, Red Grove's only banquet hall.

I leaned back in my chair and closed my eyes. My fingers pressed over my lips. Relieved tears streamed down my cheeks. "Is he—"

"Breathing on his own? Yes. They've just kept him under so he could heal. But it's time. Dr. Hastings said I could tell you, but he'll call you later."

"Thank you. I'm so relieved."

Michelle frowned. "We won't know the neurological damage until he's awake," she muttered.

"I know."

"Are you sure you want to do this now?" she asked.

"If we don't decide on a menu today, it won't get done," I said, poking at my cucumber and tomato salad. It was the first course in our tasting menu. "I made this appointment before Dad's attack. It just makes sense to keep it."

Michelle nodded. She poked at the salad but didn't take a bite. Taking a deep breath as if she wanted to say something, she opened her mouth and paused. I looked at her pointedly. "On the topic of the fast approaching wedding date." She lowered her voice. "Are you worried Tabetha will kill Logan after what went on with the vampires?"

I blinked at her, my fork hovering over my neglected salad. "Seriously? Of course I'm worried, but there's nothing I can do. I tried to talk to him, but it's like he's completely brainwashed. He thinks he's in love with her."

"But she's threatened to *kill* him, Grateful."

"I know." I pressed my lips together. "Listen, Tabetha requested I turn over my territory by the spring equinox. I doubt she'll kill him before then. If she does, she'll lose all of her leverage. I have time. I'll figure out a way—a spell, or enchantment—to keep him safe."

Michelle chased a tomato around her plate and popped it into her mouth. As she chewed, I got the sense she'd tasted the salad to get out of responding to me. I scooped up a bite and did the same. What could I say? Logan was an adult and he knew what he was getting himself into. There were limits to what I could do.

"This is awful," she admitted. "The cucumber is mushy and the tomatoes are flavorless."

I shrugged. "The Gilded Rooster is the only reception hall in Red Grove."

Michelle leaned her cheek into her fist and lowered her fork to her plate. "You've got a lot going on, Grateful. Maybe …"

"Maybe what?"

"Maybe you should consider delaying the wedding."

I shook my head. "No. I am not going to let Tabetha ruin this for me. I am getting married to Rick on the spring equinox. The wedding will be beautiful, and let's face it, none of us will be there for the food." I set my fork down, and a boy in suspenders and a bow tie swept by and removed our plates.

"This place is a barn," Michelle said. "A literal barn … with folding tables." She leaned toward me. "You only get to do this once … well, in this lifetime. It should be special."

For a moment, I just stared at her, then I burst into laughter. "Believe me, Michelle, my relationship with Rick is special." I smiled. "I wanted to have it at Valentine's, but Logan was booked. And it would be awkward now with everything that's happened."

The bow-tie boy returned with two plates. "The chicken," he said, setting the plates down in front of us.

"How is this prepared?" Michelle asked.

The boy gave a little nod and said quite seriously, "In an oven."

I watched him walk away, my mouth hanging open. Michelle broke into belly laughs, and I joined her. I poked experimentally at the chicken. The rebound of my fork off the meat only made us laugh harder. As our laughter petered out, Michelle rested one hand on mine.

She closed her eyes and took a deep breath. When she opened them again, she made a blatant statement of the obvious. "March twentieth is just more than a month away."

With a deep sigh, I slammed my fork down on the table. "You don't get it, Michelle. I know this isn't the best time to be married. I know my father might not be able to walk me down the aisle, the food might taste like rubber, and my dress might not fit perfectly. But you don't understand."

"Make me," she said, folding her arms across her chest.

"This is my life now. It's not going to stop. There's never going to be a good time to get married because there will always be a bad guy around every corner."

Michelle shook her head.

"It's true! In my life, the marriage is much more important than the wedding. The spring equinox is the magical apex of new beginnings. If this marriage is going to work, I need all the help I can get."

She narrowed her eyes at me. "You're worried it won't happen if you wait."

My mouth flapped open and closed. "Don't be silly. I can't wait to marry Rick. We've never been more in love."

"At Gertrude's you told me you weren't afraid of marriage, you were afraid the relationship would fail. You want to seal the deal before anything can go wrong. You're afraid of abandonment."

I bit my lip and stared at the painted concrete floor. "Stop psychoanalyzing me," I said.

"Grateful, marriage, even on the equinox, is not a magical binding spell. If Rick wanted to leave you, he could do it with or without the marriage license."

Anxiously, I tapped my foot. Why was I worried? Rick was mine in every possible way. But deep inside I knew why. He'd almost left me once. For Tabetha. He said it wasn't romantic on his part, but time and circumstance could have changed that. What if Rick tired of me?

My worries were irrational. We'd been together for lifetimes. He wasn't going to leave me. Still, Michelle was right. The fear was there, as illogical as it was.

"If it makes you feel better, you're right."

Michelle grinned smugly.

"But it's my wedding. I'll do it my way." With some effort, I cut off a slice of rubbery chicken and popped it into my mouth. The sauce was indescribable. I think it was supposed to be sweet and sour, but it had the aftertaste of lime gelatin. A facial tic started under my right eye as I forced myself to swallow.

Raising her loaded fork to her mouth, Michelle paused to say, "It's your party." She popped the bite between her teeth, chewed twice, and then promptly spit it into her paper napkin.

* * * * *

"Welcome back, Dad." I stood by my father's bed while he blinked up at me trying to speak. His neck wound was healing nicely and his vitals were normal, but having your neck shredded and then a tube down your throat doesn't do much for your voice. Dr. Hastings and Michelle had stopped the medication that afternoon, and Dad had been in and out ever since.

He worked his lips and rasped, "Grateful?"

I squeezed his hand. "Yeah, it's me. Your voice will come back. Just give it time." I brought the straw of the white Styrofoam cup on his bedside table to his lips, and he drank greedily.

"Need to talk," he said, although the words came out mostly air.

"Are you in pain?"

He shook his head and patted his throat. Becoming agitated, his eyes darted around the room. They stopped on the whiteboard hanging on the wall with the date and the names of his nurses. With effort, he raised a hand and pointed at it.

"You want a whiteboard? To write on?"

He nodded.

The one he'd pointed to was permanently screwed into the wall, but they usually kept a small one for patient use in the cabinet under the window. I retrieved it, popped the cap off the marker, and arranged both in his hands.

Danger, he scrawled. Each letter was a slow struggle. His hand shook.

"You're safe here, Dad. I won't let anyone hurt you."

He shook his head and wrote, *You are in* above the word *danger.*

"I'm in danger? Why?"

He erased the board with the small eraser that came with the board. *Not animal attack,* he scrawled.

"You weren't attacked by an animal," I said to show him I understood. "Do you know what attacked you?"

He wiped the slate clean. *Vampires,* he wrote. Tears spilled from his eyes. *Not crazy.* He underlined the words three times.

"Oh, Dad," I said, wiping his tears away. "I know you're not crazy. I know all about vampires."

He stopped, searched my face. Then erased the board. *How?* he scribbled.

I looked down at my fingers resting on his blanket. "It's a long story."

Crooking the fingers of one hand, he motioned for me to tell him. "I'm a witch," I whispered. "And my job is to make sure vampires who do this to humans are punished."

A raspy scoff broke my father's lips. He shook his head.

"I'm not teasing you." I met his eyes and held out my hand, right over his whiteboard. Muttering a spell under my breath, I conjured a tiny blue star over my palm. "I'd produce a full flame for you, but we're in a hospital. Fire and oxygen don't mix."

My father rubbed his eyes. *Not real,* he wrote.

"I don't want it to be real either, but it is. It's time you knew. As my only family, I'm afraid this attack won't be the last."

Dad leaned back into his pillow and stared at the ceiling.

"You're tired. This is too much. But I need to know. What did the vampire who bit you look like?"

His eyes flipped open, and he lifted the marker. *Tribal tattoo.*

I nodded. Good. Gary was right. Kace did this, and Kace was already dead.

My father scribbled on the board again. *Cleopatra.*

A chill traveled the course of my spine. "Cleopatra? Do you mean … Was there a woman with Kace who looked like Cleopatra?"

Hired me.

"She hired you to show her houses, and then Kace attacked you?"

He nodded.

Tabetha. I ground my teeth. Even I could put two and two together. Tabetha learned who my father was from Logan and used Kace to try to kill him, to distract me from the vampire challenge. No doubt Gary was a surprise to her. She wouldn't expect I'd have a vampire supporter on the inside. And all to pressure me to turn over my territory.

I placed a hand on my father's shoulder. "Rest now. You're safe here. I won't let anything like this happen to you again."

He closed his eyes, obviously overwhelmed with our conversation. He'd expected to blow me away with his revelation of the existence of vampires. Instead, his message backfired. His daughter was a witch.

I kissed him on the forehead. "Try not to think on it. There will be plenty of time to talk about this when you're better."

He blinked at me, his eyes glazing. I grabbed the remote. "How about some TV? No sense being in the hospital if you can't rot your brain." I had a wedding to plan and a friend to protect from a murderous witch, but family first. I put my feet up and flipped to a rerun of *Modern Family*.

The hint of a smile crossed his lips.

CHAPTER 22
The Book of Light

"Show me how to protect Logan from Tabetha." Hand hovering over *The Book of Light*, I commanded my grimoire to give me the answer.

The book lit up from the spine, the pages flipping in an almost imperceptible wind. The tome was huge. Hundreds of pages. It took more than a minute to flip through every page and when it was through the entire book, it simply flipped them all in the opposite direction. Usually this process would end with the book opening to the page that would help answer my question. This time the book closed itself.

I stared at it for a moment in confusion. Was there something wrong with the book? Or something wrong with me? I tried again. Thrusting my hand over the cover I stated in a firm, commanding voice, "Show me how to protect Logan from Tabetha."

Again the light, the flipping, and the concluding slam of the cover. "Ugh, this is so frustrating," I yelled.

Poe flew into the attic through his pet door. "What seems to be the problem, Spamwitch?"

"Spamwitch? Really? That's the name you come up with today of all days? Spam is a processed luncheon meat. Do I look like a processed, canned magical entity to you?" I pointed at myself defensively.

"Somebody woke up on the wrong side of the grimoire," he said, arching his feathery brows. "Sorry, *Grateful,* is there something I can assist you with today? You appear frustrated."

His forced formality almost pulled me out of my foul mood. Almost.

"I've asked *The Book of Light* a question, twice, and it just keeps closing itself."

"Usually that means it doesn't have an answer. Try changing the way you phrase the question."

I thrust my hand over the book again. "Show me how to hide Logan from Tabetha."

Light. Flipping pages. Slamming cover. No answers.

"That's your problem," Poe said. "You're asking the wrong questions. Tabetha is an ancient and powerful witch. There isn't any spell or enchantment you can put on Logan that she can't muscle through with her own spell or enchantment. The book doesn't have an answer for you."

"Then how do I protect Logan?"

Poe contemplated the window for a moment. "Maybe the answer lies not in protecting Logan but in preserving him?"

I narrowed my eyes. "Show me how to save Logan from death," I asked the book.

This time my grimoire fell open to a page near the end. I groaned and rubbed my eyes with the heels of my palms.

"What is it?" Poe asked, fluttering to my side.

"The caretaker spell. It wants me to make him immortal."

"Oi."

"No shit. Not gonna happen." I tucked my hair behind my ears and tried to think. Pacing the attic, I rubbed my hands together. Every bad guy had an Achilles heel. What was Tabetha's? "Maybe the answer is not in making Logan stronger, but keeping Tabetha away."

Poe bobbed his head. "Sounds promising."

I approached the book again and extended my hand. "Show me Tabetha's vulnerability."

Light poured from the pages, the flipping faster than before. The book landed on a page decorated with a scarab beetle. I cleared my throat and read the page to Poe.

"Scarabaeus sacer, also known as the dung beetle, has been used for centuries as an amulet of immortality. Popularized by the witches of ancient Egypt, the amulet is said to foster eternal life. History. In ancient Egyptian culture, the god Khepri was believed to renew the sun every day before rolling it into the sky. Scarabs roll dung into balls to store as food or as an incubator for their eggs. Thus, it was commonly believed that scarabs held magical properties related to renewal. During the centuries, Hecates have used scarabs to amplify spells and enchantments meant to draw on power external to themselves. The best specimens are sealed inside precious metal or amber."

"She's channeling power using the scarab." Poe said, fluffing his feathers.

"So, it's not just jewelry. She always wears it because it's keeping her strong. Hecate told me Tabetha's power was not her own."

"It won't be enough to destroy the scarab," Poe said. "The amulet might strengthen the connection, but if you want to stop her, you'd need to find the source of power and eliminate it."

I shook my head. "A source she likely protects at all costs. Let's hope it doesn't come to that. Maybe there's another way."

I turned back to the book and tried again.

CHAPTER 23
In Like a Lion

"This tastes like ass." My dad held up the glass of green healing tonic I'd poured for him.

I laughed. "Nice language. You talk that way in front of your daughter?"

"Sorry. This tastes like *butt*." He grinned. Despite the deep scar at his throat, my father was as handsome as ever, with straight teeth and a full head of dark hair, peppered with gray. I was sure he'd be back to his job as a real estate agent in no time.

"I can't argue. My friend Logan said the same thing when I gave it to him." I snatched the next invitation off the stack on Dad's dining room table and began to address it. He forced himself to take another gulp of the green juice. Sadly, Logan wouldn't agree with me on the "friend" label. Technically, we weren't even on speaking terms. But Dad didn't need to know that.

He swallowed, face contorting. "Butt or not, it's working. My voice is better, and I'm getting around okay. Doctors say it's a miracle how fast I've recovered."

"Right. A miracle."

"Or magic," Dad murmured.

I stopped writing and nodded.

"When I was in the hospital, before you brought me home, you told me you were a witch."

"I did." A week had passed since my confession, but this was the first time he'd mentioned it.

"This health tonic ... it's a potion, isn't it? It's magic."

"Yes."

He pressed his lips together and stared at the remainder of the drink, swirling it in his glass. "Thank you," he said finally. "I am going to walk you down the aisle, and this is going to make it happen."

I smiled.

"So, about Rick. Is he a witch too?"

I cleared my throat. "Sort of. He's a caretaker. A caretaker is a mystical being that takes care of his witch. Rick takes care of me."

Dad stared at me for a moment. "Then he's a good match for you."

I snorted. "Yes. Possibly the only match for me."

"I'd thought Seraphina was my match," Dad murmured. "But now she's gone."

The crushing weight of guilt pressed into my chest. I'd murdered Seraphina in self-defense. My dad had never quite gotten over it. Maybe it was time I helped him. "There's something you should know about Seraphina," I said.

Dad sighed and closed his eyes. "I was afraid you might say that. Was she a vampire?"

I laughed. I couldn't help it. "No, a shifter."

He raised his head and furrowed his brow. "Like a werewolf?"

"No. A fork-tailed cat."

Dad's eyebrows shot up. "Just say it, Grateful. There's something more about her, isn't there?"

"Seraphina wanted me dead, Dad. I think she was dating you to get to me."

I expected him to deny it, maybe to throw me out of his house in anger. But he didn't. With tears in his eyes, he nodded.

"I suspected she was something *other* near the end. I loved her. I really did. But her behavior got to be … suspicious. She pulled away from me. She never seemed to eat or sleep. I guess it was a good thing about the car accident. It could have been worse."

I glanced at my toes and remembered sinking my sword into her heart. "Yeah. I think you're right."

His face fell, and he sighed deeply. "Your mother was the last great love of my life. It was wishful thinking to hope for that again."

"Nonsense. You could meet someone else. Someone human."

He scoffed and drank the rest of the green juice.

I finished addressing the last invitation and placed a stamp in the upper right corner. "Done." I stacked the finished invites and stood from the table. Kissing him on the forehead, I asked, "Do you need anything before I go? You want me to heat something up for you for dinner?"

"No," he said too quickly.

I scowled. I couldn't cook, but the offer should be worth something. "Ha, ha, ha," I said cynically. "You're on your own then." I shrugged on my new coat, a black wool trench trimmed in leather. I gathered the invitations into my arms, and we said our goodbyes.

On the sidewalk in front of Dad's brownstone, I glanced up and down the street, remembering there was a blue postbox around the corner. The sun had set, but his street was well lit by picturesque old-timey lampposts that cast elongated pools of yellow light across the sidewalk and adjoining street. I started left, gripping the lapels of my coat tightly around my neck to keep out the chill. When I turned the corner, I dumped the invitations into the blue box with relief, anxious to get home and spend some time with Rick before our night's work.

"I hope mine is in there." Gary appeared beside me, grinning confidently.

I'd startled slightly at his voice and smoothed my hair and coat as I recovered. I shook my head a little. "It's during the day. Noon, actually."

"Right. Might be dangerous for you after dark," he said.

I took a good look at him. "You're wearing a suit. I thought you hated suits."

He smoothed the charcoal gray wool over his chest. "Got to play the part. I'm the king now."

"Guess so." I smiled. "And I trust you will be keeping your coven in line? Because if another vamp so much as touches my dad, I'm going to be using your head as a footstool."

"Ho! Jeez, Grateful. That was uncalled for." He rubbed the base of his neck. "Of course I'm reining them in. Everyone in the coven knows there will be no mercy for anyone feeding on unwilling humans."

"Good. Nice to see you again." Hands in pockets, I turned to walk back to my car.

"Wait," he called.

I stopped and glanced over my shoulder at him.

"Thanks for helping me. I wouldn't have survived three minutes in that ring without your magic. I can promise you, if Bathory comes back seeking revenge, she'll get no help from me."

With a deep breath, I told him what I'd learned. "Bathory is missing."

He narrowed his eyes at me. "Uh, yeah, she's been on the lam since you beat her ass."

"No. I mean, really missing. I found Naill, and he said she'd been gone since just after the solstice. He'd been living in a hole in the mountains. He'd assumed I'd found her and sentenced her."

"Hmm. Maybe she had a run-in with a pack of weres?"

"Possible." I shrugged. "It might be wishful thinking, but I don't believe Bathory will be a problem again. She never went far without Naill. I don't think she'd abandon him on purpose. If she's not dead, she's permanently missing."

"Like Julius," Gary murmured. The corners of his mouth dipped. He took a step forward and tentatively rested a hand on my shoulder. I allowed it. "Tell me the truth. Do you think I'm in danger, Grateful?"

"Why would you be in danger?"

"First Bathory goes missing, then Julius. Someone has it out for powerful vampires. Normally, I'd assume that was you. But it isn't."

I raised an eyebrow. "You think the two are related?"

"Don't you?"

"No. Bathory was living in the woods when she went missing. Julius was living at the Thames. The disappearances were weeks apart. There's no reason to believe the two were related."

Gary folded his arms across his chest, unease tightening his features and then disappearing behind a mask of ice. "What do you know about the Witch of Salem?"

"What about her?" I asked defensively.

"What does she want with the coven? She must have sought out Kace. No vampire would be stupid enough to propose such a thing to a witch."

Did I trust Gary enough to tell him the truth? The answer was no. Still, I'd let him into my home. I'd given him power. Perhaps he'd earned my trust. More importantly, when it came to Tabetha, it might be in my best interest to have another ally.

"Tabetha wants my territory." I kept the reason why to myself. "I'm sure she approached Kace because it would serve her purposes to control your coven."

He snorted. "I guess vampires don't have a monopoly on power plays."

"No." I tucked my hair behind my ear and met Gary's eyes. "I don't think I need to tell you that it would not be in you or your coven's best interest if Tabetha succeeded."

"Understood."

"I have a favor to ask."

Gary stilled, all hint of humor fading from his demeanor. "Go ahead."

"Tabetha has threatened to kill Logan Valentine if I don't hand over my territory by the equinox. I need you to make sure that doesn't happen."

"How do you propose I do that?"

I glanced down at the toes of my boots. What I was about to ask Gary to do went against everything I believed in regarding personal freedom and human rights. But desperate times called for desperate measures. I'd tried to do things the proper way and failed.

"The day before my wedding, I want you to hunt down Logan and abduct him. Take him somewhere safe."

CHAPTER 24

Confessions

"Try this one," I said, slipping a bite of cake into Rick's mouth. We were picking out our wedding cake, a task I'd left to the very last minute.

"I like it the same as the other two options," he said. Technically, Rick didn't have to eat. He could sustain himself on sex and blood. He even gained power from ingesting supernaturals and sending them to hell. Mostly, he ate for my benefit. The wedding cake tasting was definitely for my benefit.

"We'll take the devil's food with the chocolate glaze," I told the baker's assistant.

She raised her eyebrows. "I thought you said this was for a wedding. Our chocolate glaze only comes in brown. We can do a white chocolate frosting though, if you'd like."

"I want the brown. Dark chocolate glaze. The florist will add flowers on the tiers."

The girl opened and closed her mouth, then gave a little giggle. "Okay. We will have it ready for you on the twentieth."

"Deliver it to the Gilded Rooster in Red Grove."

She bobbed her head and disappeared into the back.

"She's back there laughing with the baker about our dark wedding cake," I said, pushing the door open. "If she only knew how dark the bride could be. Mwahahaha."

"You are not evil, *mi cielo*."

"Of course not. Simply a sorceress of the dead and guardian of a hellmouth. I'm sure every wedding cake maker knows the difference. We should go back and have a groom's cake made in the shape of a ring of skulls."

He grinned. "Cherry filling?"

"What else? And maybe we could add a door to the top tier with a couple of torches and a snake."

Rick stopped abruptly on the square of sidewalk, right outside the Carlton City drugstore. His body stiffened and his normally Mediterranean complexion paled. "Why would you request such a thing?"

"Because that's how Hecate appeared to me," I said. "I think doorways are kind of her trademark."

"When did Hecate appear to you?" A muscle in his jaw twitched with restraint.

"Maybe a week after the dinner at Tabetha's. Sorry I didn't tell you about it. It slipped my mind after everything that happened with Dad."

"The goddess visited you and it slipped your mind?"

Obviously, a visit from the goddess was a big deal. I'm not sure why I hadn't told Rick immediately. Sure, I was distracted with my father's emergency hospitalization, but this was The Goddess. The dream was important enough to discuss at the earliest convenience. I searched my emotional grid for any reason I might have withheld the information and came up short. "I guess I was distracted." I led him to a bench at the end of the strip mall.

"Tell me everything," he said.

"She came to me in a dream."

"What did she look like?"

"At first it looked like she had three heads." I laughed. "Kinda spooky."

"Human heads or animal heads?"

I giggled, but he was serious. "Human. Women." I frowned. I did not even know the goddess could have animal heads.

"Which female form did she use to present herself to you? The maiden, the mother, or the crone?"

"Uh, hmm. By maiden, you must mean the young woman. I guess the mother. It wasn't the crone. It was the middle-aged one. Why?"

"The mother is the creator and the destroyer. I was hoping she'd come as the crone, to give you wisdom regarding your circumstances. If she came as the mother, it was either to warn you or to empower you. Which was it?"

I shrugged. "She warned me that Tabetha was after the five elements and that if she succeeded in obtaining them, the results would be disastrous. She didn't pontificate on what those disastrous results might be, but she did mention that Tabetha has become less human since absorbing Polina's power. She ordered me not to turn over my territory."

"Did she give you any idea of how to stop Tabetha from taking it?"

I decided not to mention her suggestion that I allow her to kill Logan. Rick would agree, and it was absolutely unacceptable to me. I jumped straight to the ending. "She gave me permission to kill Tabetha."

"She said that? Specifically? 'I give you permission.'"

"Yes, to kill Tabetha."

"That's very rare, and potentially problematic."

"Why?" I frowned. I didn't like the sound of that.

"Did she have dogs with her when she said the words?"

"No. A snake. She was playing with a snake at the time."

He grimaced.

I shrugged. "There was also a toucan and a butterfly. We were in the jungle."

"But when she said the words, she was holding a snake?" he clarified.

"Yes."

"The snake is a symbol of her divine heritage. She's a chthonian, a goddess of the underworld. Why would she want to draw your attention to her family tree? Did she say anything about how you could kill Tabetha? She's immortal."

"Yes," I said. "She said to remember Kronos. She also said that Tabetha's power is no longer her own and to kill her I must use the source of her power against her."

"Kronos? You're sure?"

"Yeah. Who the hell is Kronos anyway?"

"Legend has it that Kronos was the son of the earth and the sky—the god of time and of the ages in some lexicons. If you believe folklore, he was Hecate's great uncle. It is said Kronos was dismantled by his own children and imprisoned in hell for centuries."

"Children of Kronos? Like in Greek mythology? Zeus, Hera, Hades."

"Hecate is said to be the daughter of the Titans Asteria and Perses."

I laughed. "Is that real?" The idea that Greek mythology had even a hint of truth to it disturbed me to my core.

Rick tipped his head back and forth. "What is true? True is what exists. All of the stories are interpretations, folklore. What is important is Hecate is real, and her reference to Kronos clearly is a hint that Tabetha can be destroyed as Kronos was destroyed."

"That doesn't make sense. I'm supposed to use Tabetha's progeny to bring her down? She doesn't have any children."

"No. None that I know of."

"Hecate also said Tabetha's power is not her own. What do you think that means?"

He shook his head.

I sighed. "She's a wood witch. Maybe I should stock up on weed killer." I laughed. Rick did not join in. "What's bothering you?" I asked him.

"If Hecate gave you permission to kill Tabetha, it means the goddess is threatened by the idea of one of her children acquiring the five elements." Rick leaned his elbows on his knees.

"And?"

"And if you kill Tabetha, you will inherit wood and metal. You already have air and have access to earth through me. That only leaves water."

"I'd be just as powerful as Tabetha," I said, confused. "Why would she allow that?"

Rick rubbed his temples for a moment with his thumb and forefinger. "I can think of only three possible reasons."

"And they are?"

"First, it could be a test. Hecate wants to know she can trust you. She gives you permission to kill Tabetha but expects you to renounce the territories you stand to inherit. When she told you about Kronos and held out the snake, she was challenging you to remember your heritage and refuse the role of the power-hungry Zeus. The snake and Kronos were a warning to refuse additional power."

"Okay. So if I kill Tabetha, I refuse her territory. Check."

"The second interpretation is that she was baiting you. She gave you a ridiculous and impossible solution to a complex problem. Perhaps her goal was to force you to default to a simpler solution."

"Like?"

"I think you know, *mi cielo*." Rick stared at the sidewalk and did not say it. We both knew what he was thinking.

"Allowing her to kill Logan."

Rick gave a curt nod.

"And the third possibility?"

"She expects you to succeed, and when you do, she plans to kill you herself and anoint new Hecates to take your place."

"Can she do that?"

"Hecate has an appetite for human men. Her children number in the thousands. She only awakens the power within some of them. Others die never knowing."

"Great." I leaned back against the park bench. "I could have a goddamned Greek-goddess bull's-eye tattooed on my chest right now. Well, I sure as hell am not going to accept any new territories." I crossed my arms over my chest. "Frankly, I'm hoping to get out of the entire kill-Tabetha scenario."

"How do you plan to do that?"

"I think I've found a way to keep Logan alive. If I get him out of the picture, she'll be forced to come to me directly if she wants my territory. She's already experienced how that will turn out. I kicked her ass at the vampire challenge. Maybe she'll come to her senses and give up on the entire thing."

Rick straightened. "You don't actually believe she'll give up?"

"Maybe not right away, but I think she might turn her attention elsewhere."

He rubbed the stubble on his chin skeptically.

"How do you plan to protect Logan?"

I thought of the promise Gary had made me. "Maybe the less you know, the better." I raised an eyebrow.

"Too late, *mi cielo*. I can hear your thoughts," Rick said, a ghost of a smile crossing his face. "Do you think you can trust Gary?"

"No," I said.

"As long as you're clear on that."

I sighed and stretched my legs out in front of me. Not only did I not trust Gary, I was positive Tabetha could find Logan if she tried hard enough. I was also sure she could blow through a legion of vampires to get to him. Our success depended on two things: first, that Tabetha would wait until the last possible moment to kill Logan, and second, that Gary would succeed in keeping Logan in my territory. My only hope of defeating Tabetha was luring her here. It was a long shot, but it was my only shot.

For a long moment, we sat shoulder to shoulder, staring at the cars passing by on the street. It was a cold day, but for the first time that year the sky was blue and sunny. I crept my hand across the space between us and threaded my fingers with his. I had no idea how to stop Tabetha and was grasping at a thread of hope that I could save Logan, but somehow, I felt like everything would be okay as long as Rick and I were together.

"You wanna get lunch? There's a place a few blocks from here with wicked-good falafel."

"I was just thinking nothing would make this day complete like a good falafel."

"You have no idea what a falafel is, do you?"

He flashed me a half-grin. "No."

We looked at each other and chuckled. Hand in hand, we rose from the bench and meandered toward lunch as if we had all the time in the world, as if an evil witch didn't want us dead, as if nothing could ever touch us.

CHAPTER 25
Wedding Day

"It's done." Gary's voice was low and steady.

"Good. And you're sure Logan is in a place Tabetha won't find him?"

"Positive."

I didn't ask for details. "I'll be in touch after the ceremony." I tapped the end call button on my phone.

Light streamed through my window, and I smiled. The big day was finally here. I was getting married. And what a beautiful day it was. I'd heard it said that March came in like a lion and went out like a lamb. Today was all lamb. Sunny. Sixty degrees. Not a cloud in the pristinely blue sky.

Poe landed on the branch of the oak tree outside my window and tapped his beak on the glass. I flipped open the locks and slid the panel up so he could fly inside.

"Good morning, dear witch. You will be pleased to know that your father and bridesmaids are pulling into the drive."

I glanced at the time on my phone and smiled. "Right on schedule."

Flying down the stairs, I unlocked the door. My father kissed me on the cheek by way of hello. Soleil and Michelle swept passed me into the foyer, arms laden with dress bags and packages. They pulled me by the elbows into the kitchen on a sea of babbling girl talk. A scent-cloud of perfume, fresh nail polish, and face cream followed them inside.

Michelle handed me a breakfast sandwich and a cup of coffee, while Soleil messed with the tangle on my head. "Your hair needs work," she said.

"I haven't even showered yet," I said, biting into breakfast.

Michelle's mouth dropped open. I noticed her hair was already professionally styled with a purple orchid pinning up a swag of her bangs. "You're getting married in three hours, Grateful. Maybe you should get a move on."

I took another bite of sandwich. My dad was already in his tux, but Michelle and Soleil were still in street clothes. "You guys aren't dressed yet."

Soleil frowned. "All we have to do is zip on our dresses and we're ready. The photographer is going to be here in thirty minutes.

"Photographer? What photographer?"

Soleil just shook her head. "The one I hired to photograph your wedding as a gift for you. Now, unless you would like to be memorialized in your pajamas, may I suggest you get on with it?"

I popped in the last bite of sandwich and burned my tongue washing it down with the coffee. "I'm on it," I said, smiling. On the way upstairs, I grabbed the bag from Evenrose Bridal emporium out of the closet and took it with me.

After a long, hot shower, Soleil put my hair up while Michelle did my nails. I did my makeup, light and natural; Rick liked it that way. When it was time to put on the dress, Michelle audibly inhaled.

"What's wrong?" I asked, holding the dress in my hands.

"You still haven't tried it on," she accused.

"No," I admitted. "But I have a feeling." In front of my full-length mirror, I stepped into the dress and pulled it over my shoulders.

Michelle, already in her violet-colored halter dress, zipped the back over Nightshade. "Oh, Grateful."

Antique lace arced high on the back of my neck and then plunged into a deep vee that revealed a tasteful amount of cleavage. The dress skimmed over my waist and hips, straight down, sheath style, a modest train sweeping around the back. The dress was sleeveless but with a full back that easily concealed Nightshade. The lace was old, but the style was new, as was the designer. The dress was a perfect metaphor for Rick and me.

"It is exquisite," Soleil said.

"How?" Michelle asked. "It looks like it was made for you."

Poe coasted into the room and landed on the edge of the mirror. "I think it was," he said softly. "That lace looks familiar."

"This was designed last year, Poe."

"Maybe the dress itself, but the material ..." He shook his head. "Uncanny."

I shrugged. "There's only one person who will remember for sure, and he's waiting for me at the end of the aisle."

I turned sideways to get a good look at the row of buttons running along my spine and glimpsed my dad in the reflection. He stood in the doorway to my bedroom, eyes misty. I turned my head to face him as he approached and put his hands on my shoulders.

"You're gorgeous, inside and out. Your mother would be proud of the woman you've become."

Tears rolled over his cheeks, and a lump formed in my throat at the sight. My lids held back a pool of emotions.

"Stop, Dad. You're going to ruin my makeup," I said through a smile. "No crying."

He wiped his face and grinned, taking my hands in his. "Your dress is new and your engagement ring is blue, so that leaves old and borrowed, right?"

I nodded.

Dad pulled a triple-strand pearl bracelet from his pocket. "It was your mother's. She wore it the day we were wed. I know she'd want you to wear it today."

There was no stopping the tears this time. I watched as he fastened the delicate bracelet around my wrist. Feminine and elegant, it embodied how I envisioned the mother I'd never met, the mother who gave her life bringing me into this world. "Thank you," I said, throwing my arms around his neck. He gave me a firm hug in return.

The doorbell rang.

"That would be the photographer," Soleil said. "Freshen up and meet us downstairs."

By "freshen up," she meant "clean up the black trail of mascara winding down your cheeks." I did and met everyone at the bottom of the stairs where Soleil was passing out the nosegay-style bouquets. The flowers were the same as the ones Rick had bought for me: roses, lilies, and exotic flowers. Michelle and Soleil's were colorful versions of my white bouquet.

For the next hour, I posed and smiled while a man with hair the color of Concord grapes and webbed fingers clicked away on his camera. The smell of fresh, running water followed him from room to room. I didn't ask what kind of fae he was. I didn't want to be rude.

We posed on the stairs, in the wine cellar, even in the front yard, which was cold but graciously free of snow for the first time all winter. My smile was genuine. It was all I could do not to ruin my makeup with more tears.

Finally, I heard Soleil say, "It appears it is time to go." Her sunny disposition filled the lawn with warmth, and I followed her line of sight up the street to a horse-drawn carriage trotting toward us.

"Is this for me?" I asked.

"My treat," Michelle said. "Believe it or not, Red Grove has one. Same guy who owns the Gilded Rooster."

A giant white horse pulled a carriage into my driveway, an old man in a stovepipe hat at the reins. The driver hopped down and opened the door for us. I held up one finger and rushed inside for my bag, a beaded white clutch the size of a brick. The four of us climbed in to the carriage and took seats on velvet-covered benches that smelled of hay and burning leaves.

"I can't believe this is actually happening," I said, as the carriage jolted to a roll. "Nothing has felt this easy for so long."

"Don't jinx it," Michelle said softly. Her eyes darted to Soleil's and then back to me. No one needed to say her name. We were all thinking of Tabetha. When would she strike? How would she exact her revenge now that Logan was out of her clutches?

Nightshade shivered against my spine. I brushed the curtains aside to see why she was humming. We'd crossed through the gate to the cemetery—my cemetery—the source of my power. Nightshade was saying, "Hello again." Tabetha wouldn't dare cross me here. She'd be stupid to try.

"Relax, Michelle," I said, lifting my chin. "I'm the queen of Monk's Hill, and nobody messes with the queen."

She laughed and raised her eyebrows. "No one with half a brain in his or her head."

The carriage pulled to a stop and the driver hopped down to help us all out. Dad opened the door to the chapel for me. I entered to the sound of a solo violin playing at the front of the church.

Michelle took my purse. "I'll store this in the bride's room for you." Soleil fluffed my short train.

The pews were filled with friends and their families, most of them human, except for Silas who stood at the front in the best man's position. Michelle's husband, Manny, stood behind him, looking equally dapper in a tuxedo with a violet cummerbund.

And then from a door to the right, Rick emerged. His dark waves were slightly more tamed than usual above his collar, although the line of his jaw and slope of his nose were just as sharp. The way the material of his tuxedo jacket stretched across his shoulders made me inhale deeply. I couldn't wait to unwrap him after all was said and done, to pull the end of his bow tie like I was untying the ribbon on a present. His eyes met mine. I smiled.

Rick didn't smile back. Oddly, he looked nervous.

"Ready?" Dad asked. Michelle was back, and she and Soleil took their places ahead of me.

"Yes," I said enthusiastically. I positioned my bouquet. The song came to a conclusion, and the violinist gave

Soleil a small nod. She began again, Vivaldi's Spring, and Soleil processed forward, meeting Silas near the front before moving to their position off to the side. Michelle was next. At the front, Manny took her hand, and she joined him behind Silas and Soleil. Then it was my turn.

Everyone stood up. I kept my eyes on Rick as I stepped forward. Step, together. Step, together. With a beaming smile, I endured the flash of novice photographers as I moved in step with Dad toward my destiny. But as I grew closer, I could see something was wrong. Rick was slightly pale and ... sweating. I'd never seen him sweat, not ever. His eyes were gray but vacant, and the closer I got, the more his expression looked *tortured*.

After what seemed like an eternity, Dad and I reached the front, the point where Rick was supposed to come forward to take my hand from my father, but Rick didn't move. The pastor cleared his throat. Rick still didn't move. The music came to an end, and still Rick did not move. I reached out to him through our metaphysical connection, but I couldn't get inside his head. He was blocking me. That's when I knew something was wrong, really wrong.

"Rick?" I said.

With a deep breath, he shook his head. "I need to talk to you."

I glanced at my father, who had a murderous expression on his face, squarely directed at Rick, and then at Michelle and Soleil who looked more confused than angry. Turning toward the now murmuring guests, I said, "Please excuse us for one moment."

The pastor looked concerned as Rick led the way into a small room behind the altar. A plate of communion wafers and a goblet of wine rested on a small table with shallow drawers. The rest of the room was plain, aside from a few crosses on stands in the corner and an uncomfortable-looking chair. This was the sacristy.

"I'm not sure we're supposed to be in here," I said reverently.

"The room will be sufficient." He coupled his hands behind his back and stared at a water stain on the wall.

"What's going on, Rick?" My voice shook more than I wanted it to. I couldn't help it. A crushing weight settled over my heart, growing heavier with every second he didn't look at me.

"I can't do this," he said toward the wall.

"Can't do what?"

"Marry you."

I laughed, although there was nothing funny about his words. It was my body's way of dealing with the pressure and pain that threatened to eviscerate my heart. "You've wanted to marry me since the day we met."

"Not anymore."

I swayed on my feet. "What changed since last night?" I asked, my words thready and barely audible. Concentrating, I focused on our connection, forcing my way into his head. Was it Tabetha? A vampire mind trick? Had he made a deal with someone to protect me? I forced my way into his consciousness, and what I saw inside his head turned my blood to ice. As far as I could tell, his thoughts were his own.

He licked his lips and faced me. "I just now realized how you've used me. I'm a tool to you. A means to an end."

"That's not true."

"I need time. I need to prove to myself that you don't own me."

"Time. You're asking for time now, on our wedding day." Okay, now I was angry. I was the president of the asking-for-time club. I would have been happy to indulge his sincere desire to wait. But this was not the time for doubts. This was the I-am-totally-ready-for-this part.

He narrowed his eyes at me. "Better now than after."

My mouth dropped open. His expression was frigid. "Why are you doing this?" I asked. "Did something happen? Are you trying to protect me?" I'd seen his thoughts. He meant every word he said. I just couldn't bring myself to believe it.

He shook his head. "I'm sorry."

"But you love me. How could you do this to me?" My words were sharp, meant to hurt.

Again he shook his head, and this time he walked away.

"Don't walk away from me. You owe me more of an explanation than this. Rick?" I tried to follow him, but he exited through the back door and slammed it in my face.

"Rick? Rick!" I glanced down at the bouquet I was still holding and caught sight of my mother's pearl bracelet.

What a waste of a good gift. What would she think of me now? I dropped my bouquet. Watched the fresh flowers bounce and roll on the wood floor. The head of a white rose broke from its stem and separated, decapitated, from the arrangement.

My father approached from behind. Good thing, because I collapsed. My tears swelled and spilled, and my body went lax. To the sound of Soleil asking for the attention of the guests in the pews, my father and a swearing Michelle ushered me out of the church and took me home.

CHAPTER 26
Fallout

Time slipped through my fingers. I was in the carriage and then being undressed and helped into bed. Sleep was an escape my mind dove toward, and I embraced the darkness. I willed myself deeper into the abyss. Who would want to wake up? Who would want to live after an experience like that? The surface of consciousness was a painful place. No, I fought to stay asleep, wrapped in darkness and blissful unconsciousness. Was this what death would feel like? To be swept away into the depths of a dark and endless ocean?

Unfortunately, time and light forced me to the surface. As well as Poe, who stood on my chest with his hooked beak pressed into the bridge of my nose. Michelle sat by my bedside, no longer in her bridesmaid's dress but in jeans and a sweatshirt.

"Grateful?" she asked uncertainly.

I opened my mouth to say something and nothing came out but a sob. She brushed Poe aside and pulled me into her arms. I cried on her shoulder until I couldn't cry anymore.

"I'm so sorry, sweetheart," Michelle said, stroking my hair.

"He left me," I gasped. My throat felt bone dry, my whole body drained of every ounce of energy. "How could he leave me?"

"I don't know," Michelle said.

Poe found his voice. "I, for one, didn't think it was possible for a caretaker to leave his witch."

This only made me cry harder.

Michelle stroked the back of my head. "Grateful, we can talk about this more, but first you need to eat something. You've been asleep for almost twenty-four hours."

"I'm not hungry."

"I don't care, hon. You need to eat." Michelle's voice changed from pleading to commanding. She pulled back the covers and helped me out of bed. A bathroom visit later, I was sitting at the kitchen island while she made me Cream of Wheat. Poe stared at me sympathetically, which was as annoying as it was worrisome. If the situation wasn't dire, he'd be his regular snarky self.

"Did Rick give you any indication he didn't want to be married?"

"No," I said. A sob erupted from my throat, but no tears fell. Was it possible to run out of tears? "We were together last ni—" I caught myself. I'd been in bed an entire night and day. "I mean, the night before we were supposed to get married. Everything seemed fine."

"What exactly did he say before he left the church?"

"He said I was using him. That he felt like he was my tool. He needs time to figure out if he loves me outside of our magical relationship."

Poe straightened his neck. "That does not sound like our caretaker." His beady eyes narrowed.

Michelle poured the hot Cream of Wheat into a bowl from the cupboard and added butter and brown sugar. She skimmed the meal across the counter to me.

"Thanks. Where'd you get butter and brown sugar?"

"The same place I got the Cream of Wheat. My house. You seriously need to go grocery shopping."

My stomach growled in anticipation, and I spooned a heap into my mouth.

"Something is wrong about this situation," Poe said.

"I was just left at the altar by my own caretaker. Everything is wrong with this situation." I tipped forward and slammed my forehead into the counter, banging it repeatedly. Michelle took me by the shoulders and sat me back up.

"You. Eat," she said, pointing at me, then at the bowl. "You." She pointed at Poe. "Be more helpful."

Poe swayed his neck. "I don't mean to hurt you, dear witch, but I must ask the question. Why would Rick choose the worst possible time to announce his change of heart? Why would he break things off with you in the most painful way?"

"I don't know. Wedding jitters." I shrugged and shoveled in another bite of Cream of Wheat. I was hungrier than I thought I was and made short work of it.

Poe shook his head. "The magic that makes him your caretaker forces him to protect you. He saved you from Julius in the fall despite thinking you were leaving him for Logan. What he did and how he did it was ... uncharacteristic, for lack of a better word."

My spoon hit the bottom of the empty bowl with a loud clank. "But he did it, Poe. I was there. He was right in front of me, in the middle of our cemetery. I didn't think it was possible either, but he stood not two feet away from me and said he didn't want to marry me. He's not sure he loves me."

"Where is he now?" Poe asked.

"I don't know. I've been asleep for the last twenty-four hours, remember?"

"Your dad, Soleil, and I went to his house after the wedding," Michelle said. "Your dad wanted to give him a piece of his mind. I wanted to show him a close-up of my fist. He was already gone by the time we got there. He hasn't been back since."

"Use your connection," Poe said. "Call for him." I'd never seen Poe so resolute.

Closing my eyes, I reached out, grasping at the magical ribbon that linked Rick and me. But the stretch extended into a misty fog within my mind. "He's blocking me," I said.

"*Someone's* blocking you," Poe muttered.

"We could check his cottage again? Or call Silas. He's a detective," Michelle said.

I lifted an eyebrow. "No. I have a better way." I looked right, then left. "Did you bring my purse when you helped me home?"

"Not initially, but I went back to get it." She moved across the foyer to the hall closet and emerged with a large shopping bag full of stuff. I saw my bouquet peeking from the top and dug through some decorative items that probably belonged to the florist to reach my white beaded bag. Inside was my phone.

I poked the Find-a-Buddy app, entered my password, and clicked on Rick's number while I slowly walked back toward the kitchen island. A map of the United States appeared on the screen while a glowing bar circled a bull's-eye, narrowing Rick's location to east of the Mississippi, then to the Northeast, and then finally to New Hampshire and the surrounding states.

A white flag appeared over Rick's location. I dropped the phone. My knees gave out, and my ass slammed into the hardwood.

"Jesus, Grateful!" Michelle rushed to my side, cradling my shoulders and placing a palm over my forehead. "What is it? Are you faint?" she asked.

I swallowed and licked my lips. With a shaking hand, I swept my bangs from my eyes before answering in an infirm voice. "Rick's in Salem, Massachusetts."

"Tabetha," Poe hissed. "He was taken, abducted as payment for the damned candle."

"He was not taken!" I spread my hands in frustration. "I watched him walk out of the church. I had a lucid conversation with him in Monk's Hill Chapel. I saw inside his head!"

"Then some kind of mind control," Poe said.

Michelle agreed. "He'd never go to her willingly. I had a hard enough time believing he left you. This is too much. Tabetha did this." She helped me from the floor.

I frowned. "How? We were in the middle of Monk's Hill Cemetery. Even presuming I was too distracted to sense her power, I knew every face in that church. She wasn't there."

Poe sighed. "Perhaps she hexed him before the ceremony."

"Or he left me for her." A part of me yelled that it couldn't be true, but another part, a large, defeated part, wondered if this was karma calling. Maybe I didn't deserve Rick. Maybe my long history of failed relationships was repeating itself.

I squatted to retrieve my phone from the floor, thankful the screen was still intact. The red bubble next to my messages icon displayed a number in the double digits. I tapped it absently and scrolled through the names of wedding attendees expressing their condolences and offering encouragement.

He's a dick! Kathleen from ICU wrote.

You can do better, Silas fumed.

I didn't open all of them. When I reached the end of the list, my eyebrows knit.

"Rick sent me a text the morning of the wedding," I said.

"What? I thought you said he didn't know how to text?" Michelle asked.

I blinked at the screen, disorientation making my eyes blur. "He doesn't." I tapped on his name. "It says, 'Gracias, *mi cielo*. I adore new beginnings only slightly less than I adore you.'"

"What was he thanking you for?" Michelle asked.

Perturbed, I shook my head. "I have no idea."

Slowly, I stood from the floor, a hot, hungry nebula of rage forming inside me, demanding to be fed. Why was Rick with Tabetha? Why did he leave me the way he did? I wanted to believe Tabetha had made him do it, but how?

"I've got to go to Salem." I started for the stairs.

"She'll be stronger than you within her territory," Poe said matter-of-factly. "Perhaps a spell or incantation to draw him out?"

I shook my head. "She'd never let him go, even if he wanted to leave. No matter how she lured him there, if I know Tabetha, she's sunk her claws in and won't let go until I cut them off."

Michelle widened her eyes. "After everything you've told me about her, you can't just walk up to her front door and ask for Rick back. She'll kill you."

I took one more look at Rick's text. He hated to text. Despised it. That text proved that at nine ten on the morning of March twentieth, Rick loved me. I had to know what happened between then and now. I had to know if the disaster that was my wedding day was real or manipulated by my nemesis. It was worth my life to know the truth.

I paused, one foot on the steps, and met Michelle's eyes. "I am going to Salem, and I am confronting Tabetha." I shook my head. "I have to know if what happened to me in that church was because of Rick or because of magic. If it's magic, you better believe I will take my caretaker back or die trying." My voice cracked.

"But—"

I shook my head. "It doesn't matter. Nothing matters until I know why, one way or another."

CHAPTER 27
Things You Can't Unsee

I parked in the street and walked to the gate of Tabetha's residence, the same way Rick and I had. Only, I didn't have Rick to give me a ride over this time.

"Poe, fly over and see if there's a button or something to open the gate."

He flew from my shoulder and circled around inside. Without thinking, I placed my hands on the bars and gave the gate a little push while I was waiting. The wrought iron moved easily under my hand.

Poe flew back to my shoulder. "It's open," he said with concern.

"She's expecting me."

The gate squealed as I allowed it to close behind me. I didn't think it was possible for the driveway to be creepier than it was the last time, but the tendrils of fog that wrapped around the trunks of the fruit trees writhed like they had a life of their own. The animals were back. To my left, the herd of albino deer stood like ghosts, half buried in the fog and partially concealed by the trunks of the grove of trees.

Closer to us, an albino buck was feeding on fallen fruit. He raised his branched horns to look at me, lips stained purple from his feast, a harsh color against his bright white coat. The deer's red eyes bore into me. It looked dead, or undead. The pulse in its neck throbbed as it trotted a few feet away inside the tree line in response to my presence. Not a vampire deer. Still, weird. It stopped a few feet inside the tree line, not far enough to be safe if I was a true predator, but then the deer seemed to know I wasn't a threat.

"Is this stuff good?" I asked the deer, crouching down to wave the fog away from the half-eaten fruit. The peel was bright red, but inside was purple with green seeds. I'd never seen fruit like that, although something about it gave me déjà vu. What would it taste like? I stood and reached for a low-hanging specimen, breaking it open between my fingers. The smell of sex wafted to my nose and blood rushed to my crotch.

"Hmm," I said to the buck watching me. "Is that why you like this? Does it make you horny, baby?" I did my best Austin Powers impression.

Poe leaned over for a whiff. "That is definitely genetically modified."

I inspected the fruit, the leathery red skin, the kiwi-like texture. An odd tingling began in my palms where the juice touched my skin. I dropped the fruit and wiped the juice on my pants. Better.

"It makes you horny *and* numb," I said to Poe. "No wonder the animals love it."

"May I suggest you focus on the task at hand?" Poe said. "The gate was open. She knows we're here." I nodded and turned back toward the house, refocusing on my mission

"Poe, I don't want you to come in with me. I need you to wait and watch at a safe distance, in case I need you. This could be a trap."

He took to the air and circled over my right shoulder. "If you insist."

I couldn't blame him for not arguing the point with me. Tabetha's house was terrifying in an abandoned-insane-asylum way.

"I insist you back me up if I need it," I said firmly. We'd reached the end of the drive, where a few feet of yard stretched to the wide steps of the stone veranda.

"You know what's weird about these trees?" Poe asked from the air.

"The fruit smells like sex and the juice numbs like lidocaine?"

"That too, but what I see from the air is it looks like she's staggered the time of the planting."

"What?" I narrowed my eyes at him.

"Bird's-eye view," he said. "From the air, it's obvious the oldest trees are near the gate, and these, near the house, are relatively new. Seems strange to landscape like that, doesn't it?"

I checked out the one closest to the house. The soil around the base of the trunk was still mounded from planting. Although, from my perspective, the tree was large enough to be called full grown. "Less fruit," I muttered. "This must be the newest one."

"And this," Poe circled over a hole prepared across from the youngest tree, "must be where the next one will go."

"What's with the planting schedule?" I asked.

"I have no idea," Poe admitted.

With a gesture of my head, I told Poe I was going inside and took the first steps toward Tabetha's front door. This time I avoided the large flowers on either side of the threshold, although their heads swung menacingly toward me, and their petals snapped like steel jaws. I didn't bother to knock. The gate was left open for a reason, and I was sure the door would be too.

The knob twisted under firm pressure, and I entered the foyer. A bare-chested blond man in dark pants and a bow tie smiled at me. "Greetings, Miss Knight, Mistress Tabetha is waiting for you upstairs." The man's perfectly straight teeth gleamed white as he pointed a hand toward the curved wooden staircase to my right. "Shall I get you a drink before you head up?"

"No, thank you. I'm fine," I said. My gaze drifted to the tight cling of his pants. *Damn,* Tabetha had an appetite for attractive men. This was the third I'd seen in her residence, including Logan. My stomach sank as if I'd swallowed a brick. Rick was here. What was Tabetha doing with Rick?

On shaky legs, I approached the stairwell. The rail and spindles were completely grown over with blood-red roses. The flowers were the biggest I'd seen, but so were the thorns. I positioned myself in the center of the runner, sure if I got too close, the plant would go for the jugular. On the second floor, the vines covered the walls, floor to ceiling. The roses were everywhere. Living wallpaper. The heady scent of the flowers was suffocating, intoxicating. Slightly dizzy, I had a sudden horrifying thought the smell could poison me. Enchanted roses meant to stupefy? My heart beat faster and panic gripped me by the throat. Too late. No turning back.

Whispers and light came from a room at the end of the hall. The door was open, but I couldn't see inside because of the angle. This was a trap. Definitely a trap. I took another step. I couldn't help myself. I needed to know. I needed to face what Tabetha had in store for me and confront Rick. With a deep breath, I turned into the light.

The first thing I noticed was the massive four-poster bed. The thing was castle-worthy with posts the size of tree trunks covered in red roses. The second thing I noticed was who was in the bed. Rick's broad sculpted shoulders tapered to the mounded muscles of his back, nakedness disappearing under a crisp white sheet. Tabetha's bare chest hovered over the curve of his waist. She was sitting up in bed behind him, her arms resting casually on his side, her dark eyes and red lips facing my direction. Her lipstick was the exact color of the roses growing around her. From a thick collar of gold around her neck, a matching scarab amulet dangled between her collarbones.

"Rick?" I rasped.

He looked over his shoulder, but didn't meet my eyes directly. Once he recognized who I was, he returned his head to the pillow. His expression was vacant, almost bored.

"Would you care to join us, Grateful?" Tabetha said through her teeth. She scraped the red nails of her right hand down Rick's spine.

Bile rose in my throat, and I gasped for breath. I thought I could do this, but I couldn't. I couldn't be here. I couldn't watch this for one more second. The stench of the roses burned in my throat.

"What's wrong, sister? You look like you might be sick." She lowered her lips to Rick's neck and planted a kiss on his jugular. "I'll give you one more opportunity to do something intelligent for a change. Hand over your territory, and you can have your caretaker back."

"No," I croaked.

The roses on the bed and walls snaked and twisted, tangling toward me. Threatening me. "Then you can show yourself out," she said through her teeth. "I suggest you run."

A thorny vine whipped at my throat. Head swimming from the floral stench, I turned on my heel and ran, tripping down the stairs and flying past the man in the atrium to charge the exit. No one tried to stop me. That would be beside the point. This is what she wanted. She did this to punish me, to ruin me, and she wanted me to live to remember it.

I stopped at the base of the drive and vomited, desperately inhaling great gasps of fresh air to clear the poison odor from my lungs. My entire body shook violently. My emotions were raw, yes, but the more I reacted, the more I was sure it was also the roses. I was stronger than this, wasn't I?

Poe came to rest in the tree above me. "I take it that did not go well."

"He's with her now."

Poe groaned. "She's drugged him."

"Probably. Maybe. I don't know. What if he wanted this?"

"You're confused. You know that couldn't be true."

I leaned on my knees and panted toward the mound of dirt under the tree. I was going to be sick again. This was my worst nightmare. All of my insecurities were colliding into one horrific moment. I couldn't breathe. I couldn't think. I swallowed repeatedly and spit on the ground.

Mmmmm. A muffled humming sound came to me on the wind.

"Did you hear that?" I paused my sobbing to ask Poe.

"Hear what?"

Mmmmful.

"There it is again," I said. I narrowed my eyes and tipped my head, straining my ears to listen.

Mmmmm.

"I hear it," Poe whispered. "It's coming from the tree."

Brow furrowed, I straightened my spine and took a step back, scanning the length of the trunk and the mound it was planted in.

Mmmmmful!

I searched for something to dig with. No shovels handy, of course. Evil wood witches didn't leave the tools to dig up their plants at the enemy's disposal. I improvised. Concentrating, I called on the air around me. I raised both hands and commanded a tornado to funnel down from the night sky. With a little effort, the suction of the swirling winds tore the young tree out by the roots and set it gently on the lawn. Success. I stepped to the edge of the resulting hole and looked inside.

"Oh dear God!" I said. Poe flew to my shoulder to get a better look. At the bottom, a body lay in the shadows.

"Who do you think it is?" Poe asked.

"I have no idea." I leaned over the hole, but it was too dark. "I'm going in."

I jumped into the hole. It wasn't a huge undertaking, only about five or six feet deep, but I had to straddle the body and plant my feet in the dirt to keep my balance in the irregular hole. Still too dark to see.

Drawing Nightshade, I focused the blue glow from her blade toward the body. It produced just enough light for me to make out the details of the shriveled specimen. A face worthy of a historical museum stared up at me, mummified and ancient, with pruney, parchment skin, protruding teeth, and wispy white hair. The creature's eyeteeth had elongated to wedge the jaw open.

"It used to be a vampire," I called up to Poe. "But the body is decimated. I'm not even sure I'd be able to revive it if I wanted to."

"Then come out of the scary hole," Poe said from above me.

I leaned over the body one more time. "Something doesn't make sense. These clothes, they're dirty but new. This vampire is mighty fashionable for someone who looks like he's been buried for fifty years." I shook my head. "He's completely dehydrated."

"Be careful, Grateful," Poe warned. He must've suspected what I was going to do.

I brought Nightshade's tip to my thumb and pressed. A bead of blood formed there, and I dangled it over the opening between the mummy's canines. One drip, then two fell into the mouth and rolled over the leathery tongue. The creature was too far gone to even swallow. I straightened, planning to leap from the hole. And that's when the vampire's eyes flipped open. They were blue and fixated on me with an unwavering and familiar stare. "Mmmm," came a moan from deep within the throat.

"Julius!"

CHAPTER 28
Awaken

"I'm coming out," I said to Poe. I gathered Julius in my arms. It wasn't difficult. He was a skeleton held together by shriveled skin and sinew. Maybe fifty pounds. Still, I was in an awkward position in the irregular hole. I tried to wedge my toes in the dirt, but the ground broke apart under my weight.

"You need to levitate," Poe said as if it were painfully obvious.

I scowled in the darkness and closed my eyes to get a grip on my racing thoughts. Once I had clarity, the instinct to float came from within. The air lifted me, or maybe my body became helium-light. I'd practiced this dozens of times with Rick, and it paid off. I landed gently on the lawn and laid Julius's body in a patch of grass. The vampire was emaciated. Completely empty of blood.

"He looks better than usual," Poe said, then chuckled at his own joke.

"I'm waking him up. We need to know what happened and if he can help us get Rick back."

"In the entire history of ideas, this one might be in the bottom five," Poe said. "A ravenous vampire is hardly an ally. He'll have no control."

True, Julius was ancient and dangerous. Fully fed, the vampire had almost killed me once—lost control while tasting my blood and practically drained me dry. Rick was able to bring me back from the brink of death, but Poe's warning rang true. If I wasn't careful, Julius would turn into a ravenous monster, and I would be lunch.

But the vampire had also saved me twice: once from Anna Bathory's torture chamber and once by challenging Bathory when she'd been ready to tear out my heart. The second was more of a coincidence, I supposed. I didn't owe him anything. I'd already spared him his life. Still, I needed help, and he was my best hope.

I had so many unanswered questions. All the time I'd spent searching for Julius, he'd been here under this tree. Why? How did he get here? Only one way to find out.

Drawing Nightshade, I ran the blade across my wrist. Blood gurgled out quickly, and I shot the trickle out over the gap of his shriveled lips. The wound would heal if I didn't concentrate on keeping it open. Just like Rick's teeth, my flesh moved aside for Nightshade. The magic was necessary as many of my spells required blood. I'd be a mass of scars if the cuts were the human variety. I was thankful for the phenomenon now, as control was exactly what I'd need to bring Julius back safely.

At first the ruby drops rolled over his leathered tongue and dribbled down his throat without any assistance, but eventually the muscles of his neck rippled with a swallow. *Drip, drip, drip.* His lips plumped and his parchment skin became soft and supple. Eyelids and eyelashes extended over his Caribbean blue eyes and the white tufts of hair fell out, replaced by a chocolate brown coif.

Julius flinched toward my wrist, and I pulled it away. Immediately, the flow stopped and my wrist healed. He licked his lips and opened his mouth like a baby bird, lungs not developed enough to support his desire to speak. He made a sound like a hum from his throat.

"Hold your horses, cowboy. I'll see what I can do." I lifted my gaze to the woods beyond the fallen tree. The albino buck was back, staring needfully at the fallen fruit with eerie red eyes. Or maybe it was a different buck. Now that I thought about it, this one looked younger, with a smaller rack of horns. I left Julius's side and plucked a fruit from the tree. I held it out toward the deer.

"Come," I said. The command was ordinary enough but charged with my witchy intention, it drew the animal to me. Natural magic. It wasn't *Star Trek* style. The deer wasn't caught in my tractor beam or anything. A strong breeze, coupled with a more subtle, imperceptible draw, coaxed the buck in my direction. When he was within an arm's reach, I tossed the fruit between us. The deer

stretched his graceful neck to take a bite, and I swiftly used
Nightshade to slit its throat.

I underestimated the blood. It gushed over me,
spritzing across my long-sleeved black T-shirt. Pinching
the gash with one hand, I gathered the front legs under my
arm and dragged the kill to Julius, who stretched toward
me with open lips. I released the wound over his mouth,
and in seconds, his arms were strong enough to haul the
body into his lap. Expertly, the vampire pinched arteries
and tipped limbs in a way that ensured every drop made it
into his stomach.

Poe landed on my shoulder and whispered in my ear.
"I hope you know what you're doing."

I gave him a harsh glare.

Faster than I expected, Julius tossed the drained body
of the buck aside and stood. Unlike me, he was
impressively free of blood. How did he do that? Did they
teach young vampires not to spill a drop? Or had he
spilled but extracted every bit from his skin and clothing?

However he did it, I hadn't fared as well. I was a
bloody mess.

"Grateful Knight," he said, bowing at the waist. "Of all
the people I envisioned coming to my aid, you never
crossed my mind. I am in your debt."

"Yeah. I didn't have this on my to-do list either," I
mumbled. "Plenty of time for gratitude later. How the
fuck did you end up in that hole?"

He gestured toward the tree. "The fruit is toxic.
Enchanted. Tabetha fed it to me." He gritted his teeth and

smoothed back his hair. "She came to the Thames asking for an alliance. When I refused, she offered me a slice of pie as a symbol of our continued peace." He pointed toward the fruit on the ground, its bright red skin split open to reveal the purple flesh and green seeds. His polite features morphed into something feral. "One bite of that fruit makes you her slave, and once she uses you and tires of you, she buries you here as supernatural fertilizer for her fucking magical trees."

"Used you?" I said softly. My mind drifted to Rick.

"In more ways than one," he spat. "The tree drained my life force, but as a vampire, I cannot die. I did not understand until I was in the ground that I'd become the source of her power."

I narrowed my eyes, his words sinking in slowly, like water into sand. "This is why she's so strong. She doesn't just pull power from her small cemetery; she pulls power from immortals. She feeds off others' power."

He nodded. "When *she* eats the fruit, it strengthens her. She's able to tap into the immortals buried under these roots." He pointed at the row of trees. "A legion of supernatural lovers feeding her limitless appetite."

"That's why she wants Rick," I said softly. "A caretaker would be the ultimate source of power." Rick wasn't just the man I loved. We healed each other and ruled my realm together. His blood kept me from aging. I was effectively mortal without him. If Tabetha succeeded in burying him beneath one of her trees, not only would she gain his power, but without his blood, I would slowly age and die. Then she'd move in on my territory, her ultimate goal.

Julius frowned. "She has your caretaker?"

"Yes." The word came out broken and hollow. I shook with anger.

"I am truly sorry. Her cruelty has no bounds, and I am a veteran of cruelty." His eyes flashed to mine and for a moment I saw straight into his vampire soul. He'd been both victim and perpetrator in his long life. Pain was no stranger to this vampire. He'd had to do things he didn't want to do to survive as long as he had. I felt a special kinship to that history, not because of what I'd done in the past but because of what I was about to do.

A seed of change took root within me. My human life seemed far less important then the supernatural injustice Tabetha had waged upon the vampire and me. I heard my goddess mother's voice in my head. *I give you permission to kill Tabetha.* Only this time, I didn't find the words harsh; I found them hopeful.

My eyes drifted from Julius to Tabetha's brick mansion, and a darkness stirred within my soul. I inhaled deeply through my nose.

"You will not succeed," Julius said as if he'd heard my thoughts. "It is foolishness to confront her here."

I trudged to the fallen tree and plucked one of the red orbs from the branches. "Do you think this fruit only gives Tabetha power, or any Hecate?"

Poe grew restless on my shoulder. "I don't like this. It's too risky. You could end up her slave."

Julius had a much different reaction. His eyes narrowed to slits. "Do it here, and if it intoxicates or subjugates you, I will throw you over my shoulder and care for you until it wears off."

"Don't trust him," Poe warned. "He *cares* for you the way you care for a fine wine. He'll drain you dry if he gets the chance."

"I will not," Julius insisted.

"You have before," Poe reminded him.

"That was an accident."

"Stop," I said, holding up one hand. I stared at the fruit. "I'm not leaving here without doing everything in my power to end this. I'm not leaving without Rick. Hecate said I could beat Tabetha by turning her own power against her. She implied I could use her progeny to tear her apart. There's nothing closer to Tabetha's children than these trees. I can't think of a better way to do that than this, can you?"

Julius gave Poe a smug grin. In response, Poe rotated on my shoulder so that his back was to the vampire.

"Relax, Poe. It's the best plan we have." I dug my nails into the red skin and broke the fruit open, my fingers going numb where they touched the purple flesh. I didn't let that stop me. I buried my face in the fruit, gulping down large bites. "The texture is like kiwi, but it tastes like lychee," I said around a mouthful.

"You're still speaking. That's a good sign," Julius said.

In fact, the numbness in my hands had abated, and a warm vitality filled my abdomen. I finished the fruit.

Poe lifted from my shoulder and circled above my head. "You're glowing."

"I can feel it," I said. I picked another fruit, tore it open, and ate the flesh. The fruits had to weigh a pound each, and my stomach protested near the end of the second one. I tossed the skin aside.

Juice dripped down my chin. Blood pulsed in my temples. *Lub-dub. Lub-dub.* I lifted both hands, tingling with power. The normally blue hue of my veins purpled under my skin and the muscles in my forearms bulged.

"Your eyes," Julius said. "The power is in you. Are you still of your own mind?"

"Hell yes!" My magic threatened to burst the seams of my skin, but it didn't own me. I was still me. "I've never had such clarity."

"Excellent." Julius clenched his hands into fists and looked toward the house. "Let us teach Tabetha the ultimate lesson."

"No," I said. "Tabetha is mine. Besides, I need your help with something else."

He scowled at me. "What?"

"Dig up the rest of the trees. Pull them up by the roots. Free whoever is underneath."

A smile stretched across his face. "Disconnect her power source."

"Exactly." I pointed my chin toward my familiar. "Poe, I need you to help him. Catch animals to feed whoever is buried here."

He landed in a nearby branch. "As you wish."

"While I am doing this deed, where will you be?" Julius asked.

I turned toward the house, rolling my shoulders back and drawing Nightshade. "I thought I made myself clear. I will be taking my fiancé back … and killing Tabetha."

CHAPTER 29
War and Roses

Nightshade in hand, I strode up the veranda's stone steps two at a time. Power, pure and unadulterated, pulsed aura-like around me and gave off a telltale shimmer. The air was thick and tingly. As far as I could tell, the fruit had the opposite effect on a Hecate as it did on other supernaturals—it amplified my control, made my mind sharp, and my magic more accessible.

I thanked my goddess mother I'd had the courage to try it. I'd need all the help I could get if I was going to take down Tabetha. I shivered apprehensively but shook it off. Fear was a luxury I couldn't afford.

As I approached the door, the carnivorous flowers swayed in their pots. In two swipes of my blade, I beheaded the plants, and then carefully avoided the sap as it leaked around my toes. It sizzled menacingly on the stone. I pushed through the unlocked door.

"Hello again," the bow tie-clad man said. His vacant smile took on new meaning now that I understood Tabetha's power. He wasn't an overzealous employee. This man was drugged on fruit-filled pastry. He didn't attempt to stop me as I climbed the stairs. His eyes drifted back toward the door. How long had he been standing there? How long would he stand there?

The tangle of roses grew faster as I passed, their heady perfume filling the hallway. This time, the fruit I'd eaten seemed to protect me from the neurological effects. I didn't feel dizzy or anxious in their presence. With a clear mind, I barged into Tabetha's room.

A naked Rick still lay on the bed, but he'd turned over to face the door. With a clear view of his face, I could see his eyes were glassy and his breathing as shallow as if he might be sleeping. Drugged.

Naked Tabetha drew a finger down Rick's outer arm. "You're back," she drawled. "A glutton for punishment?"

"I came for my caretaker." I clutched Nightshade in front of me with sweaty palms.

"*Your* caretaker." She scoffed. "Not anymore. You did not relinquish your territory to me, and I am due blood. He is mine now."

"You are due nothing," I hissed. "Rick didn't follow through with your spell. I offered you fair payment, a spell for a spell. It's not our fault you didn't accept."

She crawled off the bed, lifting a kimono patterned silk robe from a hook on the four-poster. She wrapped it around her shoulders and tied it at the waist, her gold scarab talisman peeking from the vee of silk at the neck. "Rick is here because he wants to be here. Right, sweetheart?"

"Yes," Rick said flatly. The word was a dagger to my heart.

"Only because you've drugged him," I said. "What did you do? How did you get him to eat the fruit, Tabetha?"

"Ah, the fruit. Frankly, I'm surprised a baby witch like you figured it out." Her features changed. She shed the pretense of Rick wanting to be there, in lieu of arrogance and ego. "Persigranates. My own personal hybrid. An act of pure magical genius on my part." She picked up her wand from the nightstand. "An endless source of power and a convenient way to dispose of enemies. You want to know how I got Rick to eat it?" She pouted at me with full red lips. "A heart-shaped tart." She giggled and rolled her eyes. "Men are so gullible. I left it on his counter with a note that it was from *you*, the witch who never cooks, in honor of your new beginning. How could he turn down such a sweet gift on your wedding day?"

"He ate it because he thought I baked it for him," I said more to myself than to her. That's why he'd sent me the text about new beginnings. A text that meant he understood how difficult it must have been for me to learn to cook. A text that implicitly promised he would work hard to learn to text. My heart clenched.

"Of course. He wouldn't eat it if he knew it was from me." She widened her eyes. "Blame yourself. I'd planned to use Logan to lure you here, but he's gone missing. Then again, I'm sure you were behind that. Can't lose your precious boy on the side. I could have found him easily enough, but he was never what I was after."

The thorny vines on the walls roiled and twisted as the magical tension between us took on the quality of cream soup. A thorny vine snaked across the floor toward my ankle. I sliced it in two and brushed it away.

"Wake Rick up. I'm taking him home."

She laughed at me and sent a blast of energy in my direction. Instinctively, I shifted Nightshade, intercepting her attack. Her magic fizzled between us.

Tabetha's face fell, genuinely confused.

I grinned. "Did I mention I had a snack of your fruit a moment ago? Interesting, the effect it has on a fellow witch."

Her lips peeled back from her teeth. "I'm still older and stronger," she said. Absently, she touched the scarab around her neck.

"We'll see about that." I attacked. Nightshade sang through the air. A blast of power from the tip of her wand blocked my blade and knocked me back six inches. I rushed her, struck again. Nightshade narrowly missed her throat.

A hex exploded next to my ear. I lurched forward. I faked a stab at her heart and instead twisted my wrist to slide my blade under her collar of gold. I caught her scarab necklace with the tip and pulled. According to *The Book of Light,* the scarab amulet was channeling and intensifying her power. I planned to level the playing field. Nightshade sliced through the gold like butter. The scarab dropped from her throat and through her clutching fingers. I kicked it toward the bed.

"You bitch," she hissed. Hexes flew from her wand, exploding around my head as I parried her attack. All the while, her roses reached for me. Thorny whips whacked at my skin. I cut them away when I could and positioned myself closer to her. Close contact meant the thorns had equal chance of tripping her up as snaring my limbs.

She grunted with the effort of dodging me as I swung with sword and fist. I kept her on the run, doubling down to avoid giving her a good shot with her wand. We circled back toward the bed. I crushed her scarab necklace under my heel. If it helped drain her power, I wouldn't know. She used the distraction to land a curse on my left shoulder. The limb went limp and rubbery. Good thing I was a righty. I rounded Nightshade toward the crown of her head. She ducked and a lock of her hair floated to the floor, sheared off by my blade.

"Uhng," she grunted, rushing forward. A flick of her wrist, and a hex landed in my stomach. I coughed and gagged, a spray of blood peppering my hand. I forced myself to attack, even as a vine erupted over my tongue.

"Thith old twick," I said around the vine. As I'd seen Gary do, I grabbed the end of the plant and tore it out of my innards without pausing my one-armed attack. I was successful, but the roots brought up more blood and fleshy chunks. I tossed the mess aside. Without the fruit, I might have bled to death, but despite the pain, I could feel myself healing.

Tabetha panted. She was winded. I suspected between the destroyed scarab and Julius digging up her trees, her power was flagging. The flat of my sword slapped her on the side, and she yelped. I tripped from the force of impact. Tabetha took advantage of my wavering balance. She rushed me, lowered her shoulder, and tackled me into the full-length mirror in the corner of her room. I braced myself for impact and shattering glass. It never came.

When she recoiled, I tried to follow. My head slapped a solid surface. I pressed my hand in front of me. Cold glass held me in place from the front and dark metal pressed into my back. Solid. Polished silver. Fuck! She'd locked me in the damned mirror.

I kicked and punched, tried to stab the glass with Nightshade, even threw my shoulder against the glass hard enough I'd have a bruise.

Tabetha shook her head. "You can't break it, sister," she said. "New trick I learned since I acquired Polina's territory. You're trapped inside the silver." She pretended to toast the air with an invisible glass. "Here's looking at you."

Bitch. I needed to concentrate. There was always a way. I thought about the pentagram of power Poe and Rick had taught me about. I was encased in metal. Certain elements fed metal; others weakened it. What weakened metal?

Closing my eyes, I tried to picture what Rick had drawn on the envelope on my kitchen counter. If I had any hope of defeating Tabetha I needed to use my natural power. Fire. Fire melted metal. I focused on my breath and the sound of my heart. I had a power that could melt silver; I just needed to call it. Eyes open again, I lowered my chin and glared at Tabetha. She gripped one of the bedposts as the winds started, her hair whipping around her head in my gathering power. An electric cloud formed near the ceiling, rumbling and crackling like an angry god. I focused, channeling every ounce of anger I felt toward Tabetha into the cloud. A bolt of lightning sliced through the air and into my silver prison. The mirror shattered around me.

In one powerful leap, I landed on my feet and drove Nightshade toward Tabetha's heart. I missed, but the blade sank into her shoulder. Her high-pitched scream rattled the room. I withdrew the blade by slashing upward, ripping through her skin. I expected to see blood and lots of it. Instead, purple fruit filling—persigranate—slopped onto the floor. Fuck! She was made of the stuff.

"Immortal, remember?" she said as the wound stitched itself up. "I wasn't stupid enough to give my immortality to a caretaker."

While I gaped at the realization she was a walking jelly-filled donut, the roses on the walls got all touchy feely. Apparently my electrical storm had woken them up, or else Tabetha was just getting serious. Thorns wrapped around my ankles. I hacked at the vines, only to have more encircle my waist and yank me back against the wall. My skull slapped the drywall. The impact was hard enough to break my concentration. The winds stopped. The electric cloud dissipated.

I wriggled and thwacked, my blade slicing again and again. The roses kept growing. Thorns dug into my wrists, my forehead, my neck. Soon I was bound spread eagle to her bedroom wall as if I were part of some warped S & M game.

My gaze darted toward Rick, still catatonic on the bed. "Rick, help. Please!" I begged.

He didn't even turn his head.

"Rick is in a much better place now," Tabetha said, her wand raised between us. "And when I'm done with him, he'll make a beautiful addition to my garden." She sauntered up to me, all attitude and swagger. She squeezed my chin. "So will you."

Rage poured out of me in a blast of wind that knocked her on her ass. I called the lightning again. A massive bolt struck the floor at my feet and fried the vines binding me. I levitated over a huge hole the strike had made in the floor and flashed a deadly stare in the direction of Tabetha's crumpled form. *Boom!* The hex flew from her wand without warning. She'd been playing dead!

I dropped like a rock, landing on the edge of the jagged hole in the floor. Unfortunately, the section I landed on gave way. I fell through the floorboards, thorns and wood scraping and poking, until I slammed into the dining room table. The wood cracked and toppled under the impact. My body bounced off a chair and landed in a heap on the stone floor of the dining room.

"Fuck!" Blood. Everywhere. I'd broken my nose and probably a leg. A bloody gash split my stretchy black shirt, and my bottom rib smarted when I tried to move. "Nightshade." I'd dropped her when I fell. I searched the rubble around me but couldn't find her.

"She bleeds," Tabetha said from the doorway. New vines wound around my throat and dragged me by the neck over the rubble and toward the fireplace. I might have screamed if I wasn't strangled silent. The vines hauled me up the brick wall where I dangled and kicked my legs. My tongue protruded from my mouth as I attempted to gasp for breath, and my fingers clawed at the strangling plants.

"You're practically human," she taunted. "Live like a human, die like a human, I always say."

Black spots danced at the corners of my vision. The light constricted like a tunnel that led straight to Tabetha. To my credit, she did not lower her wand, despite the fact I was dangling helplessly by the neck. The thought bolstered me. I *was* a threat. Darkness pressed in. I hated that she would be the last thing I saw before I died. Her and the man standing behind her. Men. Covered in dirt. Zombies? No. Whoever they were, they attacked Tabetha from behind, a mob of ripping hands and tearing limbs. Tabetha screamed and flailed her wand.

Oh. I needed oxygen. Levitation. I tried to clear my mind and call the air around me, but I was too weak. It fizzled against my skin, barely a tickle.

"This is the third time I've saved you," Julius said into my ear. He ripped the vines from my throat, and I crashed into his torso. His forearm was the only thing that kept me from crumbling to the floor. I pulled air into my lungs in greedy gulps. My throat burned.

"Come now, Hecate," Julius said. "Pull it together and take what is yours. And do it quickly. The blood on your face is almost more than I can bear."

I staggered to my feet, foot really. Only one leg worked. I extended my hand. "Nightshade," I whispered with intention. A pile of rubble to my right vibrated and spit out my blade. She flew into my hand.

Tabetha was still screaming, but she was also fighting back. The plants coiled and heaved against her captors. At least fifty former supernatural lovers had come to bring Tabetha her due. Purple flesh with green seeds bled from her wounds like sand from a sandbag, but she was immortal. She healed almost as fast as they pulled her apart.

I approached the fight with Nightshade glowing blue. "She. Is. Mine."

"She is ours," a female voice said from the other side of the crowd. The men parted, and I saw a redheaded woman, dirty with torn clothes.

"Polina," Tabetha spat. "I ... I ..."

"You are over." With a wave of the woman's hand, the metal gargoyles on either side of the fireplace leapt forward and wrapped their claws around Tabetha's legs, shackling her to the stone floor. Polina locked eyes with me. "Do it now. Mother has given you permission." She pointed to my blade.

Usually blue, Nightshade had turned onyx black, the scent of sulfur and death leaching from the sharp length of bone. Shaky, I limped forward, bloody and broken. My injuries must have been extensive because I moved at a snail's pace. My vision swam with pain and dripping blood.

Tabetha's eyes widened at the sight of my black blade. "Don't listen to her, Grateful. I could be an ally. I could give you the children you desire with Rick. A simple potion is all it would take. If you spare me, I'll help you. I am your sister." Her dark lips pouted and pleaded with me.

I pictured her an hour ago, in bed with Rick, and chuckled. Through my teeth, I said, "I'm an only child." I swung Nightshade with everything I had left and sent her head tumbling from her neck.

It was the last thing I did before my body gave out.

CHAPTER 30
Polina

"Drink of me," Rick said. He tipped his head to the side, revealing his jugular.

I straddled his lap, but unlike every other time I'd done so, he did not respond to me physically. "What's wrong?" I asked. The words came out as a mumble, gibberish with the cadence of vocabulary.

"Drink," he demanded. He pressed the back of my head firmly so that my lips hovered over his pulse.

I was woozy and in pain. Blood and other things leaked from a wound in my abdomen, and my leg hung awkwardly from my hip. Survival instinct took over, and I sank my teeth into his skin. His blood, a sweet elixir of magic and mojo, flowed down my throat, swallow after swallow. In response, the pain became more acute, then faded to pressure, then a tightness of my skin. I heard my nose snap into position. Felt my rib pop into place and my eye lift in its broken socket. A tickle along my scalp meant my hair was growing back where I supposed it had been ripped out of my head.

Lost in the pleasure of Rick's blood, I closed my eyes. When I opened them again, I was flat on my back with Rick's wrist in my mouth and a redheaded witch leaning over me. Fuck, I'd been dreaming.

"Drink," the witch said, pressing Rick's bloody wrist to my lips.

Pushing his arm away, I scrambled to a seated position. I *must* have been dreaming. I was on Tabetha's four-poster bed. *Gross*. Rick was stretched out beside me. I shook his shoulder. He looked dead, eyes glassy and distant, limbs unmoving. "Why isn't he better?"

"Eating the fruit is like being bitten by a snake. His body and mind are paralyzed until it wears off. It could be hours or days. Frankly, I've never seen anyone this unresponsive. I suspect Tabetha had to give him a large dose of persigranate to keep him under control. Probably means he had a strong will to escape. But don't concern yourself. I'm sure he will live through this and be as good as new."

"Don't concern myself?" I curled around Rick, shaking his shoulder. "Rick. Rick!" I held my wrist to his lips. Nothing.

Polina's voice softened. "I know you love him. It's been a long time since I saw a witch and her caretaker in person.

Your bond is eternal. He'll come back to you, sister. Give it time." She gently placed a hand on my shoulder.

"Don't call me sister." I shrugged off her hand. I sensed she was trying to help me, but it was too soon for me to trust another witch.

She nodded and glanced away nervously. Her body was long, reedy, as was her face, a finely featured oval with a smattering of freckles. The beauty of her eyes struck me, bright blue, not green like you might expect given the color of her hair. They stood out against the frame of the dark auburn. Caked dirt soiled her gray dress. I wondered how long she'd been buried in Tabetha's garden graveyard.

"Six months," she answered my unasked question. "I am Polina, the Smugglers' Notch Witch, and I am pleased to make your acquaintance, Grateful Knight. You have saved me. I will not forget it."

I surveyed the room. The roses still bloomed and crawled across the drywall. "Is Tabetha dead? The plants in here are still pacing like hungry leopards."

"I've always been particularly disturbed by the manifestation of Tabetha's power," Polina said. "I am a metal witch, but you don't see a stream of mercury following me everywhere. I think people who have to flaunt their power are compensating for something, don't you? If she were a man, I'd assume she had small genitalia—"

"Polina," I interrupted because it occurred to me she might not stop if I didn't. "Is Tabetha still alive?"

"Sorry, I'm rambling, aren't I? It's a bad habit caused by being alone for too long. Isolation can make you this way. I never had company in Smugglers' Notch, besides Hildegard, my familiar." She raised her eyebrows. "And then to be trapped under that tree day after day—"

I squeezed her hand. "Tabetha?"

She blushed. "She is immortal, so technically still alive, although permanently incapacitated," she said firmly. "She's like Humpty Dumpty, really had a great fall. Well, *I* thought it was great." She laughed. "I suppose all the king's men could put her back together. If you stitched her up like Frankenstein's monster, she would probably heal eventually. But who would do that? Everyone hates her. Once they ripped her apart, all of her lovers and prisoners just took off. I mean, I totally get the prisoners, but the *lovers.* Men who she'd been with tore her limb from limb. Maybe she was bad in bed—"

"Help me get Rick out of here," I interrupted.

Polina nodded. "Okay."

I rolled Rick to the edge of the bed and tried to lift him by throwing his arm over my shoulder. I was too weak.

"Let me," Polina said. She muttered an incantation under her breath and held up one hand, fingers spread like an upside-down spider. Limp as a rag doll, Rick stood and walked zombie-like toward her as she pulled invisible strings with her upturned fingers.

"That's convenient," I said.

"I promise I won't hurt him. It's just easier than trying to carry him."

"I've got to learn how to do that."

"I'll teach you," she said, concentrating on navigating Rick down the stairs. He teetered a few times but didn't fall. "I was friends with the old you, when you were called Samantha. We met in the early eighties. Do you remember?"

I shook my head. "I'm sorry. Very few things have come back to me."

"I'm sure death is a curious and confusing journey." She stopped Rick at the door and pointed a hand toward the dining room. "Do you want to see Tabetha's remains? I would want to see, if I'd killed her. Technically, it was you who brought her down. She would have just kept pulling herself together if it wasn't for your blessing to kill her—or dismember her permanently as the case may be. I was so surprised when your implement of magic turned black. Mother's signature—"

Apprehensively, I wandered down the hall. Polina's rambling voice faded as I entered the dining room. Among smashed furniture, Tabetha's parts littered the floor in a puddle of purple jelly. Her mouth opened and closed on her disembodied head, although no sound came out, detached as it was from her torso. A few feet away, her hands pulled helplessly against the stone, anchored by the remainder of her arms, and her legs were left in heaps on opposite sides of the room. She was helpless and pitiful, and I wasn't the least bit sorry for making her that way. When I thought of what she'd done to Rick, I wanted to do it all over again.

"I hope you spend eternity regretting the day you messed with me, you fucking bitch." I kicked, and her head rolled under a chair.

Satisfied, I retreated from the room and returned to Polina in the foyer.

"I need to get out of here," I said. On the floor near my toe, I noticed a bow tie. "What happened to the man who was here?"

"Killed by the mob," she explained.

I cringed. She led Rick through the door and I followed. At the bottom of the stone steps, Poe landed on my shoulder.

"Thank the goddess you are all right," my familiar said.

"Where were you, Poe?" I snapped. "Could have used some help in there when I was dangling by my neck."

Poe ruffled his feathers. "I'll have you know, I was trying to deal with a problem Julius dug up."

I frowned. "What kind of problem?"

"Bathory," Julius said from my left. "She'd revived before we realized who she was. I tried to stop her but she eluded me. Poe attempted to trace her whereabouts faster, as the bird flies." He waved a hand in the air. "I told him I'd handle saving your pretty neck."

"Bathory. All this time we thought she abducted you when Tabetha had taken you both."

"You thought Bathory took *me*?" Julius asked, pointing at his chest. He chuckled. "Bathory wouldn't stand a chance. Not even with that half-pint Naill backing her up."

"At least she won't have that to go back to. Naill's been sentenced to the hellmouth," I said.

Julius grinned. "Then she poses little risk."

"Speak for yourself. She wants me dead."

With a shrug, Julius stepped closer, his nostrils flaring as he drew in the scent of my spilled blood. "Do I need to protect you, little witch? My saving you seems to have become a habit."

I gave him a look that made his shirt smoke, literally. He patted the spot with his hand and backed away, swearing.

"Seems like I have the same habit, and considering I gave you my blood, I win the contest for the most effort."

"You gave a vampire your blood?" Polina lowered her voice and addressed me directly. She turned her back to the vampire. "You shouldn't do that. Hasn't anyone told you how dangerous it is? You could—"

Julius raised his voice. "Our new Hecate is clearly capable of taking care of herself." He tipped his head toward Tabetha's home.

Polina's brow furrowed. She opened her mouth to say more, but before she could, a snowy white owl broke through the clouds and barreled into her. "Hildie! Oh, thank the goddess." Polina buried her face into her familiar's feathers.

"Hubba-hubba," Poe whispered from my shoulder. I hushed him and turned back toward the house.

"Speaking of taking care of things, we need to finish what we started. I can't take the chance of someone reviving Tabetha." Both witch and vampire turned their attention on me. "Is everyone else out of the house?"

"Yes," Polina said. "The other supernaturals did not stay once she was destroyed. You can't blame them. Some have been buried beneath the trees for decades. There was only one servant working, and you saw his remains."

My heart sank thinking about the man in the bow tie. That could have been Logan, used and left for dead. Even Rick would have sustained horrific injuries at the hands of the bloodthirsty mob. I stared at Rick, catatonic at the base of the steps. It was my responsibility to make sure this never happened to anyone ever again.

Resolved, I took a deep breath and blew it out toward the house. It gathered strength along the way, fueled by my magic. The plants in the pots on the veranda burst into flames. I blew again, and this time I directed the heat inside the open door. The plants inside the foyer ignited.

The vines carried the flames to the curtains on the windows. The inferno raged. Great billows of black smoke escaped the front door. The windows shattered, and the brick walls scorched from licks of flame that danced out the resulting openings. Before long, the fire had engulfed the entire building.

"Oh," Polina said. "Would it be all right if I helped you contain this? I'm afraid for the trees." She glanced toward the woods.

"Please," I said, thinking of the wildlife that came here to feed.

Polina cast her hand as if rolling dice and gigantic rocks erupted around the house. They formed a barrier against the heat. "High iron content," she said.

We stood shoulder to shoulder as the roof collapsed, and the fire left Tabetha's residence looking more and more like a brick skeleton. I had an inappropriate vision of Tabetha's purple fruit blood caramelizing on the stone before it burst into flames.

"If you will both excuse me, the sun rises," Julius said.

I turned toward his voice, but he was already gone. I wondered what would happen when he got back to the Thames.

"I need to return to Smugglers' Notch and reassert my rights over my territory," Polina said. "Hildegard says Tabetha barely kept the trolls at bay. I suppose she didn't have much experience with trolls living here."

I smiled. "Thank you for helping me."

She nodded. "I hope this is the beginning of a long and prosperous friendship. Not an allegiance, mind you. Although if you want an allegiance, you can have it. I'm not against alliances, per se. But friendship goes deeper. Friendship—"

"Polina?"

"Huh?"

"Can you help me get Rick into my Jeep?"

"Oh, sure. I was rambling again, wasn't I?"

"It's okay," I said, smiling. "It's sort of growing on me."

Poe cleared his throat. "If you don't mind, I'm going to do some hunting." He eyed the forest as if it were a smorgasbord of exotic culinary delights. "Meet you back at the house?"

"Of course," I said. He took flight toward the sunrise.

Polina held up her hand and guided Rick down the long driveway to my Jeep, while the acrid scent of burning plants filled the air around us. On the way, she rambled on about the persigranate trees. I was too worried about Rick to hear a word she said.

Still, I was thankful for Polina's help, and I had a way to show it. I unlocked the glove compartment and produced the *Duck Dynasty* thermos filled with positivity potion. I'd locked it in there the day I offered it to Tabetha, waiting for the right moment to be rid of it. Frankly, I couldn't use it myself, and it was dangerous driving around with it. "I want you to have this," I said.

"What's this?"

"Just my way of saying thank you for helping me today. I hope this is the beginning of a long and beautiful friendship."

Eyebrows scrunched together, she unscrewed the cap and sniffed. Her eyes widened. "This is positivity potion. Very powerful. What are you doing with this in your glove compartment?"

"Long story. It should still work. I don't think it expires. My gift to you; do with it what you will."

Polina thanked me profusely, then launched into a long explanation of why the potion was so powerful. I strapped Rick into his seat.

She was still talking when I pulled away from the curb.

CHAPTER 31
Return To Me

I drove slowly back to Red Grove, taking the less traveled country roads at my own pace. Polina had said it was just a matter of time until Tabetha's poison wore off and Rick returned to me. Time might heal all wounds, but could it reverse magic? I hoped so. I'd seen no change in Rick. His body was with me, staring out the window and offering me the hope of an occasional blink, but his mind and soul were somewhere else.

The rumble of my Jeep's wheels on uneven pavement provided the kind of reflective environment where my thoughts could run wild. One thought came a-calling more than any other. I'd seen Rick in bed with Tabetha. Naked. There was no blissful uncertainty that came from finding out after the fact. I'd seen it with my own eyes.

My logical mind told me this act was not infidelity. Rick was used. Tabetha drugged him with an enchanted tart, abducted him, and used him. I couldn't fault him for being the victim. My heart wasn't a problem either. The love I felt for Rick trumped anything I'd seen. I was so thankful to have him back alive and was committed to nursing him to health, however long it took.

Beyond my logical mind and compassionate heart though, my emotional core was in turmoil. The amygdala of my brain, the part that controlled fight or flight, was telling me to fly, not because I blamed him but because my love for him was a gaping wound. Tabetha was the first to recognize that Rick was both my greatest strength and my ultimate weakness. He was my beginning and my end.

Love had everything to do with it. If Rick was simply a source of power, I could live without him. Power can be replaced. The sex was good, but I could find a number of men to have sex with. Even Rick acting as the vessel of my immortal soul didn't seal the deal.

It was love that ripped my heart from my chest when I saw him with Tabetha. It was love that made it impossible for me not to walk back into Tabetha's house and confront her to win Rick back. Most of all, it was love that made me vulnerable. As long as I loved Rick, and people knew that I loved him, he would be a target for anyone who wanted to hurt me.

My amygdala was telling me to run, not from Rick per se, but from love. I wanted to fight it, but as the miles passed, old walls came up again—walls I'd torn down months ago, protective walls. Didn't I deserve some walls? I'd been relationship toxic for as long as I could remember. Always rushing head first into love only to head-butt the wall at full speed.

But Rick was my answer to that. A love that was finally returned. A love that was eternal. Alas, this love was just as dangerous, just as soul crushing. *Is love worth it?* was all I could think, mile after blessed mile.

By the time I turned into my driveway, I'd flipped that thought over in my head ad nauseam. Rick wasn't any better, and I didn't have any answers or comfort. The one thing I did have was my regained strength. With a little help from the air around me, I helped Rick from the Jeep and levitated him up the stairs and into my bedroom. Only it didn't happen as smoothly as it sounds. I conked his head on the banister and dropped him half on, half off the bed. Anyway, he got there, all limbs intact. I thought that was pretty good, considering.

I crawled in next to him, pulled the covers over both of us, and curled into his side. His head rolled on the pillow toward the window. I toyed with the waves of his hair behind his ear.

"Rick? Are you in there?" I whispered.

No response.

Eventually, I slipped into an anxious and troubled sleep.

* * * * *

Tap, tap, tappity-tap. I woke to banging on the window. Poe. I got out of bed to slide the glass pane open for him. He swooped in along with a rush of cold night air.

"Why didn't you use your door in the attic?" I asked him.

"Because I wanted to talk to you, and you were on the other side of the window."

"But you could have entered through the attic and then flown down here to talk to me without waking me up."

"How could I talk to you without waking you up?" His beady black eyes bore into me.

I sighed. "Never mind. What did you want to talk to me about?"

"Logan is on his way here, and he looks pissed."

"What?"

"Just passed into Red Grove. He's alone."

The doorbell rang. I looked down at my shirt, still crusty with blood. "How do I look?"

Poe snorted. "I think you have intestines in your hair."

I scowled. "I didn't even encounter intestines tonight."

He shrugged his bird shoulders.

After a quick jog down the steps, I tentatively opened the door to an enraged Logan.

"Grateful, how could you?" he accused, storming toward me, then got a good look at me. "You look like crap."

"Thanks. Battling evil bitches—I mean, witches—will do that to you." I navigated around him to close the door and then retreated into the house. "You may not believe me, but I told you the truth. Tabetha was drugging you. She targeted you to get to me, and she intended to kill you."

He nodded his head. "So you had a vampire abduct me and hide me in ... God knows where—I still don't ... to protect me from her."

"Yeah. To be honest, it would have been easier to just let her kill you, but you've kind of grown on me."

"How could you do that after how I treated you? Your wedding was ruined because of me. You could have lost your territory."

"Huh?"

"When the fruit wore off, I remembered how I treated you, Grateful. You should have let her kill me."

"Don't be stupid."

He moved in closer, his green eyes blazing. "You saved my life. Again." *Bam.* His lips landed on mine like a fist punch, hard and quick, with a minor head grab to hold me in place. The kiss was there and gone before I could register much more than pressure and presence. When he pulled back, my mouth was hanging open.

"Thank you," Logan said insistently.

It took a few tries to find my voice again. I licked my lips and furrowed my brow. "How did you get out? I never gave the okay to Gary."

"Julius. When he came back, Gary stepped down as leader of the free coven. He told Julius what you'd done for him. Julius was impressed you'd helped Gary maintain control. Once he'd explained to me what had happened and made sure I didn't have the fruit in my system, he let me go."

"How did he check if you had fruit in your system?" I suspected how but had to ask.

Logan extended his wrist to show me two puncture wounds. "The vampire way."

We both wrinkled our noses.

"Actually, if I didn't know better, I'd say Julius has a thing for you, Grateful. The way he told the story of how you rescued him and slayed Tabetha, it was like one of those Pepe Le Pew cartoons where you could see his heart beat through his chest."

"Oh, come on."

"You're his hero." Logan grinned and raised both eyebrows. "You are a vampire *legend*."

I snorted. He laughed. And then the humor slowly drained from the room. "I'm sorry, Logan, that this happened to you. Your life has been nothing but crazy since you met me." I glanced down at the toes of my socks.

"As I recall, I was a ghost in your attic when you met me. I don't think you started the crazy."

"Maybe not," I admitted.

"Are we friends again?" he asked seriously.

I smiled. "The best there is." I held out my fist, and he bumped it with his own. "Who else would sign up for this?" I gestured toward myself.

He moved for the door. "I need to check in at the restaurant, and you …" His gaze flicked over me. "Need a shower."

I rolled my eyes. "Thanks for coming to see me. I'm relieved things are okay between us again."

He nodded. "For sure. When you reschedule your wedding, Valentine's will do the catering. Just let me know the date."

I shifted my eyes from him to the wall and bit my lip.

He paused. "You are going to reschedule, aren't you?"

I swallowed. Needles pricked the insides of my eyes, the pain of tears held back too long, denied their proper course. "I'm sure we will," I lied. "Maybe a longer engagement this time. The whole event was kind of rushed."

There was a long pause, and then Logan said, "Who could blame you for taking your time?" His eyes met mine, and he flashed me a crooked smile.

Who could blame me?

With a nod and a wave, he slipped out the door and went back to his life.

CHAPTER 32
New Beginnings

After Logan left, I checked on Rick. He'd changed positions and was curled on his side. I glanced at Poe to ask if there was any other change, but my familiar was asleep on my dresser with his head under his wing.

"Rick?" I asked. "Are you back?"

His eyelashes fluttered.

I moved to his side and squeezed his hand. He did not squeeze mine. I passed a hand in front of his face. His eyes glazed over again.

Frustrated, I decided Logan's suggestion of a shower would be a great way to wait this out. I started the water to heat it up, then in a stroke of genius, stepped back out to striptease in front of him. Nothing. He was definitely drugged. Healthy and conscious, I'd be under Rick before I could say *go*, blood or no blood.

The spell would have to break soon, wouldn't it?

I stepped into the shower, filled my palm with my tea tree-and-mint shampoo and started washing the blood, sap, and purple fruit from my hair. As I massaged my scalp, I repeated this mantra: *Rick will wake up soon. Rick will wake up soon.* I pictured him stepping into the shower with me, grabbing me from behind, and promising he'd never leave me again. Lather. Rinse. Repeat.

The water turned cold. I stepped out and dried myself off. I checked Rick. No change. I dressed and dried my hair. I put on makeup and cologne.

No change.

"Poe." I shook his raven body until he was awake.

"Oh, how mature. Are you retaliating because I woke you earlier? If you are looking for an apology ..." He rolled his eyes at me.

"No. No. Nothing like that. Rick still hasn't snapped out of it. I think something's wrong. The spell isn't wearing off."

The feathers over Poe's eyes dipped down into a sharp vee over his beak. He flapped his wings and flew to Rick's side. After nudging him repeatedly, Poe bit down on his ear.

"Hey! What are you doing?" I yelled, seeing blood bubble up from the bite.

"Trying to snap him out of it," Poe said. "He didn't even flinch."

I wiped away the blood and licked it off my thumb. Thankfully, the wound had already healed. "His caretaker power is still working. His injury healed."

"Have you fed him your blood?"

"I tried. He won't bite."

"It's been more than fourteen hours," Poe said. "Maybe longer. We don't know what she gave him or even when she fed him the last dose."

I straightened and inhaled sharply. "She'd meant to bury him and feed off his power. She might've given him anything. What did she care if she fried his brain?"

Poe huffed through his nostrils. "Try feeding him your blood. See if that wakes him up."

I drew Nightshade and scored my wrist. Blood bubbled to the surface. I lunged onto the bed and pulled Rick's head into my lap. Tipping his head back, his lips parted CPR style, and I pressed my wrist to his open mouth. Blood dribbled over his tongue. Eventually, his Adam's apple bobbed as he swallowed reflexively.

"That's it. Come on, Rick. Drink," I said, running my fingers along his hairline.

He sputtered against my wrist. "He's choking," Poe said.

I pulled my arm away. His body struggled for air, coughing and wheezing.

"Poe, what's happening?"

The raven shook his head.

Rick's body trembled violently. "He's having a seizure." I tipped him on his side while the muscle spasms rocked through him. When they finally stopped, he heaved vomit across my bed and onto the floor.

"He's throwing up my blood!" I looked to Poe in panic. "What's going on? What do we do?"

Poe shook his head again.

I helplessly rubbed Rick's back and shoulder. After some time, I risked running to the bathroom for some towels to clean up. He was done being sick, but was no less vacant. Expressionless. Zombie-like.

My blood was not the answer.

"How do you get blood out of carpet?" I asked absently, scrubbing the floor.

"Carpet cleaner," Poe said just as absently.

I sat back on my heels. "What if he stays like this?"

"Don't think that way."

Poe and I stared at each other. We were both thinking it. What he really meant was not to say it out loud.

The sound of the doorbell made me jump. "Who could that be?" A glance at my watch told me it was almost midnight.

"Only one way to find out," Poe said.

I dropped the towel I was holding and descended the stairs. A peek through the side window had me double-checking that Nightshade was on my back. Tree sprites. Were they here to exact their revenge on me for killing their queen? Carefully, I opened the door, trusting the protective ward around my house and the hum of my power in the air around me.

The sprite at my door had birch-bark hair and wore a green strapless moss dress reminiscent of Tinker Bell's. Her delicate features had an unmistakably carved quality. She blinked her eyes at me, then sank to her knees. Behind her, a dozen more of her kind did the same in my yard.

"What's going on?" I asked.

The sprite at my feet extended her hands, a tightly rolled scroll resting in her palms similar to the invitation Tabetha had sent for dinner. I didn't immediately accept it.

"Grateful Knight, daughter of Hecate, sorceress of the dead, and queen of Monk's Hill, we are here today to pay you homage and ask your just and generous hand to rule the once great territory of Salem." Her voice had the reedy quality of a woodwind and the clarity of silver bells.

"Wha—huh?" I said dumbly.

She cleared her throat and spoke again. "As the emancipator of Salem's realm from Tabetha the Great and Terrible, you are now the rightful Witch of Salem." She extended her arms another inch. "To accept your right and proper duty, simply read and sign the scroll and all that was Tabetha's shall be yours."

Poe landed on my shoulder as my hand slowly reached for the scroll.

"Don't do it. You will anger the goddess," Poe whispered. "She wasn't happy when Tabetha acquired two of the five elements of magic. What if you end up on Hecate's hit list?"

I unrolled the scroll. A quill fell out into my hand. Tucking it between my thumb and forefinger, I began to read. Poe was right. I'd promised Rick I would not accept the territory for exactly the reason that it might put me on Hecate's hit list. Of course, that was assuming I'd inherit two elements. With Polina back in power, there was just one in question.

"I get her grimoire, Poe," I said. "If I have her book of magic, maybe I can reverse the spell on Rick. It's our best hope."

"Your mother might kill you," Poe warned.

"She gave me permission to kill Tabetha. The goddess would know the consequences of that blessing."

"Are you sure you want to do this? It's a hell of a lot of responsibility."

I looked into his beady black eyes. "I don't want to do it. I have to do it."

Poe said nothing but leaned his soft feathers into my ear. It was the raven equivalent of a hand on my shoulder. I rested the scroll against the wall and lifted the quill. It scratched the parchment without leaving a mark.

"Do you have ink?" I asked the sprite.

She folded her tiny hands in front of her hips and in that childlike voice said, "It must be done with blood."

Blood. Of course. It was always blood. The point of the quill was sharp, and I stabbed it into my left hand, hard enough to break the skin. Then in sweeping red letters, I signed at the bottom of the parchment. No sooner had I crossed the T in Knight, than the parchment dissolved between my fingers, leaving me only with the quill, which transformed into a crooked branch … no, a *wand*.

I turned back toward the sprite, thinking her knees must hurt by now from kneeling. She lowered her face to the concrete. Her entire willowy body trembled with fear.

"It's okay. Stand up. I won't hurt you," I said.

Slowly, she raised her head and met my eyes. I tried to make my face soft. The sprites had been treated like slaves by Tabetha. Who could blame them for believing their new master would be the same sort of devil?

"I won't hurt you, but I need my new grimoire. Where is Tabetha's book of magic?"

She motioned toward the lawn where the rows of sprites parted and four male tree sprites moved forward, carrying the great book like pallbearers. This book was as large as *The Book of Light* but covered in tree bark with rough-hewn letters that said *Copse Magicum*.

"Forest magic," Poe translated. "In the old language."

The procession stopped at my threshold, the knees of the fae buckling under the giant tome's weight. I blew across the cover and then wrapped my magic around it to levitate the book inside. A collective "Ooooh" came from the gathering. They'd all seen wood magic but maybe never air.

Once the book was safely on my dining room table, I turned back to the waiting sprites.

"Thank you for coming. You can all go now. Rest assured, I will rule you and your territory with the same tender loving care I do my own." I gave them all a small wave and promptly shut the door.

I peeked out the side window and watched their confused faces turn toward the trees.

"Do you think I was supposed to do something else? Some sort of ceremony or something."

"I have no idea," Poe said. "In all of my lifetimes as a familiar, I have never witnessed a witch with two territories."

"Great. I'm a trailblazer."

He chuckled. "I can't think of a more qualified candidate."

"Let's see if my qualifications help me find a spell to get my caretaker back." I flipped open the bark cover and perused the first pages. No table of contents. The spells weren't even in alphabetical order. "How can a witch live this way?" I asked in frustration.

Poe groaned. "Ask it, Grateful."

"Oh, I always forget I can do that." I held my hand over the book. With a clear mind, I stated, "Show me the antidote for persigranate poisoning."

When I asked *The Book of Light* a question, the whole book glowed and the pages flipped in the wind. Not so with this book. A vine of ivy grew out of the spine and used its spade-shaped leaf to flip through the pages. When it reached the one it wanted, it laced itself along the crease, bookmark style. I leaned over the page and read the spell.

"Persigranate requires an even hand.

Too much sours the plan.
To undo the overdone,
mix one part milk thistle to two parts rum.
Add the fresh egg of a quail.
Administer raw, without fail,
before sunset at any cost.
Wait too long and suffer loss."

I looked at Poe. "The sun has already set."

Poe went statue still. "I will obtain the quail egg, my lady."

I nodded. I opened the front door, and he took flight. Once he was gone, I finally let myself cry.

* * * * *

"Drink," I said into Rick's ear. I propped him against my chest and raised the potion to his slack lips. He wasn't helping me at all. Limp-limbed, he leaned in my arms.

Poe paced on my dresser. "Just give it to him. Time is of the essence."

I placed one hand on Rick's forehead and coaxed his head back. When his lips parted, I dumped in a splash of potion, then moved my hand from forehead to chin to hold his mouth closed. After three more times with this procedure, he'd swallowed all of it.

I held him for a minute and then lowered him to the bed, our noses almost touching. As my arms started to cramp, I wondered if he'd ever come back to me. If his brain was fried, would he live out his immortal life in this empty and unresponsive state, until the mountains crumbled and the earth came apart? I couldn't stand to watch him exist like that.

An unwelcome thought wiggled at the back of my consciousness. I had Tabetha's spell book. I could make another candle. If I made Rick human again, he could die. Would it be better to let him die than live like this? Without a doubt, death was what Rick would choose if he had the choice.

But could I do it? No. Probably not. I buried my eyes in his chest and gave myself over to the surge of helplessness I'd fought valiantly since my ruined wedding. I dove head first into a sobbing, pitiful, self-indulgent wallow.

"Come back to me. Please, come back to me," I said in the squeaky, broken voice of a desperate woman.

Time stretched on.

Pressure. A hand rested on the back of my shoulder. I stopped breathing. Poe couldn't transform into anything with five fingers, and I hadn't heard footsteps enter the room. Slowly, tentatively, I raised my head from Rick's chest and tipped my face to see his.

He was looking at me. Soft gray eyes met mine, and the corner of his mouth crawled up his cheek in a jerky, measured grin.

"Hi," I said.

"How fare thee?"

His lips had moved, and he'd produced words. My heart leapt. I grinned and grabbed his face, melding my mouth with his. He stiffened and pushed me away.

According to Logan, when he came out of the effects of the persigranate he remembered everything he'd done under its influence. Perhaps Rick was remembering what happened. It would be like him to be consumed with guilt over Tabetha as well as leaving me at the altar.

I pulled back. "It's okay. It's all okay now." I smiled reassuringly.

Rick sat up, swinging his legs out from under me and over the side of the bed. The action forced me to do the same, and we ended up shoulder to shoulder on the edge of the mattress. His eyes narrowed. "What have you done to your appearance?"

I snorted. "Nothing." I looked down at myself.

His eyes darted around the room in confusion. "Isabella?" It was a question, not a statement.

With a small nod of my head, I pressed a palm into my chest. "Yes ... Well, not anymore," I said uncertainly. "Grateful now, remember?"

"I watched you burn," he whispered.

"That was hundreds of years ago, Rick—"

"Enrique," he corrected me.

Confused, I looked to Poe, who was watching silently from his perch on my dresser. "What year is it, Enrique?" Poe asked.

Rick startled. "The bird speaks? Is this your doing, Isabella?"

I placed my hand on Rick's thigh. "What year do you think it is?" I asked again.

He stared at my hand on the denim of his jeans. "It is 1698. You … died." He furrowed his brow. "I thought they all died."

I narrowed my eyes and searched his face for any indication he was joking. "Fuck. Me." I ignored the way Rick jarred at the curse and turned toward Poe. "I think he's lost more than three hundred years."

EPILOGUE

I walked alone in an alley of questionable repute, looking for a vampire with humans on his mind. This part of the city was populated with strip clubs and massage parlors. My magic mirror told me the happy ending this vampire had in mind had more to do with blood than pleasure.

Silently, I blended into shadow, out of reach of neon lights and beyond notice of the occasional smoker who lit up behind the dumpsters. My boots were enchanted not to make a sound, and Nightshade made me almost imperceptible to supernatural beings.

The thump of bass poured into the alley as the door to one of the clubs opened and a vampire exited, woman in tow. She might've been a stripper or a scantily-clad patron. I wasn't there to judge her, just the vamp.

"Come on, baby," the vampire said. "I've been waiting all night to get you alone."

She giggled. "In the alley? Wouldn't you rather take me back to your place?"

He pressed her against the brick wall. "I think here will be just perfect."

She shook her head. "I'm cold, and I don't like this." She pushed him away. "If you want to be alone, take me home."

Strike one, no consent.

The vampire growled and grabbed her by the neck.

"Hey!" she said.

He forced her to meet his eyes. "This will be fine," he stated again.

"This will be fine," she repeated.

Strike two, compulsion.

Maneuvering her behind the dumpster, he brushed her hair aside, and tipped her head to expose her jugular.

Strike three, intention to drink human blood. I drew Nightshade and prepared to move in for the judgment.

A dark fog rolled past me and lifted the vampire from the woman's body. The vamp was pulled straight up into the air at super speed and then dropped. I took a step back so the body didn't hit me in the head. When it did land, I noticed immediately that the vampire's heart had been torn out. In seconds, the body turned gray, then to dust, and became indistinguishable from the rest of the dirt on the pavement.

"Show yourself," I said.

A wind blew past me, smelling faintly of Scotch, and formed into a sharply dressed vampire sophisticate with chocolate brown hair and Caribbean blue eyes.

"Hello, Julius," I said. "Didn't expect to have *your* help tonight."

"The free coven does not allow feeding on unwilling humans, Grateful. We police our own."

I shrugged. "Good with me. One less thing on my list. Have a nice night." I sheathed Nightshade and turned to leave the alley.

Julius appeared in front of me in the blink of an eye. "Why are you out alone tonight?"

"Rick had some things he needed to do."

The vampire peered at me through suspicious, hooded eyes. "Bullshit. I saw the state he was in at Tabetha's. He hasn't recovered yet, has he?" He rubbed his chin.

I couldn't tell if Julius was smiling. His mouth was a straight line, but his eyes looked a little too happy about the idea of Rick having lasting consequences from Tabetha's poisoning.

"He's fine," I lied. The truth was Rick was far from fine. As the spell warned, Rick had lost something when Tabetha overdosed him with persigranate, namely the memory of our life together with him as my caretaker. At some level, he knew who I was, and he understood I was a witch. He even remembered the scar on his chest and how it got there. But he didn't remember my previous lives. In his mind, we'd never had sex. We'd never been married. He'd never transformed into his beast.

Julius rolled his neck. He wasn't buying my denial, but he didn't push the topic. "Are you done for the night?" he asked.

"Yeah. Heading home. The ward is safe for another twenty-four." That was an exaggeration. My magic mirror didn't catch everything. The situations it pictured were premeditated and not tampered with by sorcery.

"Would you like to come back to the Thames for a drink?" Julius arched one eyebrow. For a moment, I had the sense he was trying to be seductive. Julius was attractive by commercial standards, and vampires were predatorily gifted with charm, but I was immune to those gifts and somewhat sickened by his history.

"I'll pass, thanks," I said. I kept walking.

"After all we've been through?" He gently placed a hand on my shoulder. "Wouldn't it be nice to be friends? Allies? You might need me again someday."

I bunched my forehead. The lightbulb came on. Julius wasn't really asking if *I* wanted a drink. He was trying to offer me a drink because *he* might need something someday. Julius was kissing up to me. This was politics, not seduction.

I supposed it was important to be political, now that I was queen of multiple territories. "Okay. One short drink," I said. "At a bar. Not in your bedroom."

He agreed. I strolled from the alley shoulder to shoulder with the vampire, wondering if I was making a mistake. Then again, I had been chosen to rule, and rulers made a habit of knowing their constituents. At one point,

I'd kept Julius alive for his political position as leader of the free coven. It was only natural I foster that relationship, vampire or not.

"Here," he said, suggesting a bar called The Ocean.

"There's a line," I said. "And I'm underdressed."

He took my elbow and led me directly to the bouncer, who let us in ahead of at least fifty waiting twenty-somethings. In the back, in a quiet section called the Deep End, we took seats on velvet blue couches and had our drink orders taken by a girl in a bikini. He ordered Scotch. I ordered a blue Hawaiian. *When in Rome ...*

"Now that you're back, how's the transition going?" I asked. "Anyone giving you a hard time about jumping back in and calling yourself the king?"

Julius placed an ankle across the opposite knee and leaned his head back into a cradle of his fingers. "I'll answer that question when you tell me how you are faring with the wood witch's power."

I shrugged. "The day I signed for her territory, a plant sprouted from my floorboards. I cut it back. The next morning my entire staircase was covered in roses. I've tried everything. Chemicals, burning, clippers. There's no going back. My house is officially a rose garden."

Julius laughed.

I stared at him expectantly.

"You recently witnessed the death of the last dissenter." He grinned.

The waitress arrived and handed him his Scotch and me a blue fishbowl the size of my head with a straw sticking out of it. I had to use two hands. I set it down on the small table in front of us.

"Is that how you handle everything? Someone pisses you off and they wind up dead?"

He circled the amber liquid in the bottom of his glass. "Technically, everyone in the coven is already dead, but yes." He pointed at me. "It seems you have the same strategy."

I shook my head. "No, I'm not like you."

"No? Marcus crossed you. He's dead. The nekomata crossed you. The entire clan is dead. Bathory? Would be dead if Tabetha hadn't saved her by mummifying her under a tree. Oh, and lest I forget, Tabetha ... dead."

I picked up my fishbowl and took a long, sweet drink through the straw. I didn't know what to say to that, so I said nothing.

"It's okay, you know, to be like me," Julius said. "I've survived a long time living like I do."

"I am not like you, Julius. The people I've killed tried to kill me first. I was protecting myself."

"And I kill indiscriminately?"

I shook my head. "I couldn't begin to speculate on all the reasons you've killed."

He tossed back the remainder of his Scotch. "Oh, I think you probably could," he said softly.

"What are you getting at, Julius?"

"Despite what you say to the contrary, I suspect your caretaker isn't what he used to be—"

"He's fine."

"Your territory has grown, and you are still learning to use your power."

"I killed one of the strongest witches alive. I think I'm doing pretty well."

"I want to offer you help. I'm here for you, if you need me. My coven is at your service." He looked at me with nothing but sincerity in his eyes.

"And every service comes with a price, doesn't it, Julius?"

He nodded slowly, never breaking eye contact.

He was right. Poe and I hadn't been successful in getting Rick to shift into his beast yet, and he'd lost all memory of the supernatural knowledge he'd gained during the last three centuries. Not only had I lost my backup, he was still getting comfortable with indoor plumbing. I didn't trust Julius, not really. But I had a job to do.

I lifted my fishbowl. "To new beginnings," I said.

He toasted me with his empty glass.

* * * * *

I arrived at Rick's just after two a.m., an early night by our usual standards. When he opened the door for me, one look told me it hadn't been a good night. His face was gaunt. His skin pale.

"Your hands are shaking," I said.

He didn't exactly greet me, just opened the door a little wider.

The remnants of his dinner, what looked like rabbit stew, still sat in a bowl on his counter, cold. I wondered where he got the rabbit. A shotgun leaned against the corner. Maybe he'd killed it himself.

"Everything tasted rancid," he said. "I cannot eat. I cannot sleep."

I dumped the stew in the garbage and washed out the bowl. "I've tried to explain to you, Enrique, this isn't what your body needs anymore. You need—"

"Blood." His voice cracked. The thought sickened him.

"Or sex," I said hopefully.

He dug his fingers into his dark waves. "Blood," he said definitively.

I extended my wrist.

He shook his head.

Defeated, I retrieved a wineglass from the cupboard and drew Nightshade. My blood filled the glass. I tried not to think about how much I needed his blood. Now was not the time. He wasn't ready.

I handed him the glass.

Rick closed his eyes and took a sip. Almost immediately his color returned. He drained the last drop.

"It will get easier," I said. "Come. Sit with me."

He left the glass on the table and joined me on the sofa. After some time, I was able to coax him into my arms. With his head on my fully clothed chest, I stroked his hair until he fell asleep, and only then planted a kiss on his temple.

Life is funny. What we think is important, isn't. Things that seem in our control, aren't. And in the end, the one thing that matters is love. I planned to win Rick's love again. I planned to teach him about us and our long history. And then I planned to marry him. Because if there was one thing I'd proven to myself, it was this:

Rick was worth it.

ABOUT THE AUTHOR

Genevieve Jack grew up in a suburb of Chicago and attended a high school rumored to be haunted. She loves old cemeteries and enjoys a good ghost tour. Genevieve specializes in original, cross-genre stories with surprising twists. She lives in central Illinois with her husband, two children, and a Brittany named Riptide who holds down her feet while she writes.

Visit Genevieve at:

    http://www.GenevieveJack.com
    https://twitter.com/Genevieve_Jack
    https://www.facebook.com/AuthorGenevieveJack
    http://instagram.com/authorgenevievejack
    http://www.goodreads.com/author/show
                    /6477522.Genevieve_Jack

ACKNOWLEDGEMENTS

Queen of the Hill would not have been possible without the help of a few individuals who gave of their time and experience.

To my husband, A, thank you for your support and encouragement. I appreciate all those times you handled the real world while I was building a fantasy one.

To my friend MM, thanks for providing technical support.

Special thanks to Laurie Bradach, RT Wolfe, and Brenda Rothert for using their sharp eyes and ears to better an early draft of the manuscript.

Finally, huge hugs to Hollie Westring, who came on as editor with the latest editions of the series.

COMING SOON

Book 4 in the Knight Games Series, *Mother May I.*